BEAUTIFULLY CRUEL

J.T. GEISSINGER

Published by J.T. Geissinger, Inc.

www.jtgeissinger.com

ISBN: 978-1-7338243-6-1

Cover design by Letitia Hasser

Printed in the United States of America

PREFACE

Thank you for reading! To get new release information, please sign up for my newsletter.

For Jay, the beautiful soul who brightens my darkness.

These violent delights have violent ends
And in their triumph die, like fire and powder
Which, as they kiss, consume.

~ *Romeo and Juliet, Act II, Scene VI*

1

TRU

"Your big bad wolf is back again."

I look up from the coffee machine as my co-worker Carla pauses beside me, nudging me with her elbow and speaking under her breath. I don't need to turn and follow her gaze across the diner to know who she's talking about. The nickname and the sudden spike in my pulse are proof enough.

It's been seven weeks since the man in black last came in. Seven weeks since I've seen that thick dark hair, those big rough hands, those expensive Armani suits that do nothing to gentrify him.

You can try to dress up a lion all you want, but it'll still be obvious that he's king of the jungle.

"He's not mine," I say in the same low tone, watching coffee drip slowly into the glass carafe and feeling my heartbeat in every part of my body.

It's difficult not to turn around and look at him.

Difficult, but not surprising. I've never known another man I enjoy looking at more.

Carla scoffs. "He's been sitting at the same table in your section for a year, Tru."

Eleven months. But who's counting?

"If it's your day off when he comes in, he leaves. He's shot down every other waitress who's tried to flirt with him—including me, and these boobs *never* fail—and he damn sure doesn't come here for the food."

She makes a face at the plate in her hand. Grease oozes from a pile of corned beef hash, yellow as phlegm, already congealing. Buddy's All Night Diner isn't known for the quality of its fare.

"He doesn't talk to me, either, except to order his coffee."

Carla rolls her eyes. "Please. The man talks plenty loud with those big bad wolf eyes of his. One of these days, he's gonna gobble you up like Red Riding Hood's grandma."

I smile, shaking my head. "Sure. He's just waiting for the perfect full moon, right?"

She tilts back her head and makes a soft *owOooo* wolf cry toward the ceiling.

"Go away, crazy person. I'm trying to work here."

Hips swinging, she moves away to deliver the hash to the bald guy at table twelve. I take a moment to breathe and attempt to steady my nerves, then I grab a mug from the shelf over the coffee machine and head toward the wolf's table.

He's waiting.

Watching me.

Unsmiling as always, with burning dark eyes and the kind of focus and stillness I've only ever seen in documentaries of big cats as they lie in wait in tall grasses for a gazelle to pass.

This is always how he looks at me: in hunger and silence. But unlike an African cat on the prowl, the wolf's gaze holds something wary underneath. A kind of enforced restraint.

His hands are spread flat on the scarred table top as he watches me approach, as if that's his way of keeping control of them.

Concentrating on appearing nonchalant, I stop at his table-side, set the mug down, and pour him a coffee. He likes it the same way he seems to like everything else: black.

I say shyly, "Hi. It's nice to see you again."

Yay me, keeping my voice even despite the butterflies in my stomach and the lump in my throat. Though I've never shared an actual conversation with him, the man has always been hell on my nerves.

He murmurs, "It's nice to be seen."

Oh, that Irish brogue. I'd almost forgotten how delicious it is. Rich and throaty, with a rumble to it like a purr. Suppressing a shiver, I glance up and give him a tentative smile.

He doesn't return it.

As is my custom whenever he visits, I indulge myself with an inventory of his visible tattoos. One decorates each knuckle of his left hand. Stars. A crown. A knife plunged through a skull. Another one is a black square that looks like it might be covering something else. These fascinate me, as does the tip of the tattoo peeking above the collar of his starched white dress shirt.

I find this collection of ink interesting and mysterious, like him.

Deciding today will be the day we'll finally have a conversation, I gather my courage and take another steadying breath. "Beautiful weather we're having, isn't it?"

I tried to imbue the comment with light sarcasm—which would've been apropos considering how bad the weather is—but it came out heavy and flat, like a brick dropped onto the table between us.

The wolf gazes at me in inscrutable silence. The smallest furrow appears between his dark brows.

My cheeks heat with embarrassment. Just when I'm about to turn and leave, he says suddenly, "I love when it rains in the city. It reminds me of home."

Judging by the look on his face, he wasn't expecting that, either.

I ask tentatively, "Home is Ireland?"

He hesitates, as if deciding whether or not to answer. Then he simply nods.

I imagine rolling moors thick with purple tufts of heather, gray fingers of fog creeping through the ruins of medieval castles, charming little houses scaling the shores of a seaside cliff.

A big black wolf howling under a full moon.

Examining my expression with sharp eyes, he says, "Have you been to the old country?"

"No."

"If you like wild places, you should go."

I blurt, "I do love wild places. And wild things."

Holding my gaze, the wolf says softly, "Do you."

It isn't a question. He says it as if he's mulling it over. Considering what types of wild things I might particularly enjoy.

So of course, because I'm flustered, I start to babble.

"I meant I'm used to wild places. I'm from one. Little tiny town in Texas in the middle of nowhere where the sky is so blue it's blinding and the plains stretch out into forever and there's a million things that can kill you, from tornadoes to scorpions to venomous snakes to your half-blind, half-drunk hillbilly cousin who likes to practice target shooting in his backyard on Sunday after church when the family comes over for lunch and you're wearing the fake fur coat your granny got you for Christmas that has an unfortunate resemblance to a deer."

In the wake of that horrifying speech, all the little noises in the diner seem painfully loud. The rain on the roof sounds like a hail of bullets.

The wolf stares at me, rapt.

He's never seen such a train wreck before.

"Well," I say brightly. "I'll leave you to your coffee. Cheerio!"

Cheeks burning, I hurry back into the kitchen. Unfortunately, it's an open style format, so patrons can see straight through past the front counter to the grill and meal prep area beyond. I have to round the corner to the back where the big walk-in cooler is so I can cry in private.

Diego, the short order cook, sends me a questioning look as I sail past.

Carla finds me thirty seconds later, standing there whimpering with the coffee pot still clutched in my hand.

She says, "What are you doing?"

"Praying for a brain aneurysm. Unless that's painful, then I'll settle for some kind of natural disaster that will kill me quickly and leave a decent-looking corpse."

Carla thinks for a moment. "I'd say a flash flood, but you'd have a lot of bloating."

"Plus, drowning would be too scary. What's more peaceful than that?"

She purses her lips, thinking. "Maybe the building could collapse on top of you?"

I consider it. "Yeah, but then I'd be flattened. I can't look like a pancake when they pull me out of the rubble."

"What difference would it make what you'd look like? You'd be dead."

My sigh is heavy and hopeless. "The only thing my mother loves more than Dolly Parton are beauty pageants and Mary Kay cosmetics. If she saw her daughter looking like roadkill, even in death, it would be the end of her."

"You're exaggerating."

"You don't know my mother."

"And I'm counting myself lucky. Anyway, the guy on twelve wants a refill of his coffee."

"Why can't you give it to him?"

Carla looks at the carafe in my hand.

"Shit. Why doesn't Buddy buy another coffee machine for this dump?"

"Because they cost money. You know this. Now go refill twelve."

"I can't. I'm hiding."

"Why the hell are you hiding?"

"I know this is hard for you to understand because you don't have the kind of personality that can turn a sixty-second conversation into an exercise in personal humiliation, but I can't show my face in the dining room again until the big bad wolf leaves."

Carla scrunches up her nose. She already knows it's bad. "Oh no. What did you say to him?"

"Are you ready for this? *Cheerio.* Like I'm channeling my inner Julie Andrews."

"You didn't."

My laugh is full of dark despair. "Oh, yes, I sure did. And that was *after* I shared a witty anecdote about the time my cousin Bubba Joe shot me."

Carla stares at me in horror. "Please tell me you don't really have a cousin named Bubba Joe."

"Hand on the bible. I couldn't make this stuff up."

"Wow. My condolences. And he shot you?"

"I was fine, but that idiot peppered up the back of my fake fur with so much bird shot it looked like moths had gotten to it. By the way, thanks for being more shocked about his name than him shooting me. I appreciate the support."

"You'll live. Now go refill the guy on twelve. And try not to talk. I can't have you costing me my tip."

She turns and leaves, the heartless wench.

Squaring my shoulders, I promise myself I won't speak to the wolf again. My crippling social anxiety has humiliated me enough for one evening.

Life is unfairly hard for introverts. Something as common as interacting with another breathing human can knock us off kilter for days. In fact, I'm not sure socializing has even one tangible benefit. If I didn't have to work for a living, I'd never leave my apartment.

Unfortunately, I'm often mistaken for an extrovert because when I'm nervous, I chatter on and on. I can't count how many times I've had to duck into a bathroom stall and do deep breathing exercises to try to calm down.

I return to the dining room without looking in the wolf's direction. When I get to the bald guy at table twelve, he grunts his thanks around a mouthful of hash as I refill his coffee.

Then I feel a strange crackle over my skin. It's like a current of electricity, prickling hot and stinging. I glance up.

The wolf stares across the room at me as if he's got me in the sights of a gun.

Nervously tucking a strand of hair behind my ear, I hurry back to the counter and return the coffee carafe to the machine, then start wiping things down and tidying up. It's late, and there are only two customers—one of whom isn't eating—so there's not much for me to do except busy work as I wonder what the wolf's real name is, if he's married, and if this is the last time I'll ever see him.

He's probably on his phone right now trying to find a new place for coffee that employs mentally functioning waitresses.

After a moment, a deep voice from behind me says, "I was shot by a half-blind, half-drunk hillbilly once."

Startled, I jump and whirl around.

There he is, standing on the other side of the counter, dark and fierce and gorgeous, looking at me like nothing else exists in the diner. The city. The world.

"Except he wasn't a hillbilly. Or half-drunk." He pauses meaningfully. "Or half-blind, either."

His dark eyes transmit a warning I receive loud and clear: *I'm dangerous. Stay away.*

Too late. His hungry eyes and hypnotic voice have already

snared me. Despite my promise to myself, I have to know more. "So we've both been shot."

"Aye. It's an interesting thing to have in common, don't you think?"

As if I could think at the moment, what with his blistering masculinity wreaking havoc on my brain. But I'm pretty sure his question was rhetorical, so I stay quiet.

His gaze drops to my nametag. "Tru," he reads. "Is that short for something?"

I hesitate, but decide to go ahead and tell him the story. "It's short for Truvy. I was named after Dolly Parton's character in the movie *Steel Magnolias*. She ran a beauty parlor."

The wolf tilts his head, waiting for me to provide an explanation that might actually make sense.

He'll have to wait a long time for that.

"My mom's a huge Dolly fan. All her daughters are named after a character in one of Dolly's movies."

It sounds even worse out loud. My nerves get the best of me, and I start to babble.

"My oldest sister is Doralee, who was a sassy secretary in *Nine to Five*. Then there's Mona, the second oldest, who was named after the madam who ran a brothel called The Chicken Ranch in *The Best Little Whorehouse in Texas*. I would feel sorry for Mona about that, but honestly, she's a bit of a pill, very judgmental and self-righteous, so it serves her right to be named after a prostitute. Or maybe she's self-righteous and judgmental *because* she's named after a prostitute? I never thought of that.

"Anyway, then there's Louisa. She's another *Steel Magnolias* character, because that's my mother's all-time favorite movie. The name fits because the character was grouchy and short-tempered, and so is my sister.

"Finally, there's me. Truvy. The baby." I clear my throat. "I have four brothers, too, but my dad got to name them. Fortunately, he's not a Dolly fan."

As if everything I've just disclosed is completely normal, the wolf nods. "That's something else we have in common. I'm one of eight, too."

My self-consciousness disappears because I'm too busy being shocked. "You're kidding."

"My parents were Irish Catholic. Old school. For them, birth control was a mortal sin."

I say drily, "I wish my parents had a religious excuse. I'm pretty sure they were just too poor to afford birth control."

The wolf stares at me like I'm an alien. I'm sure I've said something wrong, until he says, "And that's number four."

Number four? What does that mean? "Um..."

"I come from a poor family. So do you. That's the fourth thing we have in common."

He seems disturbed by that fact. I don't blame him. Time to make a joke.

"If you tell me next that your favorite ice cream flavor is pistachio, we're probably destined to be together forever."

Dear God, those words actually just came out of my mouth.

As the devastatingly gorgeous man I just spoke that horrifying sentence to stares at me silently, I will the floor to open up and swallow me.

Alas, it doesn't. Time to salvage what's left of my self-respect.

"Well, it's been great chatting with you, but I should get back to work."

He studies me with unblinking intensity. Neither of us moves. We simply stare at each other.

Heat suffuses my cheeks.

A muscle flexes in his jaw.

I'm ninety percent certain he knows my nipples are hardening.

Finally, he moves. Never taking his gaze off my face, he reaches into his coat, pulls out his wallet, removes a few bills, and sets them down onto the counter. He closes the wallet and slips it back inside his coat pocket.

For a moment, he looks like he's trying to decide about something, his brow furrowed and his expression pensive. Then he exhales a slow breath.

"Are you working tomorrow night?"

I don't dare open my mouth again, so I simply nod.

The wolf nods, too. For some strange reason, it feels like we've made a date. When he turns and starts to walk away, I nearly slide to the floor in relief.

But then he turns around and pins me in one of his signature hungry stares.

In a low, husky voice, he says, "By the way, lass...my favorite ice cream flavor *is* pistachio."

He holds my gaze just long enough for me to have a heart attack, then he turns around and walks out, disappearing into the rainy night as if it swallowed him.

2

LIAM

*G*oddammit. Goddammit all to hell.

I knew I shouldn't have come here tonight. I promised myself I'd stay away this time. Meant it, too, until the wheels touched down on the tarmac at Logan and my resolve vanished as quick as two fingers snapping.

Just one more look, I reassured myself as I instructed Declan to make a detour from our planned route. One more chance to stare into those big green eyes and it'll be over. All I need is a final glimpse before I put this unhealthy obsession behind me once and for all.

And I actually believed it.

What a bloody fucking idiot I am.

From the warmth of the back seat of the Escalade, I stare through the window. Across the boulevard, beyond the rain and lanes of passing cars, the bright lights of Buddy's Diner shine out like beacons in the dark. She's there inside, talking to her co-worker the busty brunette, making her look like a pigeon standing next to a Picasso.

Tru.

The girl named after a character in a movie.

The shy beauty with the gentle Southern twang, eyes the color of sea glass, and a smile that could almost make a man like me believe in god.

"We're late, boss," says Declan quietly from the driver's seat.

"I know it."

If my voice is irritated, it's only because I'm mad at myself, not him.

Eleven months of denying myself something I want very badly has taken its toll on my temper.

I watch for a moment longer, wishing I had the talent to draw. I'd sketch her face a thousand ways. Try to capture the softness in her eyes when she looks up at me from under those long, dark lashes. The flash of heat as her gaze drifts to my mouth.

But my hands were made for things much more brutal than drawing pictures of a bashful, beautiful girl.

Do the right thing, Liam. Stay away from her. It's a stupid coincidence that you both come from big families and like pistachio ice cream. It doesn't mean anything that she likes wild places, too, and grew up in a tiny town, too, and looks at you like you're the most fascinating thing she's ever seen.

She's not for you.

Your life would devour her and leave nothing but bones.

I tear my gaze away from the window, drag my hand through my hair, and tell Declan to drive, and be quick about it.

The sooner I get away from here, the better.

3

TRU

*B*y the time I get home from work, it's after one a.m., it's raining harder than it was earlier, and I'm in such a state about what might happen when—if?—the wolf comes into the diner on my next shift that I need to pour myself a glass of wine to calm down.

Leaning against the kitchen counter and staring out into the rain, I picture him.

He's everything I'm not. Sophisticated. Interesting. Self-assured.

Older. Ten years at least, maybe fifteen.

I suppose it should strike me as odd that someone like him might take an interest in someone like me, but I get the feeling he's the kind of man who notices things other people don't.

He doesn't just look. He *sees*.

Maybe what he sees when he looks at me are the things I try so hard to hide from everyone else. All my restlessness and dark longings, all the chafing at my seams.

Or maybe that's just wishful thinking.

I'm finishing off my last swallow of cheap chardonnay when I hear the muffled sound of crying.

"Oh, sweetie," I say to the empty kitchen, sighing. "What did he do this time?"

Leaving the wine glass on the counter, I pad barefoot across the apartment and knock gently on my roommate's door. "Hey, Elliebellie. You need anything?"

There's some sniffling, then the sound of Ellie shuffling toward the door.

Opening up, she rubs a fist into a red and swollen eye. Her short black hair sticks up crazily all over the place. Her room smells like dirty socks and lost dreams. "I'm f-f-fine," she says, hiccupping. "I was just watching *A Dog's Purpose*. That fucking movie should have a trigger warning."

"I've never seen it. What's it about?"

"It's about this dog who keeps dying and getting reincarnated with all its memories of its previous lives and is trying over and over to find life's purpose, until finally he's reunited with his original owner who was a little boy when the dog was euthanized in his first incarnation, but now the boy is an old man, and at the end the dog narrates that the true meaning of life is finding that one person you're supposed to be with.

"How awful is that?" she wails. "Even a *fictional dog* can find true love!"

Ellie recently went through a bad breakup with her ex. It was their fourth—or tenth, I can't keep track. Every time they break up, she swears she's done with him. But within weeks they're back together and she's conveniently forgotten all the ways he hurt her before. All the indifference, all the lies, all the other girls he'd been running around with.

I'll never understand it.

When my ex cheated on me six months after we moved to Boston together, I threw all his clothes into a big pile in the middle of the sidewalk and lit the pile on fire.

I might be an introvert, but I've got a temper, and I hold a grudge like nobody's business.

But, as Ellie's friend, it's not my job to judge. "You want some ice cream? I picked up a pint on the way home."

"You're sweet," she says mournfully. "But I think I'm just gonna watch a rerun of Seinfeld and rub one out."

I grimace. "Thank you for over sharing. I'm scarred for life."

"Anyway, g'night."

She closes the door. I head straight for my own room before I can hear any battery-operated devices roar to life and lock myself in for the night.

It's raining again the next day, dumping on me as I run from my last class to the parking structure. My head stays dry, but that's about it. From the waist down, I'm soaked.

I throw the umbrella onto the back seat of my beat up Corolla, set my laptop and books on the passenger seat, dig my keys from my purse, and start the car. Though it's May, spring in Boston is unpredictable. There's been a nasty cold snap recently. I'm freezing my ass off, shivering like mad. The air conditioner never worked, but luckily the heater's a champ, blowing warm air onto my icy cheeks after only a few minutes.

I make a quick stop at the apartment to change into my uniform and grab a bite to eat, then I head out again, this time in galoshes, my heavy winter coat zipped all the way up to my chin.

When I walk through the door of Buddy's, Carla takes one look at me and starts to laugh.

"You look like you're going on an expedition to the Arctic."

I send her a withering scowl. "You're from here. Yankees have an unfair advantage in the cold."

"You've lived in Boston almost two years, kiddo. Your thin Southern blood should've thickened up by now."

"Yeah, yeah," I mutter, waving her off and wishing I'd had the good sense to apply to law school in Florida or California. I could have a tan and blonde highlights right now, instead of being soggy and frostbitten.

In the kitchen, Diego's at the grill, flipping a burger. He jerks his chin at me in a hello as I pass. His white teeth flash as he smiles. "You're almost late again, chica."

"I'm almost a lot of things, Diego."

His smile grows wider. "Almost in love with me?"

This is our ongoing joke. I actually think it's his ongoing joke with every female under seventy years old, but he gets away with flirting outrageously because otherwise he's gentle and sweet, not lecherous.

"Not quite yet, but I'll let you know if it happens."

"Ah, you're breaking my heart!" He clutches his chest dramatically, then flips the burger and starts to whistle, instantly forgetting about his pain.

He's hot in a way that creeps up on you. At first glance, he seems ordinary. Not tall or short, not stocky or thin, just an average, brown-haired, brown-eyed, twenty-something guy.

Then one day you'll notice he has a great smile. A few weeks later you'll realize that his ordinary brown eyes have quite the irresistible sparkle. Then at some point he'll surprise you by lifting something heavy and you'll notice the impressive flex of muscles underneath his white T-shirt.

That's when the whole picture becomes clear and you think, *Huh, he's cute.*

But then you dismiss that thought because you don't sleep with co-workers, and the last thing you need is another relationship distracting you from your own damn goals.

Goals, for instance, like graduating from the law school you can't afford but are killing yourself to complete so following your ex halfway across the country where he was starting his pre-med program wasn't a total waste of time.

In the employee break room, I stash my purse and coat in my locker and leave my dripping galoshes near the back door. I change into the comfy shoes I keep here and wind my hair into a messy low bun with an elastic, then tie a fresh white apron around the waist of my uniform.

It's the classic diner waitress dress, complete with short skirt, starched white collar, and white cuffs on the sleeves, but in black, instead of the typical pink or blue gingham.

So instead of looking like "kiss my grits" Flo from that old TV show *Alice*, I look like a hotel maid.

I think Carla makes twice the tips I do because of her big boobs and her willingness to lean over and stick 'em right in a guy's face when she leaves him the bill, but I do okay. Plus the owner, Buddy, is flexible with my school schedule and lets me have as much time off as I need.

The first few hours of my shift are busy. It's dinner time, and we have lots of regulars. By the time ten o'clock rolls around, however, the crowd has thinned. By eleven, there's only one guy sitting at the end of the counter, staring glumly into his coffee. By midnight, he's gone, too.

Then it's just me, Carla, Diego, and my growing certainty that I'll never see the wolf again.

I scared him off with my terrifying tales of rural Texas. He probably thinks my favorite hobbies include shooting at woodpeckers in my underwear, getting into fist fights at NASCAR races, and making beer runs to the convenience store with my pet goats riding in the back of my pickup truck.

Just when I've given up all hope, the bell over the front door jingles, and there he is.

The tall, dark, and handsome stranger who can unsettle me with a look and hasn't told me his name once in eleven months of coming here.

He stops a foot inside the door and stares at me, standing frozen behind the counter.

He makes no move to come closer or sit down. Dressed in his usual black suit and tie, his hair slicked back, his beautiful dark eyes burning as they drink me in, he looks like a supermodel assassin.

I'm gripped by an insane urge to run across the restaurant and throw myself into his arms.

Carla sails past with the coffee carafe in one hand and a mug in the other. Under her breath, she says, "*OwOooo!*"

My heart in need of a defibrillator, I watch breathlessly as Carla approaches the wolf. She says something to him, gesturing to a table in her section. Still staring at me, he shakes his head. She glances at me over her shoulder, grins, then turns back to him and says something else, too low for me to hear.

He glances back and forth between the two of us, hesitating, then licks his lips.

It's such a simple, mindless gesture, but so sexy I almost groan out loud.

Carla feels it, too. She rocks back on her heels. When she turns around and heads towards me, her jaw is slack and she has the glassy-eyed look of someone who's been hypnotized.

This time when she sails past me, her voice is unsteady. Her words come out in a breathy rush.

"I told him I'd send you over, my ovaries just exploded, great buckets of owl shit, I need to go lie down, that man is *fire*."

"Carla."

She stops and looks at me.

"Give me the coffee pot."

She looks down at it in her hand like she has no recollection of picking it up.

I know the feeling.

She thrusts it at me, along with the mug. Then she heads to the back, probably to lock herself into a stall in the ladies room for a vigorous session of self-pleasuring.

I can't blame her. I haven't even exchanged a word with him yet and my panties are already smoking.

Heat throbbing in my cheeks, I approach him, stopping a few

feel away and trying desperately not to glow with self-conscious-ness. "Hi."

"Hullo."

His voice is husky. His expression is somber. He looks like he's not entirely sure exchanging this simple greeting with me is a good idea.

But I've been examined under the gazes of enough men to know that whatever the cause of his ambivalence, however deep it might run, he'll stay and talk to me.

I know desire when I see it. He kept it in check before, but he's off leash now.

This wolf wants me.

More troublesome is that I want him, too, and I know I shouldn't. Wolves might mate for life, but they're still dangerous wild animals.

I'm as likely to get bitten as kissed.

I wordlessly gesture to the booth he normally sits in. He hesi-tates a moment longer, then runs a hand down the front of his suit jacket and sits. I pour coffee into his mug, feeling his gaze on me, feeling elated and nervous and a little bit scared.

"Can I get you anything else?"

His eyes flash. When he looks at my mouth and sinks his teeth into his lower lip, I almost topple over.

His voice low, he says, "I shouldn't be here."

I have no idea how to respond to that. "Um...okay?"

"I'm supposed to be on the other side of the city right now, taking care of business. Business I can't afford to put aside. Instead, I'm here. You understand?"

I'm about to say no, but I rethink it. A dangerous kind of adrenaline has begun to work its way through my blood, weaving magic in my veins, making me feel like anything is possible.

Making me bold.

My heart pounding, I look him in the eye and say quietly, "Yes. You have important things to do, but you came here to see me, even though you wish you didn't want to, and it's against your better judgment. For the record, I like you, too."

Jaw working, he stares at me in blistering silence.

I've surprised him. I like that I've surprised him. He doesn't seem like a man who's taken aback by much of anything.

"You don't have a man, then."

Wow. How he managed to make that sound like, "Bend over the table and lift up your skirt," I'll never know. Carla was right: the man *is* fire.

I clear my throat, shifting my weight from foot to foot, painfully aware of the flush of heat spreading down from my cheeks to my neck. "No. I'm single." I glance at his left hand, at his bare ring finger. "You?"

He says gruffly, "I don't...a relationship wouldn't...fit my lifestyle."

The boldness still flowing through me, I say tartly, "So you're only into one night stands?"

"No. I'm not into anything. I mean, I wasn't."

He stares hungrily at me. I hear the unspoken *Until you*, and the flesh on my arms rises in goose bumps.

I set the coffee pot on the table, slide into the booth across from him, fold my hands in my lap, and say, "I think now might be a good time to tell me your name. I can't keep calling you 'the wolf' in my head forever."

A faint smile lifts the corners of his mouth. I'm amusing him.

But instead of playing along, he issues a startling command. "Take your hair down."

I arch my brows. "Excuse me?"

"Your hair. Take it out of the bun."

Okay, so he's got the whole alpha male thing going on. He's probably used to issuing orders and having his minions peep in terror and scatter to do his bidding. Unfortunately for him, I'm just as stubborn as I am hot-tempered and grudge-holding.

The only orders I take are for food.

"First things first. Tell me your name. Then maybe we'll exchange phone numbers. Then maybe we'll go on a date. You don't really look like a guy who goes miniature golfing, so... dinner? Yes. Dinner. You'll take me somewhere nice, I'll laugh at all your jokes, we'll get to know each other. Then maybe at some point down the line after a few more dates, I'll take down my hair for you.

"But that's something you earn. I don't know what kind of women you're used to, but my mother didn't raise a worker bee. She raised a queen." I stare at him without smiling. "And I don't give away the honey for free."

He's silent for so long it gets uncomfortable. But then he leans over the table, threads his fingers together, and looks me in the eyes. His own are fierce and burning.

"And here I thought you were shy."

"I am," I say, nodding. "Especially with strangers. Tongue-tied and awkward, too. That doesn't mean I'm a pushover. I live most of my life in my head, but the knives come out when necessary."

The wolf stares at me. I have never, ever, been looked at with such intensity.

He says, "How old are you?"

"Twenty-four. How old are you?"

"Older than that."

"By how much?"

"Enough to know I shouldn't be doing this."

"Doing what? Having a conversation in a shitty diner in the middle of the night?"

He licks his lips again. I imagine a lion smacking his chops over a fresh kill. His gaze drifts leisurely over my face. His voice comes out thick.

"Indulging myself."

A little shiver goes through me. It's my body's acknowledgment that though this man I'm sitting across from is wearing a couture suit and a watch that could probably pay off my student loans, he's anything but civilized.

My pulse flying, I whisper, "Why are you, then?"

For a moment, he's all heat and hunger, so focused on me I think he's about to lunge across the table and eat me whole. Nothing else in the world exists, just me and him and this crackle of attraction electrifying the air between us. This weird little bubble of wanting and need.

He opens his mouth to say something...but stops.

His full lips tighten. His mouth takes on a ruthless slant. The warmth leaches from his eyes until he's staring back at me in flinty coldness. It's like watching a door slam closed.

He stands abruptly and stares down at me, his gaze flat and dark. "It was a pleasure to meet you, Tru. I hope you have a nice life."

Understanding that's a goodbye, I sag back against the booth and stare up at him for a moment in disbelief. Then I huff out a small laugh. "You, too. It's been real."

He takes one long, final look at my face before he turns around and walks out.

4

TRU

*A*s I rise from the table and make my way toward the counter, Diego watches from the kitchen with a frown. Before I get even halfway across the dining room, Carla rushes over.

The Spanish Inquisition begins.

"Holy shit, girl, what did he say to you? What did you say to him? What's his name? Did he tell you why he's been coming here so long without asking you out? Did you get his number? Did he get your number? Did you make a date? Why the hell aren't you saying anything, I'm dying here!"

I snort. "Oh, is it my turn to talk now?"

Following me as I walk, Carla pinches my arm. "Quit being ugly. *What did he say*?"

Back at the counter, I shove the coffee pot into the machine and wipe my hands on my apron. "Cliff Notes version—he said hi, I shouldn't be here, do you have a boyfriend, take down your hair, it's been nice knowing you, so long. Then he left."

She groans in exasperation. "Oh no. You talked about your family again, didn't you?"

"Not even a little bit. He ran away all on his own."

From the kitchen, Diego calls out, "Good riddance. That guy's bad news."

We ignore him. Looking puzzled, Carla says, "Wait—he asked you to take down your hair?"

"Yeah."

She eyeballs me. "And you *didn't*?"

"Of course not. I don't even know the man's name."

"Pfft. I don't know his name, either, but I'd still take down my hair for him if he asked. I'd take off all my clothes and lie down spread eagle in the middle of the dining room floor if he asked."

"Charming."

She shrugs. "Big Daddy's been slacking in the bedroom department, if you know what I mean. My lady garden hasn't been fertilized in forever."

Big Daddy is Carla's nickname for her husband, Dave. I'm not sure if it's a real daddy sex fetish thing, or if she just enjoys watching people squirm when she says it, but I am sure I'm not going to ask.

They're an attractive couple, but I don't need to be haunted by details of my friends' sex lives. My imagination is vivid enough without visual aids. My best friend in high school once mentioned her mother was a screamer, and I could never look the woman in the eye again.

I start a fresh pot of coffee, actively ignoring Carla as she launches into a gripe fest about her sexual dry spell. Eventually, she gets bored with my inattention and wanders away to help the elderly couple who drifted in while she was busy cross-examining me about the wolf.

"Chica."

I look up to find Diego standing on the other side of the counter. He's leaning with his arms on the stainless steel shelf where he puts the plates when they're ready to be served, looking at me with concern in his eyes.

"I don't like that guy."

"Carla's husband?"

"No, knucklehead. That *vato* in black who just left."

I'm about to tell him he doesn't have to worry about it because we'll never be seeing him again, but curiosity gets the best of me. "Why not?"

He shakes his head. "I know guys like him."

I wait, but he doesn't add more. "I see. Thanks for that detailed explanation. That helps a lot."

Sighing, he pushes off the shelf. Then he folds his arms over his chest and gives me a sour look.

"Fine. You wanna know? I'll tell you. I wasn't always this good boy you see now. In the barrio where I grew up, they called me a *matón. El pandillero.*"

I say drily, "How fascinating. If I spoke Spanish, I'm sure I'd be very impressed."

Diego's gaze grows serious. "It means thug, Tru. Troublemaker."

Thug. I think of the tattoos on the wolf's knuckles, and that shiver of recognition passes through me again.

But that's silly. Tattoos being something only for thugs is an outdated prejudice. These days, it's more likely a guy with lots of tats is a chef at a trendy restaurant who makes a heavenly short rib poutine served with a side of truffle mac and cheese.

Also, I don't see a single tattoo on Diego, who just claimed to be a former thug himself.

"You haven't ever spoken a word to the man, Diego. It's not fair to make a judgment on his character."

"Fair's got nothing to do with it. A shark can always smell another shark, no matter how far apart they're swimming in the ocean."

I smile at him. "So you're a shark now."

He grins. "Great white, baby. You in love with me yet?"

"Any minute."

"Okay, you let me know." He turns back to the grill, calling out over his shoulder. "By the way, could you take out the trash in the lounge bathroom? There's a bunch of Carla's girl stuff in there. I don't wanna touch it."

I know by "girl stuff" he means tampons. If Buddy would ever buy a trashcan with a lid on it for the employee restroom, Diego wouldn't have to be traumatized by these kinds of things, but here we are.

"Will do."

"Thanks."

I head to the tiny break room in back, which we ironically call "the VIP lounge." Four hideous plastic lawn chairs surround a folding card table. An ancient microwave sits atop a rickety TV stand. There's a college-dorm-sized refrigerator in one corner, a cracked mirror on the wall, and a water cooler that constantly leaks standing next to the row of battered lockers.

The walls are painted the ugliest shade of yellow you can imagine. It's like being inside the apartment of a three-pack-a-day smoker who hasn't left the place in forty years.

I use the restroom, wash my hands, and take the plastic bag out of the trashcan. I tie the ends into a knot and replace it with a new bag, then head to the larger aluminum garbage bins stacked along the wall in the corridor leading to the alley behind Buddy's where the big Dumpsters are kept.

When I get to the corridor, it's a mess.

Reeking bags full of trash and food scraps are stacked all around the aluminum bins, which themselves are full to overflowing. Keeping this area clean is the job of the dishwasher, but he quit a few days ago and hasn't yet been replaced.

"Great," I mutter.

Diego has been taking care of the dish situation while Buddy tries to find a new dishwasher, but he obviously thinks trash duty is beneath him.

It's not beneath me. Growing up, I was responsible for

mucking out the horse stalls and pig pens on the homestead. I'm no stranger to smelly, gross chores.

I go back into the lounge, put on my heavy coat and galoshes, then head to the corridor again. Propping open the door to the alley, I grab two of the bags on the floor and go outside.

The heavy rain has tapered off to a lighter, but steady, drizzle. The Dumpster is only a few feet away from the door, so I only have to walk several short steps to get to it. Unfortunately, the top is closed. It's a heavy metal hinged flap that has to be lifted and held open long enough to shove a trash bag through.

I drop the bags on the ground next to the Dumpster and throw the lid up and back, toward the building. My push is hard enough that the lid flies all the way up. It comes to rest against the wall with a clatter.

I toss the two bags in, then trudge back inside to get two more. Then I do it again, determined to at least make a dent in the mess before I get too cold and wet to continue.

On my fourth trip, someone grabs me from behind.

I'm yanked so violently away from the Dumpster that I lose my balance. I stagger back and crash into a solid form—a chest. When I scream, an arm clamps around my throat. The tip of something ice cold and sharp jabs into the soft hollow beneath my jaw.

"Scream again and I'll cut out your fuckin' tongue."

The voice is low, male, and deadly serious.

I stiffen in terror. Instinctively, I grab the arm clamped around my throat. It's covered by a jacket made of a thin layer of nylon, through which I feel sinews and muscle, hard as stone.

My pulse crashes so loud in my ears it drowns out the patter of rain and the distant sounds of traffic. Gasping in fear, I start to shake.

Don't panic don't panic oh god he's going to kill me I'm going to die.

Two more men emerge from the shadows on the far side of the Dumpster. Their heads are covered by hoodies, so I can't see their faces in the dark, but they're both broad and hulking, and both carry guns in their hands.

When I whimper in fear, the one behind me gives me a hard shake, so hard my teeth clatter.

"Here's what's gonna happen," he hisses into my ear. "We're gonna go inside. You're gonna show us where the safe is and give us the combo. Then we're gonna take whatever's in the register, and we'll be on our way. Do as I say and nobody gets hurt. Got it?"

He has a heavy Boston accent. His breath is hot against my cheek, steaming white in the frigid night air. He sounds young and feels very strong, and I know in my bones that if I do anything he doesn't like, he won't hesitate to slit my throat.

There's only one problem: Buddy's doesn't have a safe.

Buddy's wife comes every day at four to take cash from the register, then goes straight to the bank. Our credit card machine deposits charges automatically to the account. These guys would be better off hitting a Laundromat if they want easy cash.

But he's already pushing me toward the open door.

"There's no safe!" My voice is high and panicked. My fingers claw at his arm. "Only the register has cash, and there's not much in it!"

"Don't you fuckin' lie to me, bitch," he snarls into my ear, shaking me again. "I know that old prick has a safe in his office. Heard him braggin' about it myself."

My mind flies at a million miles per hour. I can't think straight, can't scream, can't run. Something warm and wet trickles in a wavering path down my throat.

Blood.

I'm bleeding.

This asshole cut me.

Something in my brain snaps. Terror turns to rage. The rage incinerates the fear and takes my brain hostage so all thoughts of cooperation vanish, leaving me a snarling animal operating on instinct alone.

I turn my head and bite down as hard as I can into the crook of his bent elbow, clamping my jaw and digging my teeth through that thin layer of nylon right into his soft, unprotected flesh.

He jerks and howls, staggering back a step. Before he can recover from the surprise, I move my hips to one side and swing my arm back as hard as I can, driving my closed fist directly into his balls.

He grunts in pain, bends forward, and drops the knife.

I twist away from him, leaping out of his grasp. Then I bolt.

My heart hammers against my ribcage as I run as fast as I can down the alley, pumping my legs and arms and gulping air like I'm drowning.

I make it almost to the street before they catch me again.

This time I'm grabbed by the hair, so hard it lifts me off my feet. I'm airborne for a moment, then my back and head slam against wet cement. All my breath is knocked out of me.

Gasping, I roll to one side to try to get my feet back under me, but am stopped by a hard kick to my stomach.

Then another to my face.

I collapse onto my side again. Coughing and wheezing, fighting the urge to vomit, I curl into a protective ball. The concrete is wet against my cheek. Everything looks watery and wavering. There's a high pitched ringing in my ears.

Get away. Get away. Hurry up and get to your feet and GET AWAY!

They drag me back farther into the alley and throw me up against the wall. The one I bit, who seems to be the leader, crouches down next to me and grabs my jaw.

"We got ourselves a fighter, boys." He sneers, fingers digging into my face.

One of the others snickers and rubs the heel of his palm against his crotch. "That could be fun."

All three of them laugh. Low, nasty chuckles that spread like a virus through my veins.

It seems they might be in the mood for a little playtime before they go back to Buddy's to get what they came for.

My lip throbbing, my eye beginning to swell, my liver screaming from the kick it took, I look up into the face of the guy bending over me.

He's got a hoodie on, too, but this close I can see his blue eyes glinting, see his crooked nose and his crooked grin and the trail of inked teardrops beneath his left eye.

I know what those teardrops mean, and it's not that he's prone to weeping.

I say hoarsely, "My name's Tru. Remember that. It'll come back to haunt you."

He scoffs. "Aw, you gonna sic your hound dog on me, Alabama?"

I answer him through gritted teeth. "No, because I'm gonna kick your ass when I see you in hell. And it's *Texas*, you inbred idiot."

With the last of my strength, I punch him in his Adam's apple.

His head snaps back. He makes a loud gagging noise, falls back onto his ass, and grabs his throat, coughing.

His companions are stunned for all of about two seconds, until one of them says angrily, "What the *fuck*?"

He delivers another savage kick to my stomach, then lifts his arm and points his gun at my face.

I throw my hand up instinctively and close my eyes, my whole body clenched as it waits for the loud crack of gunfire.

It doesn't come.

Instead, I hear a startled yelp, the dull thud of fists hitting flesh, then a cartoonish series of grunts and groans. There's some scuffling and angry cursing. Something big hits the side of the Dumpster with a loud metallic clang—then the sickening sound of bones crunching echoes down the alley, along with a piercing cry of agony. More thuds, more grunts, a heavy groan, then it falls quiet.

I lift my head and look around, squinting to see through the shadows.

When I can focus, I see two men lying unmoving on their backs on the ground a few feet away from me, eyes closed, bloody faces upturned to the rain.

Standing over them is a man dressed all in black like an undertaker. He stares at me with no expression. His empty hands hang loosely by his sides.

It's the wolf.

Movement from behind him distracts me. The one who put a knife to my throat is trying to scramble to his feet. His eyes roll wildly as he staggers and coughs. He spots one of the guns his companions carried lying a few feet away on the ground and lunges for it.

He doesn't make it.

The wolf spins around, grabs the robber's head, and gives it a hard, violent twist to one side. He slides to his knees, topples to his side, then lies still.

I know by the sickening *snap* his neck made that the knife-wielding robber who called me Alabama won't ever be calling me that again.

The rain falls harder. Somewhere off in the distance thunder booms. Jagged white fingers of lightning crackle through the night sky.

The wolf kneels down next to me and gently touches my face. Looking me over, he curses.

"How badly are you hurt? Talk to me, lass. Can you stand?"

His voice is low and urgent. His eyes blaze with fury. His face is shadowed in the hollows, dark hair dripping water from the ends.

He looks beautiful and terrifying, like an avenging angel coming to lay waste to the entire world.

I try to speak, but the sound that comes out isn't a word. It almost doesn't sound human.

He whips his cell phone from his suit pocket, jabs at it, puts it to his ear. He tells the operator he needs an ambulance and gives the address.

The last thing I see before I pass out is him staring down at me, his big rough hand cradling my face.

5

TRU

I wake up in a hospital bed with a needle in the back of my hand and a pleasant fuzziness in my head. Sunlight streams through the windows. Birds chirp in the trees outside.

I have no idea what's happening.

Pain pokes vaguely at the edges of my awareness, but it's being held in check by whatever wonderful mix of meds are flowing through my veins, courtesy of the needle. It's attached by a line to a clear plastic bag of liquid hanging from a metal stand. A beeping machine nearby displays a variety of nonsensical readings in cheerful yellow numbers.

Snatches of memory drift by like clouds: Sirens. Rainfall. The ride to the hospital in an ambulance going much too fast, judging by all the uncontrolled swerving.

The wolf on the seat opposite my cot, gazing at me in stone-faced silence.

His hand gripping mine.

I must've gone in and out of consciousness, because I have no recollection of how I came to be in this room or this bed. I have impressions of people as they leaned over me, faces blurry, lips moving without sound, and of being wheeled to different rooms, the seams of the ceiling tiles passing by overhead like lines on a freeway. There must have been tests, X-rays or such, but I don't remember those, either.

What I remember most clearly is believing I was about to die —horribly, painfully—but I didn't.

My big bad wolf saved me.

It's a testament to just how hopped up I am on pain medication that the thought makes me smile.

"You're awake."

The low voice comes from my right. When I turn my head in that direction, the wolf rises from a chair next to my bed. Tall and imposing, he stands looking down at me, his eyes dark and unreadable, his black suit and tie unwrinkled, not a hair out of place.

The only evidence of last night's carnage is the single telltale spot of red on his starched white dress shirt collar and the bruising on the knuckles of his right hand.

When I moisten my lips, he grabs a cup from the nightstand beside the chair and holds the bent straw to my mouth so I can drink. I sip, cool water sliding over my tongue and down my throat, gazing up at him as I swallow.

He watches me with perfect focus. The slightest tension tightens the corners of his mouth.

Finished with the water, I relax back against the pillows and blink lazily at him, trying to determine if my lack of fear for this dangerous man looking at me with such grave intensity is courage or stupidity.

I decide it's stupidity. My hormones have taken control of my brain. If he looked like a troll, I'd already be screaming for security.

I say, "I bet that helps in your line of work."

His dark brows draw together. "What's that?"

"Being so hot and inscrutable. It distracts people. Catches

them off guard. Are you going to tell me your name now that you've saved my life, or should I just assume The Batman is real and you're some billionaire with a fetish for latex suits and macho technology who roams the streets at night fighting crime?"

He stares at me in silence.

I sigh. "Okay. Bruce Wayne it is. Though I gotta tell you, you don't look much like a Bruce to me. I would've pegged you more as an Apollo or something."

"Apollo is a Greek name."

"Oh. Right. Not exactly Irish."

He adds, "It means 'destroyer.'"

"So there you go! Is there an Irish name for destroyer? What does Connor mean? I always thought that sounded like a hot badass name. Are you an assassin?"

He gazes at me pensively for a moment, then touches my forehead with the backs of his fingers.

"I'm not delirious," I say, enjoying the feel of him touching me way too much. "I'm a little loopy from whatever they're pumping into me from that bag, but my brain is mostly working. Like ninety percent. Okay, probably more like fifty percent, but my point is that I'd really like to know your name and also what you do for a living because I'm thinking both of those are important details for this relationship going forward."

He turns his hand over and trails his fingertips slowly down my temple and over my cheekbone, pausing to caress my jaw with his thumb.

His voice thoughtful, he says, "We're not going to have a relationship."

I smile at him. "You're silly."

His expression is a combination of frustration, irritation, and helpless intrigue. I'm charming him, and he doesn't like it.

"I told you I don't do relationships."

"Yes, and you also sat in my section for almost a year staring at me, and tried to tell me goodbye but then saved my life, and admitted your favorite ice cream flavor was pistachio, too, *after* I said that really embarrassing thing about how if it was, it was a sign that we were meant to be together forever. So I feel like all that sort of voided your ban on relationships. Tell me I'm wrong."

His lashes lower. He stares at me with heated eyes and a clenched jaw, slowly exhaling through flared nostrils.

Hot *damn*, the man knows how to smolder.

Two policemen in uniform enter the room. They see the wolf standing at my beside, stop short, and glance at each other. The older one looks back at the wolf and nods respectfully, clearing his throat.

"Liam."

"John."

"I didn't realize, uh..." The cop looks at me.

"Yes," says the wolf, who's name apparently is Liam.

Liam. Lee-YUM. Wow, this pain medication is powerful.

Nodding again, the older cop says, "Gotcha. Well. We'll be outside if you need us."

"Thank you, John."

They retreat, leaving my brain pinwheeling. Who *is* this guy?

Before I can ask any more questions, a doctor sweeps in, nose in the air, all self-important and snooty in his blue scrubs and white coat. He stops short like the cops did, looking Liam up and down suspiciously.

He says, "Are you family?"

"I'm Liam Black."

The doctor's lips part. His eyes widen. He clasps the clipboard he's carrying to his chest like a shield and swallows, hard.

"What's the prognosis?" says Liam.

It sounds like *It better be good news or you're dead.*

When the doctor pales, I giggle. Liam rests his hand on my shoulder and gently squeezes. I fight the urge to nuzzle it and look at the doctor instead.

He's nervously licking his lips. "Yes. The prognosis. Ah..." He consults the clipboard. "There's no GI bleeding or other internal injury. The CT scan showed no bleeding on the brain. Her ribs are bruised, but not broken, and the cartilage is intact."

He looks up, ignoring me, and speaks directly to Liam. "A few days of bed rest, a week or so of limited activity, then she'll be as good as new. She's a very lucky girl."

"And the swelling?"

"Swelling?" I repeat, anxiety pricking through my cottony bubble.

The doctor finally realizes I'm in the room. He gives me a cursory once over, then turns his attention back to Liam. "It should resolve in a week to ten days. The bruising, too. Ice will speed the healing process."

"When will she be discharged?"

"I'll get the paperwork ready now. Should be less than twenty minutes."

"I think she should be kept another night for observation."

Too intimidated to argue, the doctor nods. "Yes. She should be kept another night for observation."

"When she is discharged, we'll need some pain medication to take home."

We? Home? This is getting interesting.

"Tylenol should be enough to manage the—"

"Opioids," cuts in Liam, staring hard at him.

The doctor blanches. "I'll make sure you have everything you need."

"Thank you."

Realizing he's been dismissed, the doctor turns and leaves, shoulders slumped in relief.

When Liam turns his attention back to me, I say, "Is your last name really Black, or is that just a nod to your favorite color? Inquiring minds and all."

For the first time since I've known him, something resembling a real smile curves his lips. It softens the severity of his face, giving me a glimpse of a different person, one who knows how to laugh and be happy and knows nothing at all about the various ways to maim a man.

The exact amount of torque it takes to snap a neck.

He murmurs, "I can't believe I thought you were shy. I'm usually such a good judge of character."

I like it that his voice changes when he speaks to me. It lowers. Softens. Becomes warmer and more intimate, as if we're lying in bed together side by side and he's trailing his fingers over my naked skin.

"I *am* shy. I told you that. I'm very awkward with strangers."

"I'm a stranger."

"Not anymore."

Something about that response dissatisfies him. His smile vanishes. He leans over me, planting his hands on the mattress on either side of my pillow.

He looks dangerous now. Dangerous and beautiful, all clenched jaw and burning eyes, his nose inches from mine. His voice stays soft, though, so I know he isn't angry.

"Don't mistake me for something I'm not, Tru."

"Like what?"

"A good man."

I get the feeling he wants to scare me, but he doesn't. Even if I wanted to be afraid of him, I'm not. I stare up into his burning eyes and say softly, "You saved my life."

"That doesn't make me good." His gaze drops to my mouth, and his voice grows rough. "I did it for selfish reasons."

When he looks into my eyes again, he lets me see everything. All the need, all the want, all the dark desire.

It sends a thrill straight through me, like nothing I've ever known.

I whisper, "So you're not an assassin, then. They're supposed to be incognito, right? But the cops know you. My doctor did, too.

You nearly scared the shit out of the poor guy. Maybe you really are The Batman."

Liam does another of his slow, aggravated exhales, staring at me without blinking.

He smells good, like soap and cigars and testosterone, like a midnight walk in the woods. Without thinking, I reach up and touch his face. His beard is rough and springy under my fingertips.

"You're beautiful, wolfie. Has anyone ever told you that?"

In a husky whisper, he says, "You should stop talking now."

"I've recently had a brush with death, and I'm high on pain meds. I get a pass."

When I trail my fingers across his jaw and brush his lips, he stiffens. He goes so still, I don't think he's even breathing. He looks as if he's about to bolt out of the room.

"Wait," I say, gazing at him in wonder. "This is backward. I should be afraid of you, but instead..."

"I'm not afraid *of* you," he says, his dark eyes turning coal black. "I'm afraid *for* you. For all the ways I should scare you but don't." His voice drops. "For everything I want from you that I think you just might give me if I asked, though you'd dearly regret if you did."

We stare into each other's eyes as the heartbeat monitor next to the bed goes crazy.

His phone rings, breaking the spell.

With a low oath, he reaches up and switches off the squealing monitor. Then he straightens, turns away from me, walks to the window, and pulls his cell from his suit pocket.

"Declan." He listens for a moment. "Can't be helped." Another pause. "Priorities have changed. He can wait."

He hangs up, slips the phone back into his suit pocket, folds his arms over his chest, and stares silently out the window, his shoulders tense.

"I'm making you late for something."

He turns his head at the sound of my voice. After a moment, he says, "Aye."

"You should go. I don't want to get you in trouble."

For some reason, that amuses him. He looks at me over his shoulder, dark eyes sparkling with mirth. "Get me in trouble," he murmurs. He chuckles, like I've said something really funny.

I'm distracted by how much I like the sound of that deep, amused chuckle, until I think of the two policemen who came into my room. Then a little chill goes through me.

"Those guys, last night...I'll have to give a police report. The cops will want to know what—"

"It's taken care of," he interrupts, turning around.

I squint at him. The sunlight streaming through the window behind him creates a halo of glimmering gold around his head. My medicated brain suggests this is what people see right before they die, when the angel of death comes to collect them.

"Taken care of?"

He steps closer, reaching out to caress my face, but quickly withdraws his hand, frowning as if irritated with himself for doing it.

"You don't have to talk to the police." He pauses. "Unless you want to."

I examine his face. "I take it they already know what happened."

He tilts his head, a motion both affirmative and dismissive. I can't concentrate enough at the moment to parse all the particulars of his relationship with local law enforcement, so I try to focus on my own problems.

Which, at the moment, are many.

"I've got to call my boss, let him know I'm going to miss my shift."

"He knows you're going to need some time off. It's not a problem."

I blink rapidly several times, as if it might help me understand what's happening. "You talked to Buddy?"

The head tilt again. Casual, like he's got everyone in the city on speed dial and whatever he wants of them, the answer is always yes.

"Who *are* you?"

His eyes soften. He wrestles with himself in silence for a long time, until finally he says, "Apparently, your wolf."

My wolf. My deadly protector, dark knight in Armani armor ripping to shreds those who dare to harm me.

I wonder what the Grimm brothers would have to say about him. He's way more interesting than that grandma-gobbler they created for Little Red.

A wave of fatigue passes through me, settling like a ten-pound weight on my chest. I close my eyes and yawn, fighting it. I don't want to fall asleep yet. I want him to talk to me, to answer all my questions and look at me with those searching dark eyes and smile at me again, even though he doesn't want to.

Don't leave, wolfie. Watch over me while I sleep.

I didn't realize I'd said that aloud until he murmurs, "I'm not leaving."

Feather light, his lips brush my forehead. Or is that my imagination?

I don't have time to decide before sleep pulls me close into its arms and I surrender.

6

TRU

I dream I'm running through a dense forest at night. Moonlight streams down through the boughs of tall trees, dappling the forest floor ghostly white between patches of dark undergrowth. Massive roots twist through piles of fallen leaves that I kick up as I run, my hair flying out behind me, my heart pumping hard in my chest.

Howls come from all around, rising up to the canopy in eerie echoes through the cold evening air.

All is silent except the howls, the sound of my labored breath, the thud of my feet pounding against the earth, and the dry crunch of dead leaves. I'm naked but unashamed, my body more comfortable than if constrained by clothing, my mind as free as the wind.

I'm trying to catch up with the big, dark animal loping through the trees far ahead of me.

It turns its head, looking back with eyes that flash quicksilver through the shadows. It bares sharp white teeth in a wolfish grin, then lowers its big muzzle near to the ground and lunges forward, sprinting away, leaving me calling out in frustration as it disappears into the darkness.

I awaken with a gasp and jerk up in bed, wincing at the pain that shoots through my body from the movement.

"Bad dreams?"

Liam sits calmly in the chair beside my bed with a book in his hands, one leg crossed over the other, so handsome he can't be real.

I swallow, wanting my heart to stop being a jackhammer. "No. In fact, I was dreaming of you."

He gazes at me steadily. Very softly, he says, "A nightmare, then."

It's evening now: beyond the window, all the world is dark. The lights in the room have been dimmed, too, and the noisy buzz of the daytime hospital has turned to a hush.

Either Liam left while I was asleep or someone brought him new clothing, because the telltale red dot on his shirt collar is gone.

"Do you always wear a suit and tie?"

His lips quirk. I think he enjoys my random changes in conversation. Not that he'd ever admit it.

"I'm only asking because your crime fighting would probably be a lot more comfortable if you invested in a pair of sweats."

He snaps shut the book and gives me a stern look. "Do I seem like the sort of man who would wear sweats?"

The answer is so obvious, I don't even bother with it. "But what about the tie? Doesn't that get annoying?"

"No."

"What about at home? You can't sleep in that suit. What do you wear to bed?"

Holding my gaze, he says, "Nothing."

Holy shit. Inside my body, muscles I didn't even realize I own have clenched.

He sets the book on the nightstand and folds his hands in his lap, resigned to the fact that I'm going to start grilling him about his wardrobe. But I don't want to be predictable, so I change the subject instead.

"What were you reading?"

"Proust."

I think for a minute. "I know that's a person, but that's about it."

He silently hands me the book. The cover is worn. Inside, the pages are yellowed, and many of them are dog-eared. I lift it to my nose and sniff, flipping through the pages to get that good book smell. Then I turn to the front and look at the title page.

It's in French.

"It's called *In Search of Lost Time*," says Liam.

"What's it about?"

His pause is reflective. "Life. Death. Love."

"Hmm. So nothing too deep."

He presses his lips together. I get the distinct impression he's trying not to laugh.

"That's the fourth volume of seven."

"*Seven*?" I stare at the book with new respect. "That's a bit intimidating."

"It's only six in the English translation, if that makes you feel better."

I scoff. "Oh, much. I'm going to run right out and buy them as soon as I get out of this backless gown." I set the book onto the nightstand, then look at him again. "Speaking of which, I want to go home now."

His face darkens, losing all the amusement of moments before.

"Hospitals remind me of suffering," I say softly.

When his eyes sharpen, I look away, swallowing. "Long story. Anyway. I want to go home."

Silence takes the room. I feel him looking at me, feel his keen inspection of my face, but I don't give him my eyes because I know how clearly he sees things.

He says suddenly, "When I take you home, that will be the end of it. Understood?"

By "it" he means "us." Not that there is an us, but he's obviously determined it's not even an option.

I don't want to feel hurt by that, but I do. I don't want to be so intrigued by this dangerous stranger, but I am. I know in my heart there isn't a future with him, that I'm better off staying far, far away...but he's a puzzle I've been trying to solve for so long, it's disappointing to walk away when the pieces are finally starting to come together.

"Tru. Look at me."

Instead of obeying him, I look down at my hands, almost as pale as the scratchy cotton sheets they're resting on.

I need a manicure. What a strange thing to notice at a time like this.

"Tru."

"I heard you. You don't want to see me again."

"That's not what I said. Look at me."

His voice is too seductive to ignore for long. When I glance at him, he's sitting forward in the chair with his forearms resting on his knees, hands clasped, staring at me with that blistering intensity of his.

"I wouldn't be good for you," he says, his tone soft. "I don't lead a normal life."

He means he's not domesticated, as if it isn't obvious. He only wears those beautiful suits to distract people from the vicious fangs and claws.

I say crossly, "I'm aware. Did you think I missed the part where you smashed two guy's faces in and snapped another one's neck like a twig?"

A muscle flexes in his jaw. "So we're in agreement."

Parroting him so he'll discover just how irritating it is, I say, "That's not what I said." When he narrows his eyes, I feel vindicated. "But while we're on the subject..." I lower my voice. "Did you...are all three of those guys...you know."

His answer is matter-of-fact. "Aye."

I try to work up an appropriate emotional response to his casual admission that he killed three men right in front of me, the logical horror or shock that should be forthcoming, but all I produce is curiosity, which even in my injured state I know is all wrong.

"With your hands."

He does his impression of a sphinx and stares at me, his gaze turning from blistering to coolly impenetrable. The man has perfected being enigmatic to an art.

Hoping he'll give me some clue as to how he came to be proficient in the ass-beating, neck-snapping, and life-ending sciences, I prompt, "I mean, you didn't even need to use a gun."

"I hate guns," he says instantly, his voice hard. "And stop sounding so impressed."

"Sorry, but I am. I can't even twist the top off a pickle jar without help."

He exhales slowly, like he's fighting dueling urges to jump up and shake some sense into me or kiss me raw.

I study him for a moment, all his tension and iron self-control, the way he seems to have a chokehold on the chain that's wound around his own neck. But underneath the careful control lurks resignation.

He looks like the conductor of a freight train traveling at full speed who's realized the brakes are gone and the bridge ahead has collapsed and there's not enough time to jump to safety.

"Question, Mr. Black: why are you trying so hard to stay away from me?"

"I told you. I wouldn't be good for you."

"Yet here you are. Again. Giving the suggestion of major ambivalence."

His expression sours. "Argumentative little thing, aren't you?"

"I'm studying to be an attorney. This is good practice." To prove it, I continue the argument. "Even more than a man who doesn't seem like he wears sweats, you don't seem like a man who lies to himself."

His voice turns hard. "Wanting you and taking you are two different things."

Taking you. The implications leave me breathless.

But after the breathlessness, the practical side of me buts in for a public service announcement that no matter how thirsty a horse he might be, I can't make him drink. If he's determined that this strange, intoxicating chemistry between us is a no-go, so be it.

I don't chase after men. It's undignified.

Plus, at some future point when the pain meds and probable PTSD have worn off, I might find that horror over him killing a trio of men that is now so mysteriously missing.

I turn my attention back to the scratchy sheets and say quietly, "Give me a minute to get dressed, please."

"Dressed?"

"I told you. I want to go home."

"I think you should stay here until tomorrow."

His tone is firm, but he's not the boss of me. I don't care that everyone else kowtows to him. I won't.

"It's not your decision."

Silence reigns for a long, uncomfortable moment. I wonder when the last time was that someone defied him, if ever.

Finally, he stands, buttoning his jacket. "Good for you."

He doesn't look back as he walks from the room, closing the door behind him.

Sighing heavily, I consider the needle stuck into the back of my hand. The skin around it is black and blue, and sore when I touch it. I gingerly peel off the tape holding the plastic tubing to the catheter and take a deep breath.

On a count of three, I yank the needle out.

A little pinch, a drop of blood welling up, and it's done. I toss the catheter aside and swing my legs over the side of the bed.

When I stand, it's with a low groan. Waves of pain radiate from my ribs where I was kicked, a stabbing feeling I have to grit my teeth against. The worst of it passes in a moment, and the pain settles into a dull but manageable throb. I shuffle across the cold linoleum floor to the wardrobe next to the bathroom, which is where I assume my clothes are.

When I pull open the wardrobe doors, I'm shocked to find my favorite jeans hanging there, along with my black wool coat and a black cashmere sweater I usually only wear on nice occasions. A pair of my boots are there, too, low-heeled black leather ones, along with my socks and underwear hanging from another hanger in a clear plastic bag.

The clothing I was wearing when I was attacked in the alley is nowhere to be seen.

"Interesting," I say aloud, eyeing my things.

The wolf has been to my apartment. Did Ellie let him in or did he huff and puff and blow the door down?

Or maybe he called her and had her bring my clothes here? But how would he have gotten her phone number? And if she came here, wouldn't she have stayed until I woke up?

I decide to let those questions simmer on the backburner while I attend to the more important matter of using the toilet. I'll find out the particulars later, but right now, my bladder is about to burst.

When I flick on the bathroom light and get a glimpse of myself in the mirror, I wish I'd just gotten dressed and left instead.

The left side of my face is covered in ugly purple and black splotches in the shape of boot tread. My left eye is swollen. My lower lip is split. My hair is a rat's nest of tangles, and my eyes are so bloodshot I look like I've just woken up from a bachelorette party in Vegas with no memory of how I got that huge Elvis tattoo.

I understand now why Liam thought I should stay in the hospital.

I use the toilet, wash my hands, brush my teeth with the travel brush and toothpaste set someone left on the sink, and attempt to make sense of the hysteria of my hair by running my fingers through it and patting it down. It doesn't work. So I give up and get dressed, moving gingerly because my body is doing its best to make sure I remember the trauma it recently suffered.

Though it's my mind I should be worried about.

I saw three men die mere feet away from me in that alley, yet I have a curious absence of emotion over that.

Granted, I didn't like them much.

Also, I grew up on a farm with lots of livestock who regularly became my dinner, so I'm no stranger to the ways blood can be spilled. How everyday life is underscored by a soundtrack of violence.

But still. I should feel something. Remorse or revulsion, disgust or disbelief. *Something.*

Something other than this secret sense of satisfaction.

When I open the door to my room, I'm greeted by the sight of Liam deep in conversation with the two police officers who came in earlier. Standing about fifteen feet away in front of the nurses' station, they don't notice me, which affords me the perfect opportunity to observe the Liam Effect in action.

Even when speaking to him, neither cop looks Liam in the eye. Their gazes stay fixed firmly on the toes of his shoes. They look like two well-trained dogs waiting for a command at the feet of their master.

Liam notices me standing there. He looks me over, eyes

flashing like the wolf's in my dream. Then he says something to the cops, very low so only they can hear, and walks away from them toward me.

Though his back is turned, they both tip their hats to him before turning to leave.

"How do you feel?" he asks when he reaches me. His frown tells me he doesn't approve of this plan.

"Terrible, but I'll live. I can't wait to get home and take a shower. Here—you left this in the room." I hold out the copy of *In Search of Lost Time* I grabbed on the way out, but Liam shakes his head.

"Keep it."

"I can't read French."

"Not yet."

He says it like he foresees many trips to Paris in my future. If only he knew I've never been outside the United States.

He takes my arm and gently steers me toward the elevators at the end of the hall, cradling his hand under my elbow as we walk.

The clock on the wall at the nurses' station tells me it's a quarter past midnight. The slack-jawed stare the middle-aged nurse gives Liam as we pass by tells me her panties have just gone up in smoke.

I say to him, "Don't we need to let them know I'm leaving? Check me out or something?"

"No."

Of course not. He doesn't ask permission for anything.

"But what about my pain meds?"

"I already got them."

I look at his empty hands and flat pockets. His suit is cut so perfectly and fits so well it would show the outline of a paperclip, but no bulges mar his sleek outline.

Except the one between his legs, which I'm not looking at.

"I hesitate to ask where you've stashed the bottle."

He slants me a look that I think is meant to convey amusement, but is smoldering instead.

The man can't help it. His default setting is raging inferno. Even when he tries to be circumspect, heat rolls off him in waves.

We're silent as we ride the elevator down to the first floor, silent as we walk to the entrance, silent as he helps me into the back of the black Escalade waiting for us at the curb.

It isn't until we're pulling away from the hospital entrance that he speaks, and then it's to his driver...in a foreign language.

The driver—a good-looking thirtyish guy with linebacker's shoulders, black hair, and eyes as sharp and freezing blue as icicles—glances at me in the rearview mirror before murmuring an answer in the same language.

Either he's suffering from a serious case of resting bitch face, or he doesn't like me. His energy is as cold as his eyes.

When he turns his gaze back to the road, I feel like a rabbit that's been released from a trap.

I turn my attention to the foggy night beyond the windows. "Was that Gaelic?"

"Aye," comes Liam's low response. "But we just call it Irish." The following pause feels weighted. "You know it?"

"No. But my granddad was Irish. My dad's dad. He was from Dublin. He lived to be a hundred and four. He used to sing me lullabies when I was a baby."

I turn from the window just in time to see Liam and the driver exchanging a look in the rearview mirror.

That's the end of the conversation. Liam grows more and more tense as we approach my apartment, tense and restless, occasionally flexing his hands open then clenching them to fists.

I want to ask him what that's about, but don't. I want to ask him how he knows my address, but don't. I want to ask him a lot of other things, too, but don't bother with those, either. If this is the end of our non-relationship, those details don't matter. I'm too exhausted to deal with the mysteries of the universe right now, anyway.

I'll just file everything under the general heading Secrets Wolves Keep, and pack it all away.

The moment we pull to a stop in front of my apartment building, Liam leaps out of the car and heads around to my side.

As soon as the door slams behind him, the driver speaks, his Irish accent thick. "You take care now. Boston's a dangerous city. Wouldn't want to see a nice girl like you get hurt again."

His icy gaze drills into mine.

That was a threat. He's telling me to stay away from Liam.

What a dick.

I meet his cold stare in the rearview mirror, smile, and say with all the Texas charm I can muster, "Why, bless your heart, Mr. Driver. But you don't have to worry about me. I'm only helpless when my nail polish is wet, and even then I can still pull a trigger."

Our gazes hold until Liam opens my door. Then the driver looks away, shaking his head.

I think I see a hint of a smile on his face, but I could be mistaken.

I climb out of the car, square my shoulders, and look up into Liam's face. It's a long way up: he's standing on the curb and I'm in the street, and he's a head taller than me normally.

"So. I guess this is goodbye. Thank you for saving my life. I'd repay you if I knew how, or if I thought you'd let me, but I don't, and you won't, so my appreciation will have to do. Thank you again. I hope you have a nice life."

I stick out my hand, perversely satisfied to throw the same line back at him that he used on me when he tried to say goodbye in the diner.

He looks at my outstretched hand. He mutters something in Gaelic under his breath. He takes my hand and pulls me gently up onto the sidewalk.

Then he bends over and picks me up.

When he turns around and starts heading toward the front door of my building, carrying me in his arms like a child, I say, "Wait, I'm confused. What's happening now?"

He growls, "I'm putting you and that smart mouth of yours to bed is what's happening."

With that, he seals my smart mouth shut and injects electricity straight into my bloodstream.

7

TRU

*M*y apartment is on the third floor. Liam doesn't carry me all the way there, though I've no doubt he's strong enough to if he wanted. Instead, he sets me down gently in front of the elevator doors in the lobby and stabs his finger against the call button.

We don't look at each other while we wait for the elevator to arrive, but I'm hyper aware of him standing beside me. He's heat and muscle and danger, a razorblade sheathed in silk. Then there's another silent elevator ride.

Silent but crackling with sexual tension.

I stare straight ahead, willing myself not to think of that elevator scene from *Fifty Shades of Grey* where Christian slams Ana against the wall, pins her arms overhead, and makes a meal of her. But it's a given that the harder you try not to think of something, the more you do, until you're obsessing and hating yourself for it, helpless to stop.

I imagine him hitting the emergency button and whirling on me to tear off my clothes and shove his throbbing erection inside me, growling against my neck and biting me as I cry out and scratch my fingernails down his back.

When the elevator stops and the doors slide open, I'm red-faced and sweating.

"What's wrong?" asks Liam sharply.

Of course he'd notice. He notices everything, him and his damn wolf's eyes.

I say, "Nothing."

My voice is so high it's like I've been sucking on helium.

Clutching the copy of *In Search of Lost Time*, I step out, avoiding Liam's eyes. He follows right on my heels. It isn't until I'm standing in front of my apartment door that I realize my purse is still at Buddy's, which means I don't have my keys.

Which means I'm going to have to wake up Ellie.

Sighing heavily, I lift my hand to ring the bell. Before I can, Liam catches me by the wrist.

The feel of his strong fingers wrapped around my wrist brings to mind the elevator scene again, and I blush. Deeply.

Gazing at me, he murmurs, "I have a key."

I'm sure my glowing face has raised the temperature at least ten degrees in the hallway, but we both pretend not to notice.

"How do you have a key?"

"Your roommate gave me her spare."

I blink in surprise. "Ellie gave you her spare key?"

"Aye."

"That's...strange."

"She's a sweet girl."

"Sweet? I've heard her described as abrasive, intimidating, and freakishly smart, but never sweet. I'm not sure we're talking about the same person."

He lowers his arm to his side, taking mine with it, but doesn't let go of my wrist. His big hand encircling it feels both comforting and distinctly possessive.

I don't think his plan to stay away from me is working out well.

Looking at my ruddy cheeks, he says, "People tend to do what

I ask."

"I've noticed that. What did you tell her?"

"The truth."

I lift my brows. "Which is?"

His eyes burn in that way they do, all fire and dark intensity. "That I needed it. May I open the door now?"

I don't understand anything at all. Time to give up trying. My poor brain needs a vacation. "Yes. Thank you."

He finally releases my wrist and removes a key from a pocket inside his coat. With a swift turn of the lock, he opens the door and steps inside, holding the door open and extending his hand out like he owns the place and I'm the one visiting.

I walk in, setting the book on the rickety console table in the foyer that Ellie and I bought from a flea market the week we moved in. As soon as the door swings shut behind me, Liam takes off my coat and drapes it over his arm.

We stand there staring at each other until I'm squirming and swallowing, all out of breath.

"You're thirsty," he says solemnly. "I'll get you some water."

I shake my head. "I'm fine, thanks. I'm sure you're anxious to get back to your regular schedule of roaming the nighttime city streets, thwarting assaults, and intimidating authority figures." I gesture toward the door.

He stares at me for a beat, then turns and disappears soundlessly into the kitchen.

His footsteps make only the barest whisper against the floor. It's impressive that a man so large can move so quietly. Must be all that practice creeping stealthily around in the woods on padded paws.

In the kitchen, the refrigerator door opens with a *whoosh*. Whatever he's looking for in there he won't find, unless it's leftovers from Chinese takeout or condiments in various states of decay.

I survive mostly on protein bars and canned soup, and Ellie

lives on ramen and frozen burger patties. We've got plenty of ice cream and wine—we're not uncivilized, just broke—but that's about it.

So imagine my surprise when Liam returns to the foyer with a bottle of water in his hand.

I frown at it. "Where did that come from?"

"An artesian spring in the French Alps."

And he says *I* have a smart mouth. "I don't mean originally. I mean how did it get into my apartment?"

"I carried it here." He twists off the metal cap and presses the bottle into my hand. It's glass, a ridiculous extravagance. "Drink. You need to stay hydrated."

I consider the bottle for a moment, also considering how he seems to enjoy carrying things places. Me and these ounces of designer French water have a lot in common.

He sees the wheels spinning in my brain. "Don't make it more complicated than it is, Tru. Just drink."

"Are you going to stand there and watch me?"

He inclines his head.

"What if I can't, though?"

"Does your throat hurt?"

"No, because of stage fright."

He stares at me.

I crinkle my nose. "Performance anxiety is a thing for me. I get nervous."

Eyes burning, he takes a step toward me. I take a step back. He takes another step and I nervously move back again, until my butt hits the console table and I can't retreat any farther. He leans close to me, and my heart pretends it's a racehorse and starts to gallop.

Into my ear, he says softly, "Truvy. Beautiful girl. Stubborn little queen bee. I want you to drink because water will help you heal, not because I'm trying to control you. Don't defy me just to prove to yourself that you can."

His voice is devastatingly sexy. I'm afraid I might need to grab on to his suit lapels to stop myself from sliding to the floor.

He steps back before that becomes necessary and fixes me with his piercing gaze.

I take a nice, long swallow from the fancy glass bottle, trying to keep my hand steady and my heart from bursting under the stress.

When I'm finished, he murmurs, "Thank you. Now let's get you into bed."

He takes my hand and leads me from the foyer across the living room, then down the hall toward my bedroom, not asking the way because he so clearly knows.

The light is on in Ellie's room, beaming from under her closed bedroom door. I hear low voices coming from inside as we pass, and hope she's watching something less depressing than *A Dog's Purpose* this time.

When we get to my room, Liam flicks on the light, standing aside to let me enter.

Everything is the same as I left it. I don't know why, but it feels as if there should be some evidence of what happened to me in the alley behind the restaurant. Some telling clue that my life has changed in the period between when I left and now. A visible difference.

I mean other than the wolf tracking my every movement with hungry predator's eyes.

He stands perfectly still, watching me as I set the half-empty water bottle on my dresser and run a hand through my messy hair.

"I, um..." I clear my throat. "I want to take a shower before bed."

I didn't mean it as a provocation, but damn if his eyes don't flash with desire. He looks at the bed, his lashes lowering, then back at me.

"Of course," he says, his voice husky. "I'll let myself out. I left your coat on a chair in the kitchen. Your meds are on the counter in a small white bag."

I'd almost forgotten about my medication. He must've brought it at the same time he came to pick up fresh clothes. Or was that later, or a task he assigned to his surly driver?

So many questions that will have to remain unanswered.

"And Ellie's key?"

He wordlessly removes it from the inside pocket of his suit jacket and hands it to me.

Then we stand there looking at each other. The awkwardness is crushing.

"Thank you again for what you did," I say quietly. "In the alley. And at the hospital. And for the book. Just...for everything. I know I won't see you again, but I won't ever forget you."

He glances at my mouth. He clenches his jaw. He hesitates for a moment, looking as if words are on the tip of his tongue, but then he exhales and presses his lips together, thinking better of it.

As if to himself, he says, "Maybe in another life."

Then he turns abruptly and leaves.

I listen to the sound of his footsteps fading and the faint squeak of the hinges on the front door. Then everything is quiet except the dull thud of my pulse and the sound of traffic drifting up from the street outside.

With Liam gone and my adrenaline waning, exhaustion takes over.

I get undressed and take a hot shower, wincing when the spray hits my cut lip. All the various parts of my body are either sore, stinging, or dead tired. My ribcage aches, and my stomach is tender. The IV drugs are wearing off, too, leaving me feeling as beat up as I look. All I want to do is crawl under the covers and go to sleep for a year.

But when I emerge from the bathroom, wrapped in a towel, that plan is shot.

Liam sits on the end of my bed, waiting for me.

8

TRU

I stop short, eyes widening. My pulse starts to pound all over again.

Bent over with his elbows propped on his knees and his hands steepled under his chin, Liam stares at my bedroom carpet in intense concentration.

When it becomes apparent he's not going to talk first, I say, "How'd you get back in without the key?"

"I didn't lock the door behind me."

"Why not?"

He exhales heavily, as if he was afraid I'd ask that question. He closes his eyes and drops his voice. "I knew I'd want to come back in."

This is so far beyond my realm of experience with men, I don't know how to proceed. I stand there staring at him for a moment, my heartbeat going haywire, my wet hair dripping down my back.

Then I say softly, "You can stay if you want, but, um...I'm not in any shape to...uh..."

"For fuck's sake, lass," he says through gritted teeth. "I'm a lot of bad things, but a man who takes advantage of an injured woman isn't one of them."

"I know you're not."

He lifts his head and gazes at me, his brows drawn together, thunderclouds gathering over his head. "You can't know that."

"But I do."

My confidence aggravates him. He stands, towering over me, and sends me a glare that would make any reasonable person tremble. But apparently I'm not reasonable, because he doesn't scare me one bit.

I lift my chin and meet his glare. "You're not a danger to me. Nothing you can say will convince me otherwise."

He stalks closer, eyes blazing. "You watched me kill three men."

"I also watched you try not to talk to me for almost a full year because you thought you wouldn't be good for me."

"I'm *not* good for you."

"So you've said. Wine and cheeseburgers aren't good for me either, but they're literally two of my favorite things. Also, that argument would hold more weight if you hadn't saved my life. Saving a person's life is kind of the default definition of something that's good for them. Being alive is good for me. Hence, *you* are good for me. If you want to argue that you weren't good for those three guys in the alley, well, you've got me there."

Nostrils flaring, he mutters an oath.

"You can curse all you want, wolfie. It does nothing to change the fact that I trust you."

He's appalled by that. His eyes widen and his lips part in shock. "You *trust* me," he repeats faintly.

"Don't look so horrified. Maybe I'm a good judge of character."

"Or maybe that kick you took knocked something loose in your head."

"Okay. You win. I'm delusional and you're really a monster. Leave."

He doesn't move. He's rooted to the spot as if he grew there, gazing at me in outraged disbelief. And a healthy dose of anger, too.

Anger at himself, not me.

We both know he wants to leave, but he's going to do no such thing.

I try not to sound too smug about it. "Good. Now that we've established you're staying, I'm going to change into my PJs and get into bed."

His burning gaze slashes to my bed. Miraculously, it doesn't burst into flames.

I don't wait for him to issue any more aggravating pronouncements on the dire state of my brain before nabbing my yoga pants, undies, and a sleep shirt from my dresser drawers. Then I go back into the bathroom and shut the door, leaning against it as soon as it closes behind me. I stand there breathing until my knees have stopped knocking and some semblance of order has returned to the chaos of my mind.

I dress quickly and blow-dry my hair, leaving it damp because I'm too impatient to finish the job.

Then, as if this is totally normal and I always have insanely hot, mysterious, dangerous men in black Armani suits wrestling with their consciences over for sleepovers, I calmly exit the bathroom and crawl into bed.

I curl up on my side, pull the covers up to my chin, and gaze up at Liam.

He stands in the same spot I left him, staring down at me like he can't for the life of him understand what's happening.

I whisper, "Sing me to sleep, wolfie. Sing me an Irish lullaby."

He covers his eyes with a hand and groans softly.

"If it will help, I'll pretend to be really scared of you if you're still here when I wake up. I'll scream and everything."

He drops his hand to his side and sighs. It's heavy and resigned, and I know that I've won.

If anyone is in danger here, it's definitely him.

He lowers his bulk to the edge of the mattress and sits there gingerly. I scooch aside to give him more room. I bunch up the pillow under my head and watch him struggle with himself for several silent moments, cracking his knuckles and grinding his back molars as he glares at the carpet, until I tug on his suit sleeve.

He turns his head and looks at me from under lowered lashes, his jaw set, a lock of dark hair falling into his eyes. I want to reach out and stroke it aside but manage to control myself.

Keeping my voice as soft as before, I say, "You don't really have to sing to me. You don't have to talk at all, if you don't want to. We can just be."

Looking frustrated, he says, "Are you always like this?"

I furrow my brow. "Like what?"

He thinks for a moment. "Idiotically fearless."

"I'm not fearless. I'm afraid of lots of things. Just not you."

"That's why you're an idiot."

I smile at him, not insulted even a little bit. "Excuse me, but I'm very intelligent."

"Intelligent people don't invite total strangers into their bedrooms in the middle of the night after being attacked in a dark alley."

"They do if that total stranger wasn't a total stranger but *was* the one who saved them from said attack. And not to splice hairs, but I didn't invite you. You were already here when I came out of the bathroom."

He glowers at my logic. "At the very least, it's reckless."

"Look. You charmed my scary roommate who hates mostly everyone into giving you a key. You got my medication for me. You brought me clean clothes to the hospital. You gave me a book about life, death, and love. You carried expensive French water into my refrigerator, where it probably looked around in horror and burst into tears. These are not things a bad guy would do. You're not going to convince me otherwise. Let's move on, please."

He studies me intently for a moment, then turns his attention back to the carpet. He thinks for a while. He drops his head, passes a big paw over his dark hair, squeezes the back of his neck, and sighs heavily.

Then he says in a low, rough voice, "Turn over onto your other side."

Scorching hot and violent, adrenaline explodes into my bloodstream. Heart pounding, I roll over and stare wide-eyed at the wall.

The mattress moves as Liam stands. I hear rustling and the slither of fabric, then the mattress dips with his weight.

Then he stretches out behind me and tucks his legs up under mine.

Very gently, he slides his left arm under my head until his biceps is supporting my neck and my cheek is resting on the pillow. I'm frozen except for my heart, which beats frantically.

How much of his clothing did he remove? Is he naked right now? Is the wolf lying totally naked right next to me? No—he's still got his shirt on. His arm under my neck is covered by a sleeve. But maybe he took off his slacks? Definitely his jacket. What about his tie? Shoes? Belt? Underwear?

I'm having a heart attack. This is it. Oh god. I'm going to die right here and now.

"Breathe," Liam murmurs.

I exhale in a huge gust, shuddering.

"Better."

Closing my eyes, I listen to the roar of my heartbeat for several long minutes. Behind me, Liam is silent and still. The only parts of our bodies that are touching are the front of his knees, the backs of mine, and my neck resting on his arm, but I'm excruciatingly aware of every inch of him, head to toe.

He's generating so much heat I could be snuggled against a furnace.

When my tongue remembers how to form words, I whisper, "Liam?"

"Mmm."

"I...I'm glad you're here."

His quiet exhalation stirs my hair. "Go to sleep."

He thinks I could sleep at a time like this?

I worry my lower lip with my teeth, feeling how fat and sore it is and wondering how much it'll hurt when he kisses me—because he *has* to kiss me, it's just a question of when—until I freeze again because Liam has nuzzled his nose against the bare nape of my neck...

And is gently inhaling.

Every inch of my skin breaks out in goose flesh. My nipples instantly harden. I almost groan out loud.

His big warm hand curls around my upper arm and squeezes. He murmurs, "Easy."

Maybe I did groan out loud. Hell, maybe I soaked the sheets, too. There's a distinct throbbing between my legs that's probably sending out shockwaves he can feel, like a Richter scale picking up the rumblings of an earthquake.

I turn my face to the pillow and whimper.

His voice turns thick. "I'll get you some of your pain meds."

I want to roll over and bash him with my pillow. Instead, I say, "We both know you're not that clueless."

He doesn't reply. A minute goes by. Two. I blow out a long breath through my lips, silently, counting to one hundred and back again. Eventually, I calm down.

Liam stays perfectly still the entire time, all heat and nervy tension, until he senses I'm okay. Then he exhales, too, and starts to rub his thumb slowly back and forth over my upper arm.

But then he stiffens and growls, "What's that?"

I open my eyes and cock an ear, listening for the noise to

come again. It was a dull thud, and it sounded like it came from inside the apartment.

Wait, there it is now. Repeating at an even pace...

Thud. Thud. Thud.

When I hear the muffled moan, my face turns to fire.

We listen together in crackling silence, until Liam says, "I take it your roommate has a guest."

"Her boyfriend," I whisper, nodding. "They were broken up, but they must've..."

Thud. Moan. Thud. Moan. THUD THUD THUD *MOAN*.

Over another of Ellie's full-throated moans, Liam says through gritted teeth, "Gotten back together."

We can hear him now, Ellie's on-again, off-again ex Tyler, groaning lustily toward his climax as he pounds and thrusts and plows the headboard of Ellie's bed into the wall.

Oh my god. This isn't happening.

The thumping goes on forever, until it abruptly stops. Ellie and Tyler scream simultaneously, loudly enough to make my windows rattle. The neighbors across the hall are probably picking up the phone to call the police and report a murder.

Behind me, Liam is rigid, breathing raggedly, his chest pressed against my shoulder blades so I feel how wildly his heart pounds.

Either he pulled me against his body or I flexed back, but either way, I'm flush against him now, my back against his chest and stomach, my butt against his crotch.

His heartbeat isn't the only thing I feel.

His erection is big, hot, and digging hungrily into my bottom.

When Ellie and Tyler's cries of pleasure have faded and the only sounds are our own uneven breaths, I exhale and stretch my legs restlessly under the covers.

Liam moves his hand from my arm to my hip and squeezes me there. He says roughly into my ear, "Don't move. Give me a moment."

I freeze.

We stay like that for what feels like an eternity, until he presses his cheek to the back of my neck and exhales. His warm breath fans over my skin, slipping under the collar of my shirt and skimming down my shoulder blades, lighting all my nerves on fire.

If he reached up and pinched one of my aching nipples, I think I'd come.

"Liam—"

His voice is a command. "Hush." Then, very faintly, "Fuck."

Cars pass by on the street outside. Somewhere off in the distance, a dog bays. It sounds eerily like the howl of a wolf.

Then Liam's voice comes very low. "I'm sorry. I'm not...I'm usually much better at..."

When he doesn't continue, I venture, "Being in control?"

His soft sigh sounds agitated. "Something like that."

I swallow because my mouth is desert dry. "If it makes you feel any better, I'm not very in control at the moment, either."

"I know. And it doesn't make me feel better."

He sounds like he's about to leap from the bed and run out the door. I whisper, "Please don't leave. I don't want you to leave. I want you to stay with me."

His groan is barely audible. "Tru..."

"I'll be very still and quiet. Look, I'm going to sleep. I'm asleep already." I pretend to snore.

When I hear what sounds like a chuckle, my heart leaps with hope. I have no idea why it's suddenly so imperative that he stay, except maybe that I feel safer when he's around.

Semihysterical and hormone drenched, too, but mainly safer.

His sigh stirs my hair again. I can tell he's thinking. Fighting with himself about whether to stay or go. If he does go, I'm not sure he'll come back this time. If he manages to find the strength to peel himself away from me and walk out the front door, he just might find the strength to stay away for good.

This might be my last few minutes with him. Ever.

The thought causes a little starburst of panic to explode inside my belly.

In one swift move, I turn over, slip my left arm around his waist, and tuck my head under his chin, snuggling up against his solid warmth.

He sucks in a breath and goes rigid.

We stay like that for a while, me curled into him with my eyes squeezed shut, holding my breath, and him impersonating a frozen brick wall. His heart is a jackhammer under my cheek. I don't dare breathe, or move, or make a sound.

Then, very slowly, his freeze starts to thaw.

The hand that had been squeezing my hip before I turned settles there again, just over the curve of my hipbone, fingers slightly trembling. He lowers his head to the pillow, releasing a fraction of the tension in his limbs, and draws a slow breath.

Then he wraps his arm around my back and gently pulls me closer, sliding a heavy leg over both of mine.

He still has his slacks on. I'm not sure if I'm relieved or disappointed.

The breath I've been holding comes out as a sigh. I burrow into his warmth, shivering when his breath tickles my ear. He's so big. Big and comfy and deliciously hot, his strength and maleness wrapped all around me.

I could stay like this until the end of my days.

He whispers, "This won't end well."

"I promise I won't move again. Not even an inch."

"I'm not talking about tonight."

"Can you please not be cryptic for like half a minute? I'm enjoying this."

He makes a sound low in his throat, a masculine noise of pain or pleasure, I can't tell which. He says, "Me too. That's the problem."

He's holding me so gently. Like I'm fragile, a piece of bone china he might easily break. I love it exactly as much as it annoys me.

I don't want him to manhandle me per se, especially not now since I'm sore and bruised pretty much everywhere. But when I'm healed, I hope he doesn't treat me like I'm so breakable.

In fact, I hope he maybe gets a little...I mean it might be nice if he lost some of that steely self-control and got just the tiniest bit...

Rough.

Like love bites on my neck rough. Faint bruises on my hips from his fingers rough. That lovely ache deep inside the next day after you've been had by a man who knows exactly what he's doing, how to put his hands on you and touch you in just the right way to make you moan and shudder and lose yourself to him, and love losing yourself, and beg for more.

Imagining it, a shiver goes through me. A thrill like a single violin note, singing high and sweet.

Into my ear, in a gravelly voice that sounds like he's on the outermost edge of his restraint, Liam says, "Whatever you're thinking right now, lass, *stop.*"

My ears go hot. I breathe, "Sorry."

He's tense again. A big ball of tension and nerves, his frustration seeping out with every uneven breath.

I wish I didn't find his reluctance so seductive. I wish I didn't think his ambivalence is so hot. But the harder he fights himself and denies himself what his body so obviously wants, the more intrigued I become.

I've never met a man who denied himself anything. From what I've seen, men walk around assuming the whole world is their candy jar. They delight in taking whatever they want.

But even beyond that, they assume that candy is their birthright. Their due for being born with a dick between their legs.

They think candy is what they're owed.

Not Liam Black. He wants, but he doesn't take.

"I'm not afraid of you. I'm afraid for you, for all the things I want from you that I think you just might give."

Remembering his words, I wonder what kinds of things he wants from me.

What kinds of things that would make a man like him afraid.

Liam's chest rises and falls with his sigh. "Go to sleep, lass. Get some rest."

"Will you be here when I wake up?"

He doesn't answer, but he doesn't have to. Because I whisper, "I hope so," and I hear his soft groan of despair, and in that despair I hear a surrender.

I wasn't sure before, but now I know it in my bones. Even if he's not here in the morning, he'll come back again soon enough.

The important question now is why he wishes so badly that he wouldn't.

9

LIAM

*S*he falls asleep like children do. Fighting it at first, stubbornly rebelling, until the lids droop and the breathing changes and suddenly they're gone like a light switched off and not even a bomb could disturb them.

Her arm is a dead weight as I ease it from around my body. Her mouth is slightly open, full lips parted as she draws deep, even breaths. She doesn't stir when I rise from the bed, or when I don my jacket and shoes, or when I pull the covers over her shoulders and stand staring down at her for a long, long time.

Taking that first step away from her toward the bedroom door is disturbingly difficult.

Locking the front door to her apartment behind me is even harder.

Exiting the building without turning back around is the hardest of all.

As I knew he would be, Declan is waiting for me at the curb in the Escalade. He starts the car the moment I emerge through the lobby doors and doesn't say a word as I open the door and get settled in the back seat. We pull smoothly away and drive for a while in silence.

Until I say, "Go ahead. Let's hear it."

His gaze never leaves the road. "Not my place. And you already know."

I do know. That's the problem. One of the many problems.

I drop my head back against the seat and close my eyes. I expect darkness, relief, but instead an image of Tru's smiling face appears under my lids.

Christ, those eyes are haunting.

"But..."

I open my eyes and find Declan studying me in the rearview mirror. "But?"

He tilts his head thoughtfully, looks back at the road. "Rules are made to be broken. Even if they're your own."

I huff out a laugh. "You know as well as I do how badly it could go wrong."

"I'm not sure she's as fragile as you think."

"They all are."

"Aye, and they're all afraid of you, too." He glances at me again. "Except she isn't. Wasn't afraid of me, either. That's something."

"What do you mean, she wasn't afraid of you?"

"I mean she gave me lip when I told her to be careful when I dropped you two off earlier. You know when the last time was that someone gave me lip? Never. But she did. Straight up. Told me to go fuck myself in so many words, and did it with a smile."

I stare at him, incredulous. "Are you telling me you think this is a good idea?"

"No."

"Then what?"

"I don't know. Maybe nothing."

His pause is loaded, and I know he's carefully choosing his words.

"But she was about to get shot—or worse—and she fought back. You saw it yourself. On the ground, outnumbered, beat up, gun in her face, she throws a punch instead of all the other things she could've done. Begging for mercy. Giving up. Crying."

He lets it hang there, knowing I have enough personal memories of men far stronger than she doing exactly that.

Aggravated, I yank on the knot in my tie because it suddenly feels like a noose. "So she's a fighter. That doesn't make it right."

"Aye," he agrees, nodding. "But maybe it makes it a little less wrong."

I glare out the window, muttering a curse. I can't believe he's saying this. Him, of all people. I expected him to be silently seething with disapproval, not taking her side.

Not *admiring* her.

"You've been alone a long time, Liam. If you were careful—"

My temper breaks. I glare at him and thunder, "*I won't risk her life!*"

Declan's expression doesn't change. His grip stays loose on the steering wheel, his gaze doesn't dart away in panic. He simply meets my eyes in the mirror and tells me a devastating truth.

"You say that like you haven't already."

I grit my teeth and look out the window, hating that he's right. Hating myself for letting it get this far.

I had a chance, when all I was doing was memorizing her profile while she poured me bad coffee. Before I knew the particular way she falls asleep. What her skin smells like after a shower. How her body feels pressed against mine.

How deeply satisfying it feels to protect her.

No, more than satisfying—fulfilling.

As if it were the thing I was born to do.

But I can't undo what I've done. I can't go back to that first day I saw her eleven months ago, helping an old woman cross a busy boulevard, stopping traffic by holding up her hand as the light turned from red to green. I can't unfeel what I felt when she glanced up and our eyes met through the windshield for a moment before she turned her attention back to the old woman doddering by her side.

She was beautiful, but I've seen a thousand beautiful girls.

Never one who looked so fierce, though.

With her jaw set and her mouth pinched and her brows drawn together, she looked like she'd rip the head off anyone who dared to honk his horn at the painfully slow progress she and her elderly friend were making.

She was a lioness. Even without opening her mouth, I heard her roar.

So yes, it was simple curiosity that made me tell Declan to pull over. Yes, it was on a whim that I watched her wave goodbye to the old woman when they reached the other side of the street. Yes, I fully admit it was foolish of me to follow her into Buddy's Diner, and to sit in her section that first time.

But it was sheer stupidity that I kept coming back.

As long as I was out of the country, I could tell myself I wouldn't see her again. I thought I had the strength to stay away. But as soon as I returned, the wanting rushed back. The pull to see those clear green eyes. The need to hear that lilting voice and see that shy smile and be near her, if only for a moment.

Now, because I indulged myself, I'm well and truly fucked.

Because need and want have turned into something more powerful. Something darker and far more perilous, for us both.

So now I have two options.

Option one: claim her.

Option two: give her up.

I can't bring myself to do either.

"Declan."

"Aye?"

"What do you do when you have to decide between two impossible choices?"

Our eyes meet in the mirror. He says, "Create a third."

A third.

Claim her or give her up. Those are the choices at hand. But if I created a third choice from those two, what would that look like?

My heart stops when it comes to me.

Then I exhale a hard breath and stare out into the passing night, shaken by the knowledge that this idea is mad, reckless, and incredibly dangerous.

And one Tru will agree to.

Which makes it the most selfish idea I've ever had.

But even knowing all that, how wrong it is on every level, how selfish and wrong, I'm gripped by a violent, almost overpowering need to turn the car around, kick down the door to her apartment, shake her awake, and put the idea to her *right now*.

So to prove to myself I still have a shred of self-control, I clamp my jaw shut and let Declan drive me farther and farther away from her, deeper into the night.

In a life full of dark moments and hardships, it counts as one of the hardest things I've ever done.

10

TRU

*B*efore I even open my eyes, I know he's gone.

I lie there in bed, my cheek pressed to the pillow, listening to the city's morning sounds. My body hurts a little less than it did yesterday. I can tell without touching that the swelling around my eye has gone down. But though my body feels better, my heart feels exponentially worse.

I've never encountered it before, but longing is surprisingly painful.

I roll over and look at the clock. It's Sunday, so I don't have to worry about school, but I'm feeling guilty over missing my shifts at Buddy's. We've got part-timers who can cover for me, but knowing Carla, she'll take on the shifts for the extra money.

Her husband was laid off from his job as a mechanic a few months ago. They're barely making ends meet.

So, in a way, it's good that I'll be out.

But I'm still feeling guilty about it. Growing up on a farm might not be glamorous, but it definitely gets that work ethic ingrained.

Yawning, I throw on a robe and head to the kitchen. I need

coffee before I can face the day. Especially today, when everything has been turned upside down by what happened in that alley. Everything, especially my brain. And my libido.

I can't stop thinking about the feel of Liam's body against mine.

How his fingers trembled when he touched me.

How every hair on my body stood on end when he inhaled against the nape of my neck.

"Good morning!"

I jump when Ellie greets me over her shoulder. She's frying eggs at the stove in the kitchen in her bathrobe, barefoot, her hair mussed, her back turned to me. I'd been staring at the floor, lost in thought, and didn't notice her there.

"Holy Moses, Elliebellie," I breathe, pressing a hand over my thundering heart. I shuffle into the kitchen, scowling at the back of her head. "You practically gave me a heart attack."

She snorts. "Did you forget you had a roommate?"

I say drily, "No, especially after that concert you and Ty put on last night. No wonder you're so cheerful this morning."

Poking at the frying eggs with a spatula, she laughs at my tone. "Don't hate. I can't help it that our makeup sex is so—*holy shit!*"

Noticing my face as I move beside her to open the cupboard, she gasps. "Oh my god, Tru! Are you okay?"

I wave a hand dismissively, reaching for a mug. "I'm good. It looks worse than it feels. I've always been a bruiser. It's this pasty skin."

Shaken by my appearance, she rests her free hand against the base of her throat. "Jesus. When Liam said you'd had a minor accident at work, I thought he meant like a slip and fall or something. It looks like you got punched in the face!"

The way she says Liam's name makes it sound like they're old friends. Which is odd, because she doesn't like anyone. I say absently, "Kicked, actually."

She almost drops the spatula. "*Kicked? By who?*"

Mug in hand, I lean against the counter and gaze at her. "An idiot who regretted it. Back up a sec. I'm curious. Liam knocks on the door and says to you...what? 'Hi, I'm a handsome Irishman you've never met, your roommate has had a little accident, give me your spare key?'"

She thinks about it. "I mean, in a nutshell, I guess. But in between all that, he put away the groceries."

"Wait. What?"

"The groceries," she repeats patiently, as if I didn't hear her the first time. When I just stare at her, she gestures toward the fridge. "Bags and bags of them. Took forever."

Frowning in confusion, I go to the fridge and open the door. Packed inside like sardines is a rainbow of produce, cold cuts, dairy products, drinks, snacks, deli salads, and a variety of cut fruit in square plastic containers.

And water, of course. Designer French water in glass bottles nestled in between everything else.

Ellie says, "There's a bunch of food in the pantry, too. Fancy shmancy stuff. Half of it I've never even heard of."

On a hunch, I open the freezer door.

It's full to bursting with pints of pistachio ice cream.

I turn to Ellie slowly, feeling like I'm in a dream. "So...I'm confused."

She makes a face at me. "That your rich boyfriend bought you groceries?"

My heart clenches, and my voice goes high. "He told you he was my boyfriend?"

Ellie rolls her eyes, like I'm being ridiculous with all the unnecessary questions.

"Listen, I know you're a super private person, and you don't like talking about your love life, and I don't blame you after what happened with that douche canoe ex of yours. I get it. But you've been living like a nun since we moved in together—"

When my expression sours, she adds quickly, "I'm not judging. My point is that this guy is crazy hot, has impeccable manners, brings you food, and is probably related to the royal family. You should make an effort with him. Try to open up."

I lift my brows. "The British royal family? You're aware his accent is Irish, right?"

"Ireland's a part of Great Britain, duh."

"Don't tell that to everyone in the Republic of Ireland, a sovereign nation not part of the UK, which isn't the same thing as Northern Ireland, which is."

She shrugs. "Tomato, tomahtoe. They're on the same island and they both have Ireland in their names. If they wanted people to keep it straight, they should've made that shit less complicated. We don't call Canada North America, do we?"

"Yes, we literally do, because North America is a *continent*, dummy, which Canada is part of. Are you sure you graduated from college?"

"Geography isn't my strong suit."

I muse, "You don't say?"

She rolls her eyes. "My point is that he's obviously got aristocratic genes. Plus, he's crazy hot."

"You already said that."

"It bears repeating."

I shut the fridge and freezer doors and rub my temples. "I'm so confused."

"And *you* already said *that*. What's to be confused about?"

"First and foremost, you gave him your spare key."

She frowns, like I'm speaking a foreign language.

"And you'd never met him before? Hello? You're just handing out keys to our apartment now like candy on Halloween?"

She chuckles, turning back to the eggs. "What, like he's a home invader? He thought shopping for groceries would be a good way to bribe his way in the door before he tied me to a chair and rummaged through my panty drawers for hidden jewelry? Come on. Besides, home invaders don't wear Armani suits and Patek Philippe timepieces."

It figures she'd know what brand of suits he wears. I only knew because Carla told me. And I know nothing about watches except that if they're called a timepiece, they're expensive.

"But you'd never met him before."

She slides the eggs from the frying pan onto a plate, shrugging. "I know how tight-lipped you are. You could be on your honeymoon, and I'd only find out you'd gotten married when I got a postcard in the mail. I figured you just hadn't told me about him yet."

Shooting a glance toward her bedroom door, where Ty apparently is still sleeping, she adds, "Honestly, though, if the man had rung the bell and said, 'Hello, I'm here to ravage you,' I'd have torn off all my clothes myself. He's *so* damn—"

"Hot. I'm aware. So was Ted Bundy."

I'm not sure why I'm annoyed, because Liam has the same effect on me as he has on her. And Carla. And every other woman with a pair of functioning ovaries, I'm sure. Even police officers are dazzled by him, and they're *trained* to be all kinds of suspicious.

There's just something about him that makes you lower your guard.

"So this asshole who assaulted you," Ellie says as she shakes hot sauce onto the fried eggs. "What's his story? Was he on drugs? Was he arrested?"

She stops what she's doing and turns to look me up and down. Her voice softens. "More importantly, are you sure you're okay? That looks like it hurts."

She obviously hasn't seen anything in the news or heard any local gossip about three dead guys found in the alley behind Buddy's Diner. But the police were at the hospital, which means they definitely knew something. Liam said the situation had been taken care of...but what exactly did he mean?

Like suppressing news stories taken care of?

Like paying off the cops taken care of?

Like, maybe, removing bodies from a crime scene?

"Tru?" says Ellie, sounding concerned.

"Yep. I'm okay." I say it firmly then turn away, focusing on the coffee pot. "I just really need some coffee."

"Well, let me know if you need anything else. Seriously. You should probably take a few days off, too. Let that bruising heal up a little before you go back to work."

This is when I remember that Liam has already spoken to Buddy about that very thing.

"Hey, can I borrow your cell? My purse is at work, but I want to call my boss."

"Sure." Ellie gestures toward the foyer. "My bag's on the table."

"Thanks." I pour myself a cup of coffee, then retrieve Ellie's cell from her purse. I head back into my bedroom, perch on the side of my bed, and dial the diner.

"Thanks for calling Buddy's," says a cheerful female voice. "How can I help you?"

It's Lisa, one of the girls who works day shift on weekends and occasionally subs for Carla if she's sick. "Hey, Lisa. It's Tru. Is Buddy there?"

"Hey, Tru! No, Buddy already came and went."

"Shoot. Do you have his cell number, by any chance? It's in my purse, but I left it in my locker. I need to talk to him."

"Hang on a sec." I hear her rummaging around on the other end of the line. "Yeah, I found it. You ready?"

"Let me get a pen. Okay, go ahead." She reads off the number. I scribble it on a piece of note paper, then thank her. Then I ask tentatively, "So...how are things there?"

"Ugh. Same old same old. I've got this regular who comes in every Sunday after church and lectures me over his pancakes about my relationship with god. Apparently, the butterfly tattoo on my wrist has him concerned for the state of my soul."

"The regular or god?"

She laughs. "I doubt the supreme being gives a hoot about what people ink into their skin. If he does, I'm not interested in getting into heaven. Gotta go, hun, some bearded old guy with a parrot on his shoulder is waiting to be seated."

"Good luck with that."

She drops her voice, imitating a pirate. "Ahoy, matey, there be a salty sea dog dead ahead!"

She hangs up, leaving me shaking my head as I dial Buddy's number.

Obviously, Lisa knows nothing about what happened in the alley the other night, which makes me think nobody else at Buddy's does, either. Gossip normally spreads through the place like wildfire.

Somehow, Liam managed to keep three dead guys a secret. But how?

And where do Diego and Carla think I disappeared to that night?

Hopefully, Buddy will provide me with some answers. He picks up, sounding guarded.

"Hello?"

"Hi, Buddy. It's Tru."

Thundering silence. Odd from a man who chatters non-stop to everyone and everything, including himself, random strangers, and the pigeons he feeds in the park.

"Um, did I catch you at a good time?"

"Any time you want to call me is a good time, dear."

The "dear" gives me pause. Buddy's a friendly man, but he isn't prone to endearments or pet names. I've only ever heard him call his wife by her first name, and they've been married for fifty-two years.

"Okay. Um. Great. So...I guess you already know what happened on my last shift."

More silence, this one vast and empty, like outer space. After a long time, Buddy clears his throat. He says, "Are you all right?"

Nice evasion. "Yes. A bit bruised up, but nothing that won't heal."

His exhalation sounds genuinely relieved. "Thank heavens."

I wait, but he doesn't add more or ask any other questions, which seems strange. "I will need a few days off work, though. Which I take it you already know?"

He says hastily, "Yes, yes, take as much time as you need, dear. As much time as you need. The most important thing is your health. In fact, if you feel too traumatized to return to work, I'll make sure you get disability and unemployment."

I'm not sure I could legally get both at the same time, but he's still talking.

"And anything else you need. We could even keep you on payroll until you find another job, if you prefer. I'll cover all your medical bills, of course. Just send them directly to me."

"I'm not too traumatized to come back to work."

"Oh. Well, then."

I can't decide if he sounds relieved or disappointed. This is getting weirder by the minute.

"I appreciate the offer though. About the medical bills, too. That's very generous of you." I frown. "Although, to be honest, I don't know if the hospital even knows how to contact me. Liam seemed to handle everything."

Buddy pauses. When he starts to talk again, he sounds like he's proceeding with enormous caution, carefully choosing every word.

"I'm just glad you're okay. Your well-being is the only thing that matters."

I hold the phone away from my ear and make a face at it. When I put it back against my ear, I say, "Buddy?"

"Yes, dear?"

"What's going on?"

He hesitates a hair too long. "I…don't believe I know what you mean, dear."

"I'll clarify. You've called me 'dear' four times in sixty seconds, which is four times more than the entire time I've worked for you. You offered to pay me disability, unemployment, and continuing wages if I didn't return to work, plus all my medical bills, and we both know your picture is next to the definition of frugal in the dictionary."

I try to imbue my pause with weight. "Did Liam threaten you or something?"

I hear a loud thud and wonder if Buddy fell out of his recliner.

"No! I didn't say that! Please, don't tell him I said that!"

"Sheesh, calm down. I was just asking."

On the other end of the line, he's panting like a Labrador. "Please, Tru, this is of the utmost importance. The *utmost*. It cannot get back to him that I said anything…" He gulps. "That I even *implied* anything negative. About you, or him, or—or anything."

His fear is so palpable it's reaching through the phone and squeezing a cold hand around my throat. Lowering my voice, I say, "You're afraid of him."

His exhalation is shaky. "Of course I am. The devil himself is afraid of that man."

Realizing what he's admitted, he blurts, "I didn't mean that! He's a fine individual, and I have nothing but good things to say about—"

I say firmly, "Buddy, I'm not going to repeat a word of this conversation to him. I promise you. I *swear*. Okay?"

I hear some rustling, then a heavy sigh. I imagine Buddy flattened in his recliner, passing a shaky hand over his pale face.

"Thank you," he whispers.

"But I am going to ask you more questions."

His moan is faint and full of despair. It doesn't deter me at all.

"Who is he?"

There's a pause. When he comes back on, he sounds surprised. "You don't know?"

"I know his name is Liam Black. I know he has some kind of relationship with the police, because they recognized him when he was with me at the hospital. Speaking of which, he scared the shit out of them, too, *and* my stuck-up doctor, if that helps you feel better."

Buddy makes a grudging noise, indicating it might help a little bit.

"Beyond that, I'm in the dark. How do *you* know him?"

"By reputation only," comes the solemn answer. "But that's enough."

"What is he, like, a boogeyman or something?"

I laughed when I asked the question, but Buddy doesn't echo it. His voice is dead serious. "The boogeyman wishes he were Liam Black."

"I have no idea what that means."

"And if you don't know, I can't tell you."

I say drily, "Gee, thanks, boss. That's super helpful."

"You're a smart girl, Tru. I've always thought so. Smart and tough. Mature for your age." He pauses. "Could be all that cow milking and steer riding, I don't know."

"I regret telling you anything about my childhood."

"My point is that you have eyes and a brain. Use them."

Obviously, he's not going to give me anything here. We sit in silence for a while, until I decide to go in a different direction. "What did you tell Diego and Carla?"

"The truth. That you were assaulted in the alley and a good

Samaritan found you and called an ambulance. They had a lot of questions—Diego especially—but I told them you had family with you at the hospital and I'd let them know as soon as I heard anything."

"Uh-huh. And how did you explain the bodies?"

"I don't know anything about any bodies," he says quickly. "Perhaps the police..."

He trails off, coughs, then falls silent. It's his way of letting me know he's already said too much on the subject, but he doesn't have to give more detail for me to understand him.

The cops were Liam's cleanup crew.

The plot thickens.

Buddy says, "I, uh, I also gave Carla and Diego each a nice bonus. You'll get yours too, of course."

Now I'm *really* suspicious. "Bonus? For what?"

"For...loyalty. For all your hard work. The late shift is difficult, after all. And I know it's been hard since the dishwasher left. You've all been doing extra work."

I'm quiet a moment, thinking. "In other words, it's a bribe."

"What? No!"

"You want us to keep our mouths shut about what happened that night."

He scoffs. "Now, now, let's not be theatrical."

"Buddy, you're starting to freak me out. This isn't you. You don't say 'dear' and make bribes and call people the boogeyman. What the hell is really going on?"

He takes a moment to gather his thoughts before he speaks. When he does, his voice is hushed and reverent, like you'd use in church.

"You're under the protection of Liam Black now. That's what's going on. And I only say that much because it surely must be obvious to you. I'll add nothing more, except to repeat what I've already said: you've got eyes and a brain. Use them."

He disconnects.

I sit staring at the phone in my hand, even more confused than I was before I made the call, until I hear the doorbell ring. Then Ellie's voice floats in from the other room.

"Tru? Come out here." She laughs. "You're gonna want to see this."

11

TRU

hen I enter the living room, Ellie is standing at the open front door with her arms crossed over her chest. She's grinning.

Crowded around the door in the hallway outside are three delivery guys holding gigantic bouquets of flowers.

"Go ahead guys," says Ellie, gesturing into the apartment. "Put them down wherever you can find a spot."

The delivery guys file past her. I was wrong: there are six of them, not three.

"What's this?" Bewildered, I watch them place bouquets around the room.

"Delivery for Truvy Sullivan." A tall guy wearing a baseball cap with a flower logo on it sets a bouquet of tulips on the coffee table, then straightens and turns to me. "That you?"

"Yes."

He holds out a clipboard. "Sign on number five, please."

I take the clipboard, looking around the room in disbelief. "These are all for me?"

He jerks his thumb toward the door. "We've got another load in the van."

I scribble my signature on line five, give the clipboard back to the delivery guy, and stare in wonder at a bouquet of long stemmed roses. The petals are a red so dark and velvety they're nearly black. "I've never seen roses that color before."

He grins. "They're awesome, right? It's a hybrid variety called Black Magic."

He points to the bouquet of tulips he set on the coffee table, a gorgeous deep purple, again so dark they're almost black. "Those tulips are called Queen of the Night." He points to an arrangement of black calla lilies. "And those callas are called Black Star."

I say faintly, "I'm sensing a theme."

"The irises are my favorite, though." He gestures to a bouquet on the dining table. The flowers have long, elegant stems, topped by extravagantly ruffled petals the color of midnight.

"What are those called?"

"Before the Storm."

I try not to take that as a bad omen.

The guy says, "We'll be back in a minute with the others," and ambles away, whistling. The other guys follow him out, and Ellie turns from the door.

She says, "I told you the Irish hottie was a keeper."

"Stop looking so smug. We don't know for sure they're from him."

She arches her brows. "Really? You've got another secret boyfriend you're hiding? Because these damn sure aren't from Ty. Oh, wait—there's the card."

She crosses to the bouquet of Black Magic roses and removes a small gold envelope. Flicking the envelope open with her thumbnail, she withdraws a white card and reads it aloud.

"I need to see you. L." She wrinkles her nose, flips the card over, then looks up at me. "The only other thing is a phone number."

"You look disappointed."

"I am disappointed. I wanted something juicier."

I take the card from her and look at it. The handwriting is small, slanting, and precise. I wonder if Liam wrote it himself or if one of the salesgirls from the shop did the honors, but then I catch the faintest whiff of scent.

I lift the card to my nose, sniff, and smile.

Ellie demands, "What?"

"Tell me what you smell." I wave the card back and forth under her nose.

She blinks, frowning and sniffing, then pronounces, "Testosterone."

I can't help but laugh. "So it's not my imagination."

"Give me that." She snatches the envelope from my fingertips, shoves it against her nostrils, and inhales deeply. She closes her eyes. After a pause, she says, "I think I just ovulated."

"If you put that card in your underwear, I'll smack you."

She thinks for a moment then gives me back the card. "I've got a better idea."

Without another word, she turns and disappears into her bedroom, closing the door behind her. I hear a husky male laugh, followed shortly thereafter by a low moan.

Apparently, Ty owes Liam a favor.

The flower guys come back in a few minutes and place the rest of the flowers around the living room and on the kitchen counter. I feel bad that I don't have my purse, so I can't give them a tip, until the one with the baseball cap informs me the tip was already generously handled by the customer who placed the order.

They leave me alone, wondering exactly how many varieties of black flowers there are. I think I must've received all of them.

I look at the card in my hand again. Then I return to my bedroom and pick up Ellie's phone from where I left it on my bed and dial.

It rings once before it's answered with a brusque, "Aye."

"Liam? It's Tru."

Instantly, his tone softens. "Tru. I wasn't expecting you to call so soon."

"I just got the flowers. They're amazing, thank—"

"How are you feeling? Did you sleep well? Are you taking your pills? Drinking enough water? Have you eaten anything yet?"

I laugh, flattered by the worry in his voice. "Good, yes, no, and not yet, I just got up. But I promise I'll drink more of your pricey French mountain water as soon as possible."

Feeling shy, I add softly, "And maybe gorge myself on pistachio ice cream. Thank you for that, too. And for all the other stuff. I think there's more food in this apartment right now than at the grocery store. You're very generous."

There's a pause. When he speaks again, his voice has turned husky. "I can't stop thinking about you."

My cheeks heat, but I manage to keep my voice steady. "Good. I'd hate to think this insanity was one-sided."

He starts to say something, but I cut him off. "If you're going to say something along the lines of, 'it would be better if it were,' I'll hang up on you, so don't bother."

Another pause, this one longer. "All right. I won't say it. Though I have to admit, it's disturbing that you took the words right out of my mouth."

"Don't like being predictable, hmm?"

"It's not that I don't like it. It's that it's never happened before."

"I hate to tell you, wolfie, but you're a bit of a broken record when it comes to that particular topic."

He chuckles. "Not that it's done any good."

"Once I make up my mind, I can't be budged."

"So I'm learning. I need to see you."

The sudden gruffness in his voice makes my heart start to thud. "Um...when?"

"*Now.*" His exhale is aggravated. "Except I can't get away until later tonight. I'm not sure when."

"I'm not going anywhere. Come over whenever you can."

"It might be late. Very late."

"Okay. I'll leave the door unlocked."

He groans softly.

"What's wrong?"

"You should say no to me."

I wrinkle my forehead and huff out a disbelieving laugh. "I don't think those words have ever been spoken by a man before in the whole of human history."

"It's for your own good." His voice turns dark. "Because I'm going to ask you things that you should say no to, Tru. Things you should slap me for and throw me out of your apartment for. Things that are so fucking selfish and wrong they should make you run away screaming no, no, a thousand times *no*."

After a moment of stunned silence, I clear my throat. "See, now I'm just more intrigued."

He demands, "Promise me you'll consider it."

I cover my face with my hand and laugh. "This is honestly the strangest conversation I've ever had."

"I'm not joking. I want you to give serious consideration to not only saying no to what I'm going to propose, but also to not ever seeing me again. To not letting me into your apartment later tonight. To hanging up on me right now and forgetting you ever met—"

"Liam."

"Aye, lass."

"Stop telling me what to do."

He makes a low, aggravated sound in his throat, like an animal's growl.

"Snarl at me all you want, but you're being ridiculous. The only way I can judge if what you're going to say is selfish, wrong, and slap worthy is for you to *say it*. To my face. Without all the hazard lights flashing and the fire alarms going off. Deal?"

Silence.

Then comes the sound of heavy footsteps. Half a dozen steps, a pause, half a dozen more, another pause. The steps begin again.

"Are you pacing?"

"I keep underestimating you."

"Thank you. I think. How is that related to your pacing?"

He growls, "I'm frustrated."

"Because..."

"I don't misjudge people."

I make a face. "Then I guess I'm glad to disappoint you?"

Another growl. A low, sexy, masculine sound of discontent that I would happily listen to on replay for the rest of my life.

"Liam, look. I appreciate that you're trying to keep me safe. I understand that you have a great deal of ambivalence about me, and that you think us, together, is a bad idea. What I don't understand is *why*. If you'd tell me the problem—other than an unhelpful 'I wouldn't be good for you'—I'd be in a much better position to judge the argument on its merits."

He mutters, "You're going to make a very good attorney."

"Thank you. As I was saying...just spit it out. Tell me the deal. Are you..." I try to think of something that could really put a damper on a relationship. "In the witness protection program?"

His laugh is low and dark. "I wish."

I know he won't tell me what that means, so I forge ahead. "Married?"

"Ach. *No.*"

He sounds truly appalled by the idea, so I believe him. "A spy? A drug lord? A superhero vigilante?"

He says drily, "You have a vivid imagination, lass."

"This is what happens in the absence of facts. Imagination kicks into gear to fill the vacuum and suddenly that little bump on my neck turns into an inoperable tumor rapidly metastasizing through all my vital organs, and I only have weeks left to live."

After a pause, he says, "You should stay off the internet."

"I know. I once convinced myself from reading Web MD that

the little twitch in my left hand was the early stages of MS. Don't change the subject. *What's your deal,* Liam Black?"

He says nothing for a moment. I hold my breath, gripping the phone, listening hard into the crackling silence.

"I...I'm in a very dangerous line of work."

His voice is so low it's almost inaudible. I don't dare say a word, because I can tell he had to fight himself to reveal even that much, and I want him to keep going.

He takes a breath. "The kind of work that could follow me home. Which is why I don't have anything in my life that isn't expendable."

I can't help myself. I need more. "Expendable..."

"I have to be able to walk away from everything at a moment's notice, and never look back. It's the way I live. The way I've lived for a very long time. I can't have ties, you understand? Anyone I'd be close to would become..."

When he doesn't continue, I whisper, "A target?"

"A liability," he corrects, his voice gaining an edge. "A responsibility I can't afford."

My heart hammers against my sternum, banging so wildly it's hard to catch my breath. "And this dangerous work of yours... what exactly is it?"

After a tense pause, he says darkly, "Enforcement."

Why that sounds so damn ominous, I don't know. "Like...law enforcement?"

"Aye. Exactly like that. Except outside the law." He pauses again. "Your laws, anyway."

I swallow, my pulse going gangbusters and my hands starting to shake. "Okay. This is a lot. To be honest, it sounds like you're telling me you're a criminal."

His voice softens. "You know what I'm capable of."

"The devil himself is afraid of that man." I hear Buddy's words in my head, but push them aside in frustration. "You did what you did to help me. Criminals don't put other people's well-being

before their own."

"Perhaps we have different definitions of what a criminal is."

I say hotly, "Which one of us in this conversation is going to be a criminal defense attorney, me or you?"

This pause is the longest so far. Then, softly, disbelievingly, Liam starts to laugh. "You're studying to be a *criminal defense attorney*?"

"Don't laugh. From what you're telling me, you might need me one day."

"I need you now," is his sharp, instant response. "And not for your skills in the courtroom. Which is why this is such a disaster in the making, and I keep warning you away."

We sit in tense silence for a while, until I say, "If you truly think this is such a disaster in the making, then you're the one who should stay away. I don't know all the facts. I'm lacking half the evidence. I can't make an educated decision, but you can."

His voice goes rough. "Aye. And for almost a year, I've been telling myself every time I see you that it's the last time, but it never is. So I've thought of something that might be a workable solution for us both. But you should still say no."

I think for a moment, then give up. "Okay. No."

His silence sounds surprised. That gives me a profound sense of satisfaction.

"Your move, Mr. Black."

He says my name, my full name, in this hot, frustrated, sexy-as-hell guttural tone that makes me think he'd love nothing more in this moment than to take me over his knee and spank my ass.

Which, let's be honest, would be a very satisfying outcome to the conversation.

"I'm going to hang up now, because I've reached my daily limit of growls. But my front door will be open tonight. If you don't come, don't bother contacting me again. I'm not going to play this cat and mouse game with you. I don't have the patience for it.

"And if this is really the last time we speak and I never see you again...you should know that I think you're the most interesting, aggravating, and beautiful man I've ever met. Thank you for everything. Goodbye."

I hit the End button and throw Ellie's phone over my shoulder. Then I sit on the bed, seething with discontent.

Liam Black. Criminal? Vigilante? Hit man? Warrior poet? Cultured badass?

Good guy who does bad things...or bad guy who does good things?

In the end, all my brooding gets me nowhere, so I get dressed and call a cab to take me to work.

My laptop's in my car, and I'm in the mood to do some major online sleuthing.

12

TRU

*M*y car is parked in the same spot I left it at Buddy's. When I go inside, Lisa's behind the counter, pouring coffee for a customer. She glances at me, does a double-take, and fumbles the coffee pot, almost dropping it. Coffee splashes all over the counter.

"Tru!"

"I know," I say drily. "I look like a punching bag. It looks worse than it feels."

"What happened?" Ignoring her customer, who's obviously peeved about the mess, she rushes over to me and gives me a one-armed hug.

I think it's best to be circumspect about the whole situation, especially in light of Buddy's obvious fear about anything getting back to Liam, so I shrug and say, "Long story."

She lowers her voice. "Did someone hit you?"

"Something like that. I don't really want to get into it. I just came by to get my handbag and pick up my car."

She takes me by the arm and steers me into the back, past the kitchen. Diego's not on shift yet, so there's another guy behind the grill, an older man named Tony who doesn't look up as we pass.

When Lisa and I find a quiet corner, she turns on me and says sternly, "If you're being abused by a man, I'll help you. There are a lot of resources out there—"

"If a man laid a hand on me in anger, he'd lose the hand. It's not that."

"So what then? Did you fall?"

"I was jumped. By a couple of guys I didn't know."

Her blue eyes widen. "Oh, my god. I'm so sorry, sweetie! Are you okay?"

"Yes. I got lucky." *A wolf saved my life.* "Honestly, I'm fine. I... got away from them."

"Where did this happen?"

I hesitate, because I don't want to scare her. "In the alley behind the restaurant. I was taking out the trash."

Her face pales. "Holy shit. Nobody said anything about it to us! Did the police catch the guys?"

Oh god. How do I explain this? "They're, um, looking into it."

None of these things are lies, but they're not exactly truths, either. Since I know what Buddy told Carla and Diego, I want to keep my story in line with that. And considering how spooked he was about Liam, there's no chance in hell I'm mentioning his name to anyone else.

I can't wait to see what I can find out about him online.

Lisa's customer calls out from the front. "Can someone clean up this coffee, please? It's dripping onto my lap!"

"Shit," mutters Lisa.

"Get back to work," I say, smiling at her. "And thanks for being so sweet."

She gives me another hug, tells me to get Arnica cream for the bruising and to call her if I need anything, then heads back out to the front.

I go into the break room and quickly grab my bag from the

locker, then leave through the side door that leads to the parking lot to avoid any more conversation with Lisa.

Which is where I run into Diego, who's just coming in.

He stops dead in his tracks when he sees me. His mouth falls open in disbelief.

I hold up a hand and walk closer to him. "I'm okay. Don't freak out."

He says something in Spanish, his gaze roving over my face. He's dressed in jeans, a black pea coat, and boots, his dark hair combed and his face freshly shaven.

As soon as I'm within arms' length, he pulls me into a hug.

"Chica," he says, his voice uneven. "Jesus fucking Christ."

I try to keep my voice light, because even though I told him not to freak out, he obviously is. "Good to know I'm that frightening."

He pulls away. Holding me by the shoulders, he looks me over again, his brows pulled together and his expression distraught. "Me and Carla...we didn't know what the fuck happened. One minute you were there, the next you were gone. Buddy said you got attacked? You were in the hospital?"

"Yeah. But I'm fine now. No damage, other than what you see."

I smile at him, hoping to avoid the interrogation I sense is coming.

No luck. He starts to grill me relentlessly.

"So, what happened? How many of them were there? Had you ever seen them before? What did your doctors say? What are the cops doing to help? When are you coming back to work?"

He pauses, and his voice gets strangled. "And can you ever forgive me for not taking out the fucking trash myself?"

I sigh. "There's nothing to forgive. Stop being such a drama queen. I'm fine, truly. Honestly, I just want to put the whole thing behind me."

He moistens his lips, swallows, shakes his head like he's in denial about something. "I should've never let you go outside alone so late. I should've *never*. I don't know what the fuck I was thinking. I should've—"

"Stop."

He clamps his mouth shut and stares at me.

"It wasn't your fault, Diego. There are some bad people in the world, who do bad things. This isn't on you in any way, okay?"

He pulls me into another hug, but this one feels different. More tender, somehow. He holds me like he doesn't want to let me go.

Five seconds into it, I'm uncomfortable.

I pull away, smiling awkwardly, and push my hair behind my ear. He shoves his hands into his front pockets. We stand there in silence for a moment, until he says, "I tried calling all the hospitals around, but they all said there was no Truvy Sullivan checked in."

"Really? That's strange." I have no idea what else to say.

He stares at me. "Yeah. I thought so, too."

"Maybe they thought you were saying Ruby or Trudie or something like that."

He shakes his head. "I spelled it for everybody. You weren't in anybody's computer system."

Shifting my weight from foot to foot, I glance away, trying to avoid his penetrating gaze. "Um, I don't remember much about when I checked in. I might've given them my middle name or something."

"Uh huh." Pause. "So this 'good Samaritan' Buddy said found you and called the ambulance. I'd like to thank him. Did you get the guy's name?"

"The, uh, the police probably have it. Like I said, I don't really remember much."

He's silent for a second, then says, "You know you're a shitty liar, right?"

I snap my head around and meet his level gaze. "I'm not lying!"

"You're not telling me the truth, either." When I'm silent, he challenges, "Are you?"

"Okay, you know what, Diego? This is BS. I got attacked in an alley by three thugs who wanted to rob the place. I got beat up. I went to the hospital. And now I'm out of the hospital and trying to get back to normal. Why are you giving me grief about this?"

He takes a step closer. His voice lowers. "Because I've never seen Buddy act as weird as he did when he told me and Carla what happened. He looked like he was about to shit his pants or leave town for good. And I could tell he wasn't being straight with us, just like I can tell you're not either."

He pauses. "This has something to do with that *vato* in black who always comes in and stares at you, doesn't it?"

I press my lips together and look away. "No."

I hear his huff of annoyance. Then he gently takes me by the chin and turns my face toward his. His gaze drills into mine. He says softly, "I'm your friend, chica. Why are you lying to me?"

Aw, shit.

I whisper, "I'm sorry." I take a breath and look at my shoes. Diego drops his hand from my face to my shoulder. "It's just that I can't...I don't exactly know how..."

I blow out a hard breath and look up at him. "It's complicated."

He examines my face for a moment, then nods. He says softly, "Okay. I won't push it. But I want you to know that I'm here for you, yeah? If shit gets more complicated, you can talk to me. I won't judge."

A lump forms in my throat. I nod wordlessly, blinking back the moisture forming in my eyes.

Diego's voice hardens. "But if I find out that *puto pendejo* hurt you, I'll kill him."

I stare at him in horror. "Diego! How can you expect me to talk to you after that?"

His brown eyes flash in anger. "So he *did* hurt you. It wasn't strangers who attacked you in the alley—it was *him*."

"No! Stop twisting this around, it was *not* him!"

He looks at me with narrowed eyes, a muscle in his jaw flexing.

"I'm not lying about that," I say, exasperated. "He was the one who helped me!"

The minute it's out of my mouth, I want to kick myself.

Of course, Diego hones in on that statement like a bloodhound.

"So the man in black is the 'good Samaritan,' huh?" Livid, he shakes his head. "Did it ever occur to you that he might have set the whole thing up?"

"That's ridiculous. Why would he do that?"

"So he could look like the good guy. Gain your trust."

"You've been watching too many crime shows."

"And you don't know the lengths a man will go for something he wants."

I close my eyes, pinch the bridge of my nose between two fingers and mutter, "I can't believe this."

"You're beautiful, chica."

Surprised, I open my eyes and look at Diego. He stares back at me with a grim set to his mouth.

"Beautiful and sweet. And smart. And funny. I've been watching guys come in here and get boners over you for two years. But I've never seen any man look at any woman the way that fucker looks at you."

I hesitate to ask, but curiosity gets the better of me. "How does he look at me?"

"Like he'll die if he doesn't."

My heartbeat is doing something strange. It's all fluttery and chaotic, banging against my ribcage like a panicked bird. I take a moment to compose myself, then say, "I'm gonna go home now. I'll be back at work in a few days."

"Tru—"

"No, Diego," I say firmly. "I appreciate your concern for me, and I value you as a friend. But we're done with this conversation."

He tips his head back and looks at me from under lowered lashes. Then he smiles a grim little smile and says, "Okay. I hear you."

"Thank you."

He leans closer and says, "But what I said stands—if I find out that fucker hurt you, I'll kill him."

He brushes past me and enters the diner, letting the door slam shut behind him.

I stand staring at the closed door with a cold shiver running down my spine.

When I get back to my apartment, I drop my purse onto the console table in the foyer, kick off my shoes, then go to the fridge for a bottle of water. I don't hear voices from Ellie's room, so I assume she and Ty are out.

Which is good, because I'm not in the mood to suffer through more of their caterwauling.

The conversation with Diego upset me. In all the time I've known him, he's been nothing but smiling, friendly, sweet. Lighthearted. But today I saw another side of him. The darker side.

He was like a different person.

Brooding on that, I take the water and my laptop and head to my bedroom. I'm anxious to look up the name Liam Black to see what I can find, but as soon as I open the door that idea goes straight out the window.

Because the man himself is inside.

Leaning against my dresser in his beautiful black suit and tie, calmly eating pistachio ice cream from the container while gazing at me with burning dark eyes.

I jerk to a stop and stand there staring at him.

My heart lurches. My stomach drops. I try to catch a breath, but can't.

In a thoughtful voice, he says, "You hung up on me." He lifts a spoonful of ice cream to his mouth and eats it, tonguing the spoon as if it's a woman's body. As if he's got his face buried between a pair of spread thighs.

I've never seen anything so carnal.

"I...I..."

"No one's ever done that before," he says, in that same thoughtful tone. He crooks his wrist and points at me with the spoon. "Except you."

Swallowing, I manage to form a complete sentence. "You deserved it."

He stares at me for a moment in crackling intensity. Then he slowly sets the ice cream aside, dropping the spoon into the container and leaving it on the dresser.

He turns his attention to me again. It's like being hit with a spotlight.

"Come here."

His voice is calm, but his eyes are wild and his nostrils are flared, as if he's about to start pawing the ground like a bull.

I feel electrocuted, like someone just plugged me into a socket. All my nerves are screaming. Gripping the water bottle and laptop, my hands start to shake.

Watching me, Liam licks his lips.

Feeling like I'm standing on the edge of a very high cliff, I whisper, "You said you couldn't get away until late."

His eyes glitter like he's running a fever. His voice drops. "Come. Here."

I'm engulfed in a wave of heat.

Trying not to hyperventilate, I slowly set the bottle of water and my laptop on the nightstand next to my bed. Smoothing my sweaty palms on the front of my jeans, I take a few tentative steps toward him.

He lifts out his hand.

I take a few more steps, sliding my hand into his. His fingers curl around mine. He gently coerces me forward, closing the distance between us.

Then he pulls me against his body, wraps an arm around my back, and cradles my head in his big hand.

He's huge, hot, and hard everywhere. His gaze locks onto mine, and I'm on fire.

"Tell me to leave," he whispers, his voice an urgent rasp. "Tell me it's over. Tell me you never want to see me again."

I flatten my shaking hands on his chest, look into his eyes, and shake my head.

He closes his eyes briefly, draws a breath, exhales in a ragged rush. Then he presses my head to his chest and brushes his lips against my forehead. "Last chance, lass."

"I can't kick you out yet. You've never even kissed me."

His chuckle is a low rumble underneath my ear. "So you've been waiting for that to end it, have you?"

"Guess you'll have to wait and see."

His arms tighten around me. I sense he's trying to be gentle, but also is having a difficult time holding back.

I tilt my head back and reach up and touch his face. "Kiss me," I whisper, my voice trembling.

His lips curve into a wry smile. "Such a bossy little thing."

"Please?"

Hearing that, his eyes darken. The smile disappears from his face. He grinds his back teeth together, hesitating.

Then he lowers his head and lightly brushes his lips against mine.

It's exquisitely soft and tender, a whisper of a thing, yet it sends a bolt of lust straight through me.

When I softly gasp and lean into him, he pulls back and gazes down at me in silence.

I drop my forehead against his chest and groan in frustration.

"You're still hurt," he murmurs.

"Somebody else is about to get hurt here, I'll tell you what."

Silent laughter rocks his chest.

I wind my arms around his broad shoulders and snuggle closer to him, closing my eyes. Then I sigh, because Liam's body has gone stiff.

I grouse, "I don't bite."

The hand cradling my head closes to a fist around my hair. He slides his arm down my back, palms my ass, and pulls me closer, so I feel his erection digging into my hip. He lowers his head and says gruffly into my ear, "But I do."

Then he opens his mouth over the pulse pounding in my neck and bites me.

It's not hard, not enough to sting or leave a mark, but it sends such a jolt of electricity through me I moan like a porn star. I sag against him, digging my fingers into his shoulders, my eyes rolling back into my head.

The bite turns into a gentle suck.

His mouth is heaven. Velvet soft lips and greedy hot tongue—I want to feel that all over me. I want his mouth to explore every inch of my skin.

I whisper, "Liam. Oh god."

He rocks his hips against mine and sucks harder.

My nipples are so hard they ache. I want his mouth on those, too. And his teeth, that gentle bite. I need to feel the scratch of his beard against my most sensitive skin, hear that low, masculine rumble of pleasure go through his chest as he manhandles me with those big rough hands, moving me this way and that on the bed, growling filthy words into my ear as he drives into me.

Picturing it, a whimper of need rises from my throat.

He pulls away from my neck, grasps my jaw in his hand, and stares down at me with burning eyes. I've seen him on the edge of his control before, but never like this.

Breathing raggedly, he says, "Twenty-eight days."

I blink in confusion. The room is spinning, I'm panting, and my heart is a hammer in my chest. *What is he saying? Does he need a calendar?*

"W-what?"

"I have to go out of the country tomorrow for three weeks. When I come back, I'm here for twenty-eight days until I leave again."

I stare at him, not understanding his point.

Until he says, "I want us to be together for those twenty-eight days. I want you to stay with me at my home. To be with me all the time. To be mine. All mine, every minute, in every way."

He pauses, then delivers the most shocking part of this proposal.

"Then we'll never see each other again."

*S*tunned, I breathe, "You want me to…"

"Move in with me."

"For…"

"Twenty-eight days. Then leave."

He stares at me with blistering intensity. A disbelieving little laugh escapes my lips.

He says, "I told you I don't do relationships."

"And this is your solution? A month of round-the-clock cohabitation, followed by permanent separation? It's a little drastic, don't you think?"

His gaze drops to my mouth. He growls, "I think it's the only way for us both to get what we want without any lasting damage."

I stare up at him. He can't be serious. "Liam—"

"Yes or no. Decide."

I arch my brows and slide my arms from around his shoulders, flattening my hands on the broad expanse of his chest. "And *I'm* the bossy one?"

"I need to know right now."

"Why? Where's the fire?"

Through gritted teeth, he says, "I can't concentrate on

anything else. Every time I see you, it gets worse. It needs to be settled."

"It?" I say archly.

"Us."

I study him for a moment, all his frustration and impatience. I don't feel a shred of pity for him, the arrogant ass.

"You know, this is how it is for normal people. The not knowing. The uncertainty. This is what most of us have to deal with in relationships all the time."

"I'm not most people," he growls. "And I don't do—"

"Relationships. So you've said."

Aggravated, I pull away from him. Turning my back, I fold my arms over my chest and glare at my bed. Why does he have to make everything so intense?

His voice comes very low from behind me. "Decide."

I roll my eyes to the ceiling. "Can you give me a minute to catch my breath?"

"No. Decide."

I turn around and look at him, standing there boiling with heat and danger, like a volcano about to blow its top. "If you want a decision right now, the answer is no."

He falls still and glowers at me.

Heat creeps up my neck. "Oh, I see. It was a foregone conclusion that I'd say yes, right?"

He presses his lips into a thin line and says nothing.

Even more aggravated now, I start to pace the length of the room. It's a small room, so I feel a little ridiculous turning around every four steps, but I have to work off some of this frustration and sexual tension somehow.

"I have a life, you know. Work. School. Friends. I can't just drop everything and disappear for a month."

"I didn't say you had to disappear. You wouldn't be cut off from the outside world."

"You said 'all mine, every minute.' I took that to mean I'd be chained to your bed."

His eyes grow hot. He likes the idea.

"No," he says, his voice husky. "I'm not asking you to be my slave."

"So I could leave?"

"Are we negotiating?"

I stop short and stare at him. He stares back at me from under lowered brows, his gaze level and unwavering.

He's never looked hotter, more intense, or more dangerous. My mouth goes dry.

I whisper, "I don't know. Maybe."

He adjusts the knot in his tie, then adjusts his cufflinks, one by one. He shifts his weight from foot to foot. He stares at me like all the mysteries of the universe can be discovered in my eyes.

"What would make you say yes? Name it."

He really wants this. He wants it so badly, he can barely stand still.

A strange feeling moves through me. It's so unfamiliar, it takes a moment for me to identify it, but then I realize what it is.

Power.

The way Liam wants me doesn't make me feel demeaned, or weak, or frightened.

It makes me feel powerful as fuck.

I say softly, "Well, for one thing, you have to kiss me, wolfie. I'm not about to spend twenty-eight days with a man who I'm not even sure can properly kiss."

He cocks a dark brow.

I fold my arms across my chest and gaze calmly at him. "Non-negotiable."

He looks me up and down slowly, eating me up with hungry eyes. When he moistens his lips, I almost groan out loud. Then he moves toward me, takes my face in his hands, and lowers his mouth to mine.

It's immediately evident that the man not only knows how to kiss, he knows how to kiss a woman senseless.

His mouth demands.

It takes.

It *owns* me.

I clutch his jacket in my fists and take short bursts of air through my nose as his tongue delves into my mouth and sweeps against mine, over and over again with the perfect amount of suction and pressure to get me squirming and rubbing my thighs restlessly together as I press against the hard length of him.

I'm vaguely aware of my lower lip stinging, but I'm drowning in his taste. In the pleasure of this kiss, the decadence of it, the way he's framing my face with his hands and holding my head in place so he can take what he wants and give me what I didn't even know I needed.

I moan into his mouth.

My heart glows like a light bulb.

I go up on my toes and kiss him back harder.

When he suddenly breaks away, I'm so dizzy, I almost fall over.

We stand there breathing raggedly, his breath hot against my cheek and his erection throbbing against my crotch, until he demands roughly, "Well?"

I say faintly, "Well...it didn't suck."

He lowers his mouth to my ear. His voice is a dark, delicious command.

"Don't toy with me."

Oh, god, all I want is to rip off my clothes and climb him like a tree. I'm delirious with desire. This can't be normal. Not that anything about the situation is normal, but I'm having hot flashes a good quarter century before menopause is due.

With my eyes closed and my hands still clutching his suit jacket, I say, "That was..."

He waits, taut and crackling with tension.

"The best damn kiss I've ever had."

Exhaling, he wraps his arms around my body, pulling me tight against him. "So it's a yes?"

I groan and bury my face in his chest. "This is so weird."

"Don't overthink it. Just go with your gut."

When I whimper, he says hotly, "Fuck. I need to hear you make that sound when I'm inside you."

He's trying to kill me. He's trying to fry my brain with a testosterone overload, so he can throw me over his shoulder and take me back to his cave and have his way with me.

So we can have our way with each other.

I have no doubt this little experiment he's proposing would be a two-way street. He'd give as much pleasure as he'd take. He'd make sure he'd send me away twenty-eight days later with crossed eyes, bowed legs, and a goofy smile on my face.

Twenty-Eight Days Later is the name of a horror movie. Coincidence or bad omen?

It could be amazing, though. It could be an absolute dream. No strings, no commitments, just constant sex with the hottest man I've ever met along with a little vacay from real life...

Oh, who am I kidding? This is insane!

I pull away and look him in the eye. "I'm incredibly tempted. But it's too out there for me. Too impractical."

Ignoring the "out there" comment, he pounces on the other reason. "Impractical—how?"

"I can't be off work for a month—"

"Yes, you can," he cuts in. "And your boss will pay for it."

I twist my lips, knowing he's right. Considering how terrified he is of Liam, Buddy would probably give me a full year's worth of paid leave if I asked.

Okay, next.

"I have school."

"The semester's over in thirteen days. You don't sit for the bar until the end of July. Which means you have two months open in the interim."

I stare at him in surprise. "How did you know that?"

"I've done my homework. Next argument, counselor?"

"No, back up. Did you investigate me or something?"

"If you count asking your roommate a few questions as investigation, then yes."

"Oh."

"Why are you frowning?"

"I'm wondering what other personal details my blabbermouth roommate provided you."

"Let's stay on topic. What other concerns do you have?"

His eyes burn with intensity. It's too distracting, so I turn and move to the other side of the room, putting a safe distance between us. I lean against the small desk where I study, fold my arms over my chest, and look at him.

"Okay, let's get to the nitty gritty. From everything you've said about your life, it's clear you think I'd be in danger if I spent any significant amount of time with you."

He waits, bristling with impatience.

"Which means if I'm staying with you, at your place—"

"You'd be protected there," he says, his voice hard. "It's a fortress."

When I lift my brows, he says, "Figuratively. There are safeguards. Technology."

He waves an impatient hand in the air to indicate a long list of safety measures he employs that he's not going to mention. "The point is you'd be safe. Much safer than you are here. You don't even have a deadbolt on your front door, for fuck's sake."

I study him.

When I'm silent too long for his patience, he demands, "Tell me."

I say softly, "You seem to have thought of everything. Except this plan of yours has one glaring issue that all your clinical problem-solving has overlooked."

"Which is?"

"Emotion."

His reply is silence, along with a slow grind of his molars.

"It's not going to be easy to break it off after a month of total immersion, Liam. If it's this intense now, and we haven't even—"

"It won't be a problem."

"You sound pretty sure."

He examines my face for a moment, then abruptly turns away to stare out the window. He drags a hand through his hair and adjusts his tie. His voice lowers.

"Falling in love is a luxury I don't allow myself."

I gaze at his profile, so handsome and hard. His expression is unreadable.

I wonder if I'll ever get to the center of this man. If he'll ever allow me to see past the black velvet curtain. That he's equally capable of violence and passion I already know, but beyond those extremes lies the dark heart of him, the mystery of who he really is.

Somewhere deep inside Liam Black is the key to all the secrets he keeps locked away, but I doubt it's a key I'll be allowed to find.

The thought makes me unspeakably sad.

I whisper, "Who said I was talking about you?"

Eyes flashing, he turns to look at me. Our locked gazes are an invisible circuit conducting electricity through the air, cycling back and forth between us on a loop. My heartbeat goes haywire.

He says gruffly, "I told you it was selfish."

"You did. You also told me I should slap you and throw you out, but you're trying very hard to convince me to do just the opposite. I'm not sure which version of you I should listen to: cupid or Dr. Doom."

Liam crosses to me slowly, his gaze never leaving mine. When he reaches me, he takes my wrists and winds my arms around his shoulders. Pulling me close, he lowers his head and murmurs into my ear.

"Listen to your heart. I won't try to convince you beyond this: I want you like I've never wanted anyone or anything. Give me twenty-eight days, and in return I'll give you everything on earth I have to give.

"I can't promise you forever, but I can promise you a month you'll remember for the rest of your life."

Then he fists a hand in my hair and kisses me.

It's hard and desperate, shockingly passionate, and rocks me with the depth of its need.

He's giving me a preview. A taste of what he's been holding back. A small window into the bottomless ocean of feeling he keeps so tightly locked inside.

What frightens me is just how addictive this one little taste is.

I cling to him and kiss him back, knowing that this is a terrible idea...and also that I'm in real danger of agreeing to it.

Liam breaks away, breathing raggedly. His voice hoarse, he says, "I leave tomorrow at six in the morning. You have my number. If I don't hear from you by six, I'll consider it a no."

He releases me and strides off, his long legs taking him away with shocking speed.

The front door to my apartment opens and closes.

Then I'm alone with my thundering heart and a million unanswered questions, wondering how on earth I'm going to make this decision. And, if I say yes to Liam, what exactly I'd be getting myself into.

I glance at my laptop lying on the nightstand next to my bed.

"Okay, Mr. Black," I mutter, headed toward it. "Let's see what we can find out about you."

14

TRU

*A*fter three hours and two-thirds of a bottle of chardonnay, the answer is: nothing.

Google helpfully provided 174,000,000 results for a search on his name. From there, I drilled down to images, social networks, and his cell phone number. I tried cross-referencing his name with the Boston PD. I tried his name plus the word "enforcement." I tried variations on the spelling of his name, I searched Irish genealogy sites and US government databases, I even paid thirty bucks for one of those background reports claiming to guarantee results.

Basically, I twisted my brain into a pretzel to find any crumb of information, but nothing worked.

Liam Black is either a ghost or a pseudonym.

I hear a knock on my closed bedroom door. Ellie calls, "Yo. You decent?"

"I try to be. Come on in."

She sticks her head in the door and looks at me, propped up on my bed with the laptop, simmering with frustration.

"You okay?"

"Define okay."

She thinks for a moment. "Having slept well, eaten well, and had an orgasm within the last eight hours."

"I aspire to your goals, my friend."

She smiles. "It's the simple things. Speaking of eating, me and Ty are gonna head over to South Creek Pizza for some pie. You in?"

"I'm kind of working."

She looks at the mostly empty bottle of wine on my nightstand, then looks back at me. "Did you eat anything today?"

"Does grape juice count?"

She makes a face, opening the door wider to stand inside my bedroom with a hand propped on her hip. Dressed in a tight black miniskirt, a short red leather jacket, and white lace baby doll socks with high heels, she looks like she's starring in an 80's music video.

"No, wino. Grape juice doesn't count. I'll bring you back some pizza."

"Don't bother. We have about six month's worth of food in the apartment. Anyone who looks in our kitchen will think we're doomsday preppers."

She struts over and plops down on the edge of my bed. Gently squeezing my ankle, she says, "Girlfriend."

Keeping my gaze on the laptop screen, I say, "Yep."

"You've got that constipated look you get when something's wrong."

When I glance up at her, she purses her lips. "You dumped the Irish hottie, didn't you?"

Sighing, I close the laptop and rub a fist into my eye. "I wish it were that simple."

"What's up?"

She turns to me eagerly, eyes alight. There's nothing Ellie loves more than gossip. Well, maybe *The Bachelor*, but other than reality TV, it's gossip.

I chew on my lip for a moment, debating what to tell her, but go with my default, "Nothing. Everything's fine."

She folds her arms over her boobs and glares at me.

I roll my eyes, pull my knees up to my chest, and wrap my arms around them. "Okay, everything *isn't* fine. It's just...so... complicated. Forget it."

When I don't add anything else, she says, "You totally suck at the girl thing, you know that?"

"What girl thing?"

"Talking. Opening up. Sharing your feelings." She makes air quotes around the word "feelings."

Because this is a failing I've been accused of before by various other people, I'm automatically defensive.

"I can't help it! I grew up on a farm! Unless you were bleeding from a major artery or one of your limbs was hanging on by a thread, no one cared about your problems!"

"You're not on a farm anymore," she says flatly. "There are no tractors, roosters, or cow teats in sight. Tell me what's going on with Liam."

I collapse back against the pillows and stare at the ceiling. I know she'll badger me until I submit, so I sum up the situation in a sentence. "He wants me to move in with him for a month then never see each other again."

There's a long pause. "So he's married. He's got a wife holed up somewhere."

I lift my head and look at her. "Worse."

"What's worse than married?"

I muse, "How to describe it?" I think for a moment, then drop my head back against the pillows. "He's...emotionally unavailable."

"Ha!" She cackles. "Dude! It comes with the testicles!"

That obviously didn't impress her. I have to give another example. "He's also very, very, very...mysterious. Enigmatic. Unfathomable."

She scoffs. "Puh. What, you want to know all the gnarly details about his private life? How often he jerks off? Plucks his nose hairs? Shaves his balls?"

My sigh is heavy. "Yeah, this girlie sharing thing is awesome. I can see why you like it so much."

"Stop being sarcastic. A little mystery in a relationship is a good thing, not a problem."

"This is more than a *little* mystery, Ellie. This is like...does-Bigfoot-exist mystery. Who-really-shot-JFK mystery. What's-the-deal-with-the-Bermuda-Triangle mystery. This is *big*."

"Or maybe you're just making it big."

"I'm not making it anything. It is what it is."

"Hmm."

She clearly doesn't believe me.

After a while of staring at me in faint disapproval, she says, "Can I point something out here without you getting offended?"

I groan. "You know when you say something like that, the person you say it to will get offended, right? Asking that question first doesn't let you off the hook for being offensive."

Ignoring that, she continues. "You need a man. Don't look at me like that, it's true. You've had one serious long-term relationship in your life—"

"Which ended very badly, let's not forget."

"—and since then, nada. It's not healthy, Tru. Your vagina is probably as shriveled up as a sun-dried tomato. You're too young for this kind of celibacy. Wait until after you've been married a few years to give up on sex, like everyone else."

Staring at the ceiling, I say without heat, "I never thought I'd be defending my sex life to my feminist roommate. Aren't women supposed to support each other's choices?"

Ellie shrugs. "Hey, I'm not judging you. I've had so many sexual partners, I stopped counting when the number equaled my age. I'm simply pointing out facts."

"Do these charming facts of yours have a purpose?"

"Yes."

I turn my head and look at her. "Which is?"

She smiles, looking smug. "A month of shacking up with Ireland's hottest export since Colin Farrell would be like winning the lottery, girlfriend. It'd be a friggin' dream come true. *And* the perfect way to ease yourself back into relationship waters without a long-term commitment. I mean, you've probably forgotten how great sex without a condom is."

"My head is spinning. How did we go from the lottery to condoms?"

She turns practical. "Well, you'd both have to get STD tests, of course."

"I don't have an STD!"

"And we want to make sure he doesn't, either. The best way to do that is to make it a condition of moving in with him."

When I only stare at her in disbelief without responding, she sighs.

"Dude. Seriously. *Look* at the man. He's got women throwing their vaginas at him from across the street."

I say sourly, "That's a lovely visual. Thank you very much."

"What I'm saying is that he's the guy who gets mad pussy. He's rich, suave, beautiful...that all equals mad pussy. He's got so much pussy, it's falling out of his pockets."

"Jesus, Ellie, when did you start talking like Snoop Dog?"

"Sorry. I've been listening to a lot of booty rap lately. Tyler's really into it. He likes to play it while he's doing me from behind."

I make a face. "Can you please leave and go get your pizza now? This sharing stuff is killing me."

She sighs dramatically, stands, and looks down at me with her hands propped on her hips.

"Give me the bottom line. What's your main argument *against* having a month-long affair with that excellent specimen of manhood?"

"Gee, where to start?" I muse. Then, dropping the sarcasm: "I don't know anything about him. I don't know his age, where he lives, what he does for a living, and if he owns any clothing other than black Armani suits. I don't know what kind of food he likes. What kind of music he listens to. What his politics are. Frankly, I don't even know if the man is actually from planet Earth."

She deadpans, "Didn't you hear? Men are from Mars."

"Oh my god." I put the laptop over my face so I don't have to look at her anymore.

"He isn't the kind of guy you marry, Tru, so don't worry about any of that stuff!"

I peek over the edge of the laptop and stare up at her.

She smiles at me. "Your hottie Irishman is the guy you have the best sex of your life with, then move on. Guys like him aren't built for the long haul."

"What do you mean, built for the long haul?"

"Example: can you picture bringing him home for Christmas?"

I think about that for a moment. Liam, elegant mystery badass, reader of dead French novelists, on the farm, in his couture Armani suit.

My mother would serve a goose she'd slaughtered that morning. My father would suggest a tour of his taxidermy collection of skunks and possums that he shot himself and keeps in the shed. My brothers would get drunk and try to wrestle him. My sisters would flirt. The bull would probably break out of the corral again, and my nana would be eager to tell the story of The Day Truvy's Pig Ate the Wash.

I slide the laptop down to my chest and say slowly, "That would be a big, fat no."

"What about doing housework? Mowing the lawn? Changing diapers?"

"No, no, and *definitely* no."

"Which is why his plan is so perfect!" She grins like she's the president of the debate club and just took home the winning trophy.

I sit up, swing my legs over the side of the bed, and sigh. "He must've hypnotized you. You never like anyone."

She shrugs. "People in general suck. But he's a bonafide, once-in-a-lifetime, fiercely smokin' hot piece of ass that you *need* to bang six ways to Sunday until your coochie is ready to fall out. And then come home and tell me every single thing."

I throw my hands in the air. "This isn't *Real Housewives*! This is my life!"

"No, it's a month of your life. But if you're not interested, tell him I'm up for it."

"Ellie!"

She rolls her eyes at my outraged expression. "Fine. I'm up for a three-way, too."

"Oh, really?" I say drily. "And what would Ty think of that plan?"

She snorts. "If I had a chance to spend even ten minutes in the sack with Liam, Ty would be dead to me, girl."

She turns and heads to my bedroom door, stopping just before she passes through it to give me a stern look. "Eat something."

"Yes, mother."

Shaking her head, she leaves.

I fall back onto the bed and think for a long time, following the cracks in the ceiling with my eyes and debating the situation.

Ultimately, it comes down to logic versus hormones.

I want him. That's an undeniable fact. Also undeniable is that our chemistry is explosive, and I'm dying of curiosity about everything to do with him. And, based on the kiss alone, I have no doubt our sex would be mind-blowing.

But.

He's dangerous. And not drives-after-a-few-drinks dangerous.

He's *lethal*, and I'd be totally vulnerable living with him at his home.

The home I don't even know the location of.

What if he decided at the end of twenty-eight days he wasn't going to let me go? He said he didn't want a slave, but isn't that exactly what you'd say if you were trying to convince someone you didn't want a slave, but you really did?

What if I wound up chained to the floor in a cage in his basement?

"Safeguards," I say to myself. "Someone has to know where I am and when I'm supposed to be coming back."

Okay. That's doable. I could make it a condition of my agreement.

Plus, I could do a daily check-in call. For instance...if Ellie didn't hear from me by ten in the morning, she'd call the police and give them Liam's address.

I think that's a great idea for all of about two seconds, until I remember the cops seem to be on his payroll. And I don't know his address.

So...she could call the news.

Or my cousin Bubba Joe.

Or whoever, the point is, Ellie could be my link to safety in case things went sideways.

No—that's wrong.

If I believe he's a danger to me in any way, I shouldn't go through with it. I should say no right now, and let that be the end of the mysterious Mr. Black.

The thing is...I know he's not a danger to me.

I *know*, without knowing how, that Liam would never hurt me. I've always felt safe with him. In fact, I believe he'd risk his own life to keep me from harm.

After all, he's already proved he would.

But still. This is not normal. This request of his isn't real life.

And let's not forget to consider the opposite scenario of him keeping me in a cage: what if he let me go without a fuss?

How would I feel at the end of twenty-eight days when he happily sent me on my way, never to see me again?

Most likely...disposable.

Forgettable.

Used.

With an aggravated grumble, I scrub my hands over my face, then spend a while longer pondering the problem.

Finally, I decide the only way to get some of my questions answered is to go directly to the source. So I send Liam a text, asking him to call me when he gets a chance.

My phone rings less than sixty seconds later.

Before I can even say hello, he demands, "Tell me it's a yes."

I curl up onto my side on the bed with the phone to my ear, close my eyes, and sigh.

"That doesn't sound like a yes."

"Can you appreciate at all how strange this is for me?"

After a beat, he answers, his voice an octave lower. "Aye, lass. I can. It's strange for me, too."

"How is it strange for *you*? This is your rodeo."

He growls, "Because I've never been obsessed with a woman the way I am with you."

The raw honesty in his voice stops me short. I whisper, "Really?"

"Aye. I feel like a filthy fucking addict."

I sit with that for a moment, enjoying it.

He says, "You're worried. You don't need to be. You have my word I'll take care of you."

I hear voices in the background. Male voices, several of them, all angry. It sounds like an argument...and it's in Gaelic.

"I have to go. I won't be able to answer the phone again for a while." His voice turns hard. "Say yes, Tru. And say it *now*."

I open my mouth to obey him, but something stops me.

It might be the tone of the voices in the background, or that I've heard one too many demands from him, or that my mind chose this exact moment to provide me with a memory of Buddy's dark warning about using my eyes and my brain.

But from one heartbeat to the next, I'm certain that agreeing to this outlandish proposal would be a mistake.

One I might never recover from.

"I'm sorry, Liam," I say quietly. "But I'm going to listen to your advice and say no."

A moment of blistering silence follows. "I see."

I exhale a pent-up breath, my heart pounding though I don't know why.

Then he adds darkly, "Let's hope I can honor that decision."

The line goes dead in my hand.

15

TRU

*O*ne week later, my bruising has faded, I'm back at work, and life has returned to normal.

I haven't heard from Liam. I don't know if I ever will again or not, but the memory of that kiss we shared in my bedroom is branded onto my mind.

So are the last words he spoke to me.

I've gone over it a thousand times in my head: his blistering pause, his dark tone, the words themselves. I don't know exactly what to make of all of it, except that he wasn't expecting it...and he wasn't sure he accepted it.

Beyond that, I haven't allowed my thoughts to wander. The terrain out there is much too dangerous.

"What're you gonna do for graduation? Are your folks coming up?"

I laugh at Carla's question. It's Sunday night, and my shift at Buddy's is over. I'm in no hurry to get home, however, because Ty and Ellie have been having so much raucous sex over the past week, my ears are bleeding.

I feel guilty for thinking it, but I'll be glad when they break up again.

In the meantime, I need to buy myself ear plugs so I can get some sleep.

"God no. They never leave Texas."

"Really? Why not?"

"My dad's claustrophobic. He can't get on a plane or he starts to bellow like an elephant. And my mom won't go anywhere and leave him home alone, because he'll either burn down the house trying to fix himself a meal or let Daisy sleep with him in their bed."

Carla stares at me for a beat. "Please tell me Daisy is a dog."

"She's a donkey."

She mutters, "How did I know that?" and walks away.

I call after her, "You asked!"

Smiling, I head into the back. Diego's at the grill in the kitchen. He lifts his chin at me as I pass, but doesn't say anything.

We haven't spoken much since I started back at work. He's kept his distance, which I'm grateful for. After that hug he gave me, along with the threat against Liam, I'm still uncomfortable around him. I think he must sense it, because his usual playfulness is gone.

In the break room, I hang my apron in my locker and change my shoes. Then I put on my coat—I still don't know what happened to the one I was wearing the night I was attacked—and grab my purse.

When I turn around, Diego is lounging against the door frame, looking at the floor.

His voice muted, he says, "I owe you an apology."

I'm so surprised, I only stare at him for a moment.

He glances up and sends me a small smile. "I was out of line. Saying that thing about the *vato* in black. You know."

About how you'd kill him? Yeah, I know. "It was, um, a little unexpected."

His smile turns wry. "It freaked you out."

I return his smile. "To be fair, I was freaked out in general."

He sighs and pushes off the door frame. "Yeah. It was bad timing. And bad manners, too. Me being a macho dick was, like, the last thing you needed to deal with. I'm really sorry."

I'm touched. He's being very sweet, and I can tell he's sincere. He looks like a little boy who got yelled at for stealing a cookie.

"Apology accepted," I say warmly. "And now let's never talk about it again."

He examines my face for a moment, then breaks into a genuine smile. "Deal."

There's a moment of awkward silence before he asks, "You headed home?"

I nod. "Yes, but not to bed, unfortunately. I've got a paper due tomorrow that I totally spaced on."

He crinkles his forehead. "Didn't you already have finals?"

My chuckle is dry. "Yeah, but there's one professor who thinks he's not doing his job unless his students are miserable. We're going to be working like dogs straight up until the last minute of the last day of class on Friday."

"That sucks. When's your graduation ceremony?"

"The week after. But I'm not going."

Diego looks surprised. "Why not? You've worked so hard."

"For one thing, I hate big crowds. They give me hives. I skipped my college graduation, too. All that fuss and attention…" I shudder. "And my family isn't coming out, so there's really no point."

He furrows his brow. "Well, that's not right. We have to celebrate your accomplishment. Why don't we get dinner? Make it a special night."

I freeze. Then I start to panic, my stomach twisting and my mouth going dry. "Um…Diego, I hope this doesn't offend you, but I don't think that would be a good idea. You and I—"

He says smoothly, "I meant with Carla and Buddy. Your roommate, too, if you want. The more the merrier, right?"

I say hesitantly, "That sounds nice."

He grins, flashing a set of perfect white teeth. "Cool. You let me know where and how many, and I'll make the reservation."

"Thanks, Diego."

"Anything for you, chica."

He turns and saunters off, leaving me staring after him with a strange tightness in my chest and the feeling that a group date wasn't what he had in mind at all.

I was right: the last week of school is grueling.

I don't have time to do anything other than study, work, go to classes, and study some more. I apply for several different internships at local law firms because I'm not 100% sure I'll pass the bar the first time, and the experience would be good for my resume.

Thoughts of Liam linger in the back of my head, but I'm busy enough that I can mostly ignore them.

Except at night.

Lying in bed, I stare at the ceiling and listen to Ellie and Tyler have wild sex while imagining it's me and Liam.

It's torture. I wonder if I'm being punished for something terrible I did in a former life.

But she's glowing with happiness, so I act like a good friend and keep my mouth shut about how her amazing sex life is killing me. She'd just tell me I'm jealous, anyway.

She'd be right.

The Saturday after school ends is when I asked Diego to make the reservations for dinner at a local hot spot that I've never been to before. Ellie suggested the place. Carla and her husband are coming, and so are Ellie and Ty. Buddy declined, so that leaves six of us.

I ride with Ellie and Ty to the restaurant. When we arrive, we find Diego, Carla, and her husband, Dave, waiting for us in the bar. I take one look at Diego and my heart sinks.

He's wearing a suit. A nice navy blue suit with a white dress shirt, a gray tie, and black loafers polished to such a shine they could blind me.

That isn't a "we're just friends" suit.

He jolts from his chair as soon as he spots me, looks me up and down, and whistles. "You look beautiful, chica. That's some dress."

The dress in question is a sleeveless, V-neck, fitted red number with small crystal buttons all the way down the front. It reveals more skin than I'd like, but I'm wearing it under duress.

"Thank you. I borrowed it from Ellie. She said she wouldn't be seen at this place with me in my usual..." I turn to her with a quirked brow. "What did you call it?"

Hanging on Ty's arm, Ellie laughs. "Walmart chic."

"That's an oxymoron," says Ty, grinning down at Ellie.

I'm surprised he knows the definition of the word.

Ty is blond, permatan, and the kind of superficial you can spot all the way across a room. He looks exactly like what he is: the rich, popular jock from high school who's got more dick than brains and a trust fund of such a size it guarantees he'll never have to bother with developing those pesky character traits like honesty or empathy.

It's one of life's great mysteries that a woman like Ellie— smart, attractive, self-confident—would have anything to do with him.

Then again, judging by the volume of her screams, the sex is legendary.

"Hey, Tru!" A grinning Carla gives me a hug. She's wearing a leopard print minidress that looks painted on. Her cleavage is eye-popping. "You remember Dave?"

She gestures to her husband, a slab of beef of a man standing beside her.

He's a few years past his prime but is handsome in a rugged, outdoorsy way. He looks like someone you'd want with you if your plane crashed on a desert island. He'd be the guy chopping down palm trees to make huts for shelter and catching fish with his bare hands.

"Tru," he says in a rumbling baritone. "Congrats on graduating."

"Thank you, Dave. I never thought I'd make it!"

He regards me with a level look. "Carla says you're gonna be a public defender?"

"That's the plan."

"Good for you. This town needs more bright young people who're civic minded. Seems like all the young folks these days only care about takin' selfies and bein' Instagram models."

Flipping his hair, Ty laughs. "Yeah, that's 'cause Instagram influencers make *bank*. Tru's gonna have to find herself a rich husband if she wants to be able make her rent."

He winks at me. "Being civic minded doesn't pay the bills, babe."

I'm irritated by the wink, the condescension, and especially by being called "babe." I say coolly, "I'm not interested in a rich husband, but I *am* interested in helping people who can't afford decent legal representation."

He scoffs. "So basically poor criminals?"

My nostrils flare. Heat crawls up my neck. "Many of those 'poor criminals' are unjustly accused—"

Ty snorts. "Right."

"—living on the fringes of society and suffering from poverty or addiction—"

He rolls his eyes. "Totally self-inflicted."

"—who need someone to advocate for them," I finish loudly. "I want to be that someone."

Bored with the topic, Ty looks over my head to scan the crowd. "Have at it, babe. Just don't expect to ever own a decent car."

Dave glowers at Ty, Carla nervously puts her hand on Dave's

beefy forearm, and Ellie, sensing the conversation has gone off the rails, says brightly, "Let's get our table, shall we?"

She steers Ty away toward the hostess stand near the front of the bar.

Watching them go, Diego mutters under his breath, "What an asshole."

Dave grunts. "With you there, brother."

When I sigh, Carla looks at me with sympathy. "Let's get you a drink, honey."

I smile at her. "And this is why I love you."

From that inauspicious beginning, things go straight downhill.

Ty gets drunk on overpriced celebrity tequila and flirts outrageously with the simpering teenage waitress. Ellie's mouth gets more and more pinched, until it resembles a prune. Dave barely speaks, preferring instead to chug one beer after another while glaring daggers at Ty, while Carla chatters to fill the awkward silence.

Worst of all, Diego spends far too much time staring at me.

Outright staring, not even bothering to hide it.

We're seated in a table in a corner of the room away from the dance floor—had I known the place had a dance floor, I never would have come—so though the music is loud, it's not unbearable. Pretty much everything else *is* unbearable, however, from the pretentious food to the pretentious crowd to the pretentious DJ who keeps hollering, "What up, party people?" between songs.

After the dinner plates have been cleared, Ty burps loudly, gazing wistfully at the retreating waitress's ass. "Anybody wanna dance?"

"I think it's time for us to go." Dave looks at Carla, who smiles uncomfortably.

"Naw, don't go!" Tyler claps Dave on the shoulder. "Party's just gettin' started, bruh!"

Through a clenched jaw, Dave says curtly, "*Carla.*"

"Yes, time to go!" she says nervously, sending me an apologetic glance. "Thanks for a really fun dinner, Tru. This was a great idea. See you at work tomorrow!"

She and Dave rise from their chairs just as the waitress returns with dessert menus.

"Would anyone care for after dinner drinks..." She smiles at Ty. "Or something sweet?"

Ty grins like an idiot, while an obviously disgusted Dave pulls out his wallet. "Not for us, thanks. I'll take care of the bill."

I'm about to protest that that's not necessary, but the waitress says, "Oh, it's already been paid, sir."

Everyone looks at each other. When it becomes clear no one is going to take credit for it, Ellie squeals happily at Ty, "Honey! Did you do this?"

"No."

"Oh." Crestfallen, she looks at Diego. "You?"

"Nope."

The waitress says, "The owner took care of it."

Diego looks puzzled.

Ty mutters, "Woulda come here sooner if I'd known it'd be free."

Carla says hesitantly, "How nice," like she's not sure if it's nice or not.

Because Dave doesn't look happy at all about this development. And not just unhappy—furious.

He sends me a hard stare. "The owner a friend of yours?"

Feeling defensive, I lift my hands in the air. "I have no idea who owns this place. This is my first time here."

Dave and the waitress share a look. Smiling stiffly, the waitress sets the dessert menus on the edge of the table and says, "I'll just leave these here, then." She hurries off.

Carla looks confused. "That's weird. Why would the owner pay for our dinner? Are they running a contest?"

Dave grabs her upper arm and pulls her closer to him. He glances around suspiciously, like he's expecting armed gunmen to leap out from under nearby tables. "We're leaving. *Now*."

"Okay, honey, take it easy! What's gotten into you?"

"Liam Black just bought us dinner is what's gotten into me," he snaps.

My heart freezes to a stone inside my chest.

"Who?"

Carla doesn't know who Dave's talking about, but apparently Diego does, because all the blood drains from his face. He stares at me in horror.

When Ty says loudly, "Who the fuck is Liam Black?" Dave drags Carla off without another word. They're in such a hurry, they don't even say goodbye.

Still staring at me, Diego asks Ty, "You're not from around here, are you?"

"I'm from L.A.," Ty says proudly.

Diego stands and quickly scans the restaurant and dance floor. "That explains a lot." He grabs my wrist and pulls me to my feet. "Get your purse. We're outta here."

Diego knows who Liam is. Chills run down my spine.

I grab my handbag, wave goodbye to Ellie, and let Diego lead me past the dining tables and through the crowded dance floor to a pair of double doors on the other side of the restaurant. They're swinging doors, the kind with round windows at eye level.

I don't know why, but we're not going out the front...we're headed to the kitchen.

He shoves open one of the doors and pulls me inside.

The kitchen is much larger than Buddy's, with about half a dozen chefs sweating over sizzling pans and shouting directions to the line cooks and runners. Wait staff scurry around like rats, holding plates aloft. Bus boys zoom in and out, carrying armloads of dirty dishes.

It's barely-controlled chaos. No one spares us a glance.

"Diego, slow down! Why are we leaving through here?"

"So the bouncers at the front door won't stop us on the way out."

"Why would they stop us?"

Ignoring me, he tugs harder on my hand and jerks his chin in greeting at a young Latino chef standing behind a steaming six-burner stove. Diego says something to him in urgent Spanish. The chef nods and tilts his head to the right.

We turn in that direction. I assume it's an exit, but before we go ten more steps, we skid to a stop.

Because six huge men in black suits are filing through the door we were headed to.

They flank out to stand in formation, three on each side of the door, with their hands clasped at their waists and their legs spread. Bulges in various places under their suits hint at an arsenal of concealed weapons.

Unsmiling, they stare at us.

The noise and frenzied activity of the kitchen fades instantly to breathless stillness and silence.

Until Liam strolls through the door.

He stops and folds his arms over his broad chest. He looks at Diego. He looks at me.

Eyes burning, he says softly, "Good evening."

Then every cook, bus boy, and waitress in the kitchen turns around and runs out.

16

TRU

*M*y heart slams against my breastbone. Adrenaline turns my blood to fire. Beyond the swinging doors, the music thumps, but inside the kitchen, it's as silent as a tomb.

Until Diego hisses viciously, "*You.*"

Bristling at the disrespect in Diego's tone, one of the armed heavies behind Liam steps forward. When Liam lifts a hand, he reluctantly falls back into place.

Liam says, "We haven't been introduced."

His tone is calm and his posture is relaxed, but those eyes. My god. If I were Diego, I would've already passed out from terror.

His voice shaking, Diego says, "I know who you are."

"And I know who you are. But we still haven't been introduced."

From behind Diego's shoulder, I say, "This is my friend. His name is Diego. Don't hurt him."

Liam's eyes cut to me. A small smile lifts the corners of his mouth.

Diego snaps, "I don't need you to ask him for protection, Tru."

Liam glances back at Diego. His smile fades. He says, "Don't you?"

When Diego drops my hand and steps forward, every man behind Liam steps forward, too. They form a formidable line behind him, staring us down with flat, emotionless eyes.

Shit.

I step around Diego, stand in front of him, and match my posture to Liam's, folding my arms across my chest. With my chin lifted, I look him in the eye and carefully enunciate my words. "I said, *this is my friend.*"

For a while, Liam and I simply stare at each other. The silence crackles with tension. A few of the bodyguards or hit men or whatever they are glance at each other, eyebrows cocked.

Then Liam says gently, "I know. I won't hurt him."

"Your goons, either. Promise me."

Now his bodyguards are outright astonished. One of them huffs out a breath. Another's jaw drops. The rest of them wear expressions ranging from confusion to disbelief.

But Liam only smiles and keeps that same tender, indulgent tone when he speaks again.

"You have my word."

"Thank you."

"You're welcome."

His burning gaze rakes over me, head to toe then back again. "Did you enjoy dinner?"

"Honestly? It was awful."

"I'm sorry to hear that. I'll have to speak to the head chef."

"Is 'speak to' code for fire?"

"No."

"Beat up?"

"No."

"Threaten with dismemberment?"

Liam's lips twitch. "No, lass."

"Good. I don't want to be responsible for any mayhem toward

your staff. The food wasn't good—neither was the atmosphere, if you care to know—but it's not their fault. I think you'd have to speak to management about that."

The goon to Liam's right blinks. Once. Slowly. In any other circumstance, it would be comical.

Apparently, my sass toward his boss is unprecedented.

Behind me, Diego is agitated, shifting his weight from foot to foot. He mutters, "I told you he was bad news, chica. Even before I knew his name, I knew this *vato* was ..."

He says something sharp in Spanish. It sounds like a curse.

Calmly, Liam answers right back.

In Spanish.

They go back and forth for a brief, intense burst, until Diego switches back to English.

"You don't deserve her!"

He says it loudly, with force and emotion. Every man behind Liam stiffens. But Liam retains his calm demeanor when he replies.

"Careful."

"I'm not afraid of you."

"Then you're uncommonly stupid." Over his shoulder, he says, "Kieran, get him out of my sight."

The biggest brute steps forward. He grabs Diego out from behind me and drags him toward the door.

When Liam sees my expression, he adds, "And if there's so much as a bruise on the boy, I'll hold you responsible."

"Aye, boss," grunts Kieran. He releases Diego grudgingly, but gives him a small push toward the door for good measure.

"Tru!" shouts Diego. "Listen to me! Get away from him! He's dangerous! He's in the mob!"

Kieran shoves Diego out the door Liam came in. It closes behind them with a hard, chilling *thunk* that sounds eerily like the lid sliding shut on a coffin.

"He's in the mob."

So there it is.

My heart pounds so hard it hurts.

Liam gazes at me with that posture of unruffled calm. He appears totally undisturbed or surprised by Diego's accusation. He looks as cool as in control as ever.

Except for those incendiary eyes. God, how they burn.

After a moment, he says, "Just for clarity's sake, I'm not in the mafia." His voice drops an octave. "I *am* the mafia."

He stares at me. His goons stare at me. A small, semihysterical laugh escapes my lips.

I feel unstable, like the ground beneath my feet is shifting, and I'm starting to sink. I knew he was dangerous, of course. I knew he had dark secrets and led an unusual life, but nothing could have prepared me for the reality of this moment.

It all comes together like fingers interlacing. Like a key sliding into a lock.

I think of all the months he sat in my section at Buddy's, staring at me in ferocious silence, his stillness and focus that of an animal—of a predator.

I think of all the times I called him a wolf, *my* wolf, and how efficiently he killed three men for me, and how I flirted with him, and smiled at him, and begged him to stay while I slept.

I think of all the mental gymnastics I performed trying to guess what and who he was, and realize with a distant sense of horror that the darker side of my nature, the intuitive part buried deep below rational thought, the bestial part of blood, bone, and instinct...that part of me recognized him immediately.

Recognized him and wanted him without reservation.

Liam watches me in blistering silence. Blood throbs in my cheeks. When I inhale a ragged breath and cover my face with my hands, he issues a curt order in Gaelic to his men that makes them turn and walk out.

When they're gone, he says gruffly, "I told you I didn't lead a normal life. I told you I wouldn't be good for you. I tried to protect you, Tru."

I lift my head and gaze at him in anguish. "If you really wanted to protect me, you would have stayed away."

Something surfaces in his eyes. An emotion I can't identify, welling up quickly but just as quickly smothered. If I didn't know better, I'd think it was pain.

"I should have. But you knew."

I open my mouth on an automatic denial, but slowly close it again.

How could I deny it when I know he's right?

Seeing my expression, he nods, licking his lips. "You did, lass. Even if I didn't give you a hand-drawn map, you knew what I was from the first time you laid eyes on me. You knew, and you still said you trusted me."

His voice grows husky. "You knew and you wanted me anyway."

Trembling, I close my eyes. I whisper, "This is insane."

Then he's on me, closing the distance between us before I can open my eyes. He pulls me against his body and wraps his strong arms around my chest, holding me tight.

"Aye, it's fucking insane," he says hotly into my ear, pinning me against him. "And it's exactly what we both need."

He pulls my head back with his hand fisted in my hair and kisses me. It's deep, hot, and desperate, and goes on and on until I twist my head away, gasping.

I push at his chest, but it's useless. He's too strong. He won't let me go.

Instead, he picks me up in his arms and heads for the back door.

"Liam, put me down!"

"Don't bother fighting me. It's too late for that."

My mind sounds a panic bell. My pulse doubles. I cry, "Where are you taking me?"

He growls, "Home to bed."

A fleet of black SUVs awaits in the dark alley behind the restaurant, steam billowing from their tailpipes. Liam opens the back door of one of them, hustles me inside, and buckles me in.

"Stay," he orders. Then he climbs in beside me and we pull away.

The bodyguard with the icy blue eyes who told me to be careful the night I got out of the hospital is behind the wheel. He glances at me in the rearview mirror. His expression is less hostile than last time. In fact, he almost looks worried for me.

It's small comfort.

We speed off into the night. I can't catch my breath. I'm shaking all over. When we go over a bump in the road and I gasp, Liam reaches out and grasps my wrist. He holds it tightly, as if he's expecting me to leap out of the car the moment we pause at a stoplight.

I try to pick through a thousand chaotic thoughts to find something to say, but it's like trying to catch the wind.

Looking out the window, I whisper, "You're back a week early."

His voice is low and rough. "I couldn't stay away any longer."

Oh god. "How did you know where to find me?"

"I own this town."

He leaves it at that, but from that simple statement, I understand that he can find anyone he likes, anytime he likes, and there's nothing we mere mortals can do about it.

Panicking, I try to catch my breath. Taking deep breaths doesn't help. Neither does Liam's grip on my wrist, which remains steady for the duration of the drive. I stare straight ahead, pulse pounding, feeling his burning gaze on my face.

When we get into the heart of the city, the driver turns into the underground parking garage of a modern black glass high-rise. It stretches so far into the sky, I can't see the top. We park in front of a bank of private elevators flanked by two men in black suits, and Liam exits the car.

I sit still, breathing raggedly, until he comes around to my side, opens the door, and unbuckles the seat belt.

He grasps my upper arm, helps me out, and strides to the elevators with his fingers curled possessively into my flesh. One of the suits pressed the call button when we pulled in, so the elevator doors are opening as we walk up.

When we're alone inside the elevator and the doors slide shut behind us, Liam turns to me and grabs me in a rough embrace. Then he crushes his mouth to mine.

He kisses me like his life depends on it. The way Diego said he looked at me: like he'll die if he doesn't. His mouth is hot and demanding, and I'm helpless to resist.

No—I'm not helpless.

Truth be told, now that the shock is wearing off, I'm spitting mad.

I'm not a wilting flower, or a weakling, or a damn damsel in distress. I'm the daughter of an iron-willed Southern woman who turns grown men into frightened children when she gets angry. I've got her fire in my veins, her pride and self-respect, and I won't be carted off like a bag of groceries and turned to mindless mush by a bossy Irish mobster, no matter how much I like the way he kisses.

I push Liam away and slap him across the face.

He jerks back, breathing hard, and stares down at me with wild, glittering eyes.

I say, "Do you really think I'm going to fall into bed with you after you just crashed my celebration dinner, manhandled my friend, bragged about being some kind of mafia kingpin, and threw me into your car like a piece of luggage?"

"That's the plan."

"Not my plan."

He glowers at me. The elevator stops. The doors slide open. He says darkly, "We'll see."

Then he picks me up in his arms again and walks me inside his home.

It's the penthouse, huge, with floor-to-ceiling windows that showcase the glittering Boston skyline far below. Liam carries me through the apartment without a word. Automatic lights blink on, lighting the space in a muted glow. His footsteps echo off the marble floor as I cling to his shoulders, my pulse racing.

"Put me down, Liam."

"In a minute."

We enter a bedroom larger than my entire apartment. More lights flick on. The room is huge, with a fireplace at one end and a king size bed at the other. A sofa and chairs are clustered into a sitting area near one of the windows. A wet bar displays a variety of cut crystal bottles behind glass. The space is masculine and sophisticated, and decorated entirely in shades of gray and black.

Liam heads straight for the bed.

"Liam, I'm not—"

"Quiet."

He takes us down to the black silk duvet and settles his big heavy body over mine with his wolf's hungry growl. He pins my wrists over my head and takes my mouth again without speaking a word, flexing his hips into mine so I feel every inch of his arousal.

My dress is bunched up around my thighs. My skin is covered in goose bumps. My pulse is flying at a breakneck pace, I'm gasping for air, and I suddenly feel unhinged. As if I might at any moment break out into hysterical screams...or laughter.

I'm exhilarated and furious and turned on, all at once. My body is filled with so much emotion my skin feels tight, like I could burst at the seams.

I gasp, writhing. "I'm not your fuck toy, dammit!"

Liam starts to speak to me in Gaelic.

His words are guttural, muffled between greedy kisses on my mouth, neck, chest.

Though I don't know what he's saying, it's the sexiest thing I've ever heard in my life.

He holds me down with one big hand clenched around my wrists and the other running up and down my body, squeezing and exploring the curve of my waist, the rise of my ribcage, the swell of my breast.

When he pinches my hard nipple, I moan, arching into him, so out of my mind with lust and fury I think I might die.

"No, you're not my fuck toy," he says against my neck, his voice husky. "You're my queen bee. My unhealthy obsession. The reason I haven't been able to sleep in a goddamn year."

His teeth scrape over my clavicle. His lips and tongue kiss a hot path down my chest to my cleavage. He nuzzles his nose against my breasts, inhaling deeply against my skin and squeezing my nipple again, thumbing over the nubbed peak through the fabric of my dress.

I groan. "Liam. Please."

Into my ear, he says gruffly, "I'm gonna fuck you now. It's gonna be fast and hard because I've waited too long for this, but we'll go again right after, and then I'll take it slow."

He looks at me, breathing hard as he gazes into my eyes. "Ready?"

I debate with myself for a tense, breathless moment, hating myself for not saying a forceful *no* instantly. But it's not a *no* my body is feeling. It's a big, fat, unequivocal *yes.*

Damn. I'm going to regret this.

I whisper, "Yes. I'm still going to be mad at you after."

He rears back onto his knees, his legs straddling mine, and grasps the neckline of my dress. With one hard yank, he rips it wide open.

I gasp. Buttons pop and fly, scattering over the bed, clattering against the floor.

He stares wildly down at me, exposed and trembling beneath him. Except for a bra, I'm bare down to my waist.

Liam yanks again, and the dress rips open the rest of the way, down to the hem. The sound of fabric tearing and buttons popping and my own breathless gasps of shock fill the room.

He doesn't give me time to recover before he swings a leg over me and tears off my panties. Then he positions himself between my spread thighs, buries his face between my legs, and shoves his tongue deep inside me.

I arch and cry out, clenching my fingers into the blanket. He makes a low noise like a hum that reverberates all the way through me.

With his fingers digging into my ass, he fucks me with his tongue, working it in and out as I moan and rock my hips against his face.

He's still fully dressed.

I'm still wearing my heels, my bra, and the ruins of Ellie's pretty red dress.

He reaches up and pinches my swollen clitoris, then starts to stroke it, his fingers moving in time with his tongue. Pleasure ripples out from my core in waves as he eats me hungrily, making soft noises of approval at my response. Then he moves his mouth to my clit and sucks on it, hard, sliding a thick finger inside me to replace his tongue. With his other hand, he reaches up and roughly pinches one of my nipples through my bra.

His teeth scrape over my clit.

His beard scratches my thighs.

When I come, it's with a scream that claws its way out of my throat like an animal.

The contractions are violent. They rip through me like the detonation of a bomb. I writhe against the bed, raw sounds of pleasure coming out of me that I'm helpless to control.

I sink my fingers into his hair and pull on it, scratching his scalp, until the throbbing slows and I collapse back against the mattress, sobbing with relief.

Liam turns his mouth to my thigh and bites me there, like he wants to take a mouthful of my tender flesh and swallow it.

He rises to his knees and unzips his trousers. Licking his lips, he takes his jutting erection in his fist and strokes it, base to crown and back again.

It's insanely hot that he's still in his suit and tie, the only exposed part of his body a hard cock that is very obviously eager to get buried inside me.

I open my legs wider.

His eyes flare with heat. He drops down to hover over me with one hand planted on the mattress beside my head, positions his rigid cock between my thighs, and strokes his crown up and down through my soaked folds, nudging forward.

"Wait—do you have protection?"

"I'm clean."

"Me, too, but I'm not on birth con—"

With one forceful thrust, he shoves his cock deep inside me.

He's hot, hard, and invading, stretching me out, making my back arch and my body open to him. I gasp, shocked but loving how he feels.

Balancing his weight on his elbows, he grabs my head, fists his hands into my hair, and growls, "Then I'll come in your mouth."

He starts to fuck me, hard and relentlessly, driving deep, his hips pistoning, his grunts of pleasure ringing in my ears. He's all over me, all around me, his weight and his smell and his dominating masculinity, all of it laying claim to me like a raised sword and a battle cry and a line drawn in the sand—*this is mine.*

When I moan deliriously, he takes my mouth again, swallowing the sound. Every time I exhale, he breathes it in. He fucks me so hard it's like he wants to crawl inside me. Like he wants to break me apart.

Like *he's* breaking apart, and the only thing that can save him is surrender.

I hook my ankles behind his back and let him take me like he needs to, burying my face in his neck as he drives us toward the end that aches inside us, the peak of that mountain we first set foot on long ago, the moment he stepped inside Buddy's Diner's door.

"Tru." He groans, shuddering.

He's close, but I'm closer.

With a small cry, I'm over the edge again, convulsing around him, bucking wildly as pleasure consumes me. I open my mouth and suck hard on the pulse pounding in the side of his neck, scraping my teeth against his skin and clawing at his back as he groans.

The rhythm of his hips falters. "Fuck. You're coming. I can feel you coming—"

He breaks off with a low, broken moan and holds himself motionless and rigid above me.

I continue to writhe underneath him, rocking my hips, fucking myself onto his beautiful hard cock, giving myself over to the most intense pleasure I've ever felt. I use his body shamelessly as he tries to hold back, his arms shaking, low moans working from his throat.

My orgasm goes on and on, spinning out into eternity. I'm lost in it, tumbling under every crashing wave, drowning in him and loving every second.

The moment the convulsions slow to a stop and I relax under him, Liam rasps, "Give me your mouth. *Now.*"

He slides out of me, rolls to his back, and grips his stiff cock in his hand. I quickly climb over him and take him in my mouth. As soon as my lips slide over the wet, engorged crown, he sucks in a hard breath and curses.

I open my throat and slide him all the way down. His groan forms the shape of my name.

Then he spills himself inside my mouth, throbbing against my tongue, his entire body jerking.

"Take it all, baby," he rasps. He squeezes a hot, shaking hand around my throat. "Take every last drop of me." He breaks off into garbled Gaelic.

I swallow, then do it again, my lips stretched tight around his girth as he thrusts up into my mouth.

With a final shudder, he falls still, spent. His chest rises and falls with his ragged breath.

I slowly slide him out of my mouth and lick my lips. After a moment, he exhales. He lifts his head and looks at me, still holding his jutting cock in my fist.

Without a word, I climb off him, retrieve Ellie's shredded dress from the bedroom floor, and wrap it around my naked body. My head held high, I turn around and walk out.

The sound of Liam's low laughter follows me as I go.

17

LIAM

I find her in one of the guest suites, curled up on top of the bed in the fetal position in the dark.

She's wrapped in the fur throw taken from the chair near the fireplace. I know she didn't want to crawl under the covers, because that would be a commitment to staying. To falling asleep and being vulnerable.

As if she'd ever be vulnerable when she was with me. As if I wouldn't kill anyone who dared to even give her the wrong kind of look.

I try to gather her into my arms to pick her up, but she rolls to her other side, avoiding me.

I say firmly, "If you're under this roof, you're sleeping in my bed."

"Then maybe I shouldn't be under this roof."

Her voice is quiet and steady. Irritation flares inside my chest. I don't bother with more conversation because I know it will only be an argument. I simply pull her back to the edge of the bed and pick her up.

She mutters, "This is ridiculous."

But she doesn't fight. She hides her face in the crook of my neck and lets me carry her back into my bedroom, silent and sleepy, her body lush and warm against my chest.

When I set her down on the bed, she curls into a ball again and peeks up at me from under the edge of the fur throw. I know she's trying to look mad, but a woman's eyes are never as soft as when she's looking at the man who just made her come.

My lips curve. With a faint sense of surprise, I realize I'm smiling.

Loosening my tie as I gaze down at her, I say, "You screamed my name."

She rolls her eyes, then squeezes them shut. She mutters, "The ego on you."

"Both times."

"Anytime you'd like to stop talking, it would be great."

I pull my tie over my head and drop it to the floor. Then I shrug out of my suit jacket, tossing it aside. I kick off my shoes and discard my belt. As I'm unbuttoning my shirt, Tru opens her eyes again. She watches me as I pull off my shirt and let it fall from my fingertips to lie on top of the jacket.

Then she bites her lip and her eyes go wide.

I stand unmoving and allow her to look at my bare chest. The light is low in the room, but there's enough of it for her to see everything.

The tattoos. The muscles.

The scars.

She sits up abruptly. The fur throw slips off her shoulders and pools around her waist, exposing her breasts, but she doesn't notice. She's too busy staring.

After a moment, she reaches out and touches me.

With the tip of one finger, she lightly traces a scar that follows the shape of my ribcage. Though it's faded to white now, it's as thick and vicious as the day it was made.

She says, "This must've hurt."

"Aye."

She glances up at me, examines my expression for a moment, then drops her gaze back to my chest. She slides her finger down my ribs and across my stomach, to a knot of scar tissue near my waist. "And this?"

"It didn't tickle."

Her eyes flash up to meet mine. She whispers, "Don't joke."

She's solemn and still, her eyes shadowed with some bad memory that has nothing to do with the marks on my skin.

I cup her jaw and stroke my thumb over her cheekbone, wanting to make that pained look in her eyes disappear, wanting to push her back against the mattress and shove inside her again and make her cry out my name until she's hoarse.

Wanting to make her mine for good, which can never happen.

With effort, I set all those competing emotions aside. "You really want to know?"

Her voice comes very small. "Yes."

"That scar is from a wooden stake."

She jerks her hand away as if she's been burned. She repeats faintly, "*Stake*?"

She looks so horrified, I wish I'd lied. "Let's just say I didn't trip and fall onto it. We'll leave it at that."

When she just keeps staring in horror at the scar, I kneel between her knees and take her face in both my hands. "It was a long time ago. I was a boy."

"A *boy*." Her face drains of blood.

"I'm sorry. I didn't mean to upset you."

She looks at me like I'm a complete idiot.

It confuses me, until she says, "Liam. I'm not *upset*. I'm pissed off. What kind of an animal would drive a stake through a boy's stomach?" She huffs. "And please tell me he spent the rest of his life in prison."

I answer without thinking. "No. I killed him. But later on, after I'd grown up."

She looks deep into my eyes. Her own are fierce. After a silent, bristling moment, she says quietly, "Good."

Several things dawn on me at once. The first is that I continue to underestimate her. The second is that Declan was right: she's much tougher than she seems.

The third is that I lied when I told her falling in love is a luxury I don't allow myself, because I'm sliding so fast down that slippery slope it might already be too late to stop it.

When I speak, my voice is thick. "Why does that make you happy?"

"I don't know." She pauses, thinking. "Maybe because justice is so rarely served that it's really gratifying when it finally happens."

"You think what I did to him is justice for what he did to me?"

She answers without hesitation. "I think a person who would do that to a child has done much worse things that no one knows about."

She's right about that. The man who drove that stake through my body was one of the most evil people I've ever met, to this day.

Then she says suddenly, "So this 'I am the mafia' thing. Let's talk about that."

I rise, push her back against the mattress, and straddle her body, kneeling down to brace my elbows on either side of her head. "The less you know, baby, the better."

We're nose to nose, so I can see exactly how much me calling her 'baby' affects her. She adores it, but it also irritates her. That reaction is such classic Tru that I have to press my lips together to keep from chuckling.

She says, "My idea of a mob boss is that they put contracts out on their enemies, and run drug, weapons, and prostitution rings. Is that what you do?"

Her gaze is unflinching.

I feel a warm flicker of pride. She really will make an excellent attorney.

"No."

She stares at me, weighing the truth of my answer. "I feel like this might be a semantics issue. Let me rephrase. Is that what you have other people do *for* you?"

Goddamn. She's going to make an *amazing* attorney.

Why that should make my dick hard, I don't know.

"I don't get my hands dirty anymore."

"Meaning?" She waits for an explanation with one eyebrow lifted.

I drop my head and inhale against her neck, drawing the scent of her skin into my nose. When I press a soft kiss against her collarbone, she shivers. My dick grows harder.

"A CEO is concerned with the big picture. Growth. Market share. Streamlining operations to maximize profitability. He doesn't stock shelves or make deliveries."

"You make it sound so corporate."

"It is."

When I lift my head and gaze down at her, she winds her arms around my shoulders and looks into my eyes. She says quietly, "That's not all, though, is it?"

I frown. "What do you mean?"

She tilts her head, letting her gaze drift over my face before she answers. When she does, her tone is thoughtful. "There's something else you're not telling me. There are bigger secrets you keep."

I freeze. My heart stops pumping. My blood turns to ice in my veins.

Her eyes sharpen. "I'm right, aren't I?"

Calm down. She doesn't know anything. "I told you—the less you know the better. End of conversation."

"If you think this is the end of the conversation, you don't know me at all."

Damn those piercing green eyes. The woman sees everything.

I roll off her and sit on the edge of the bed.

She sits up, too, but she's not looking at my face anymore. She's looking at my bare back.

"Liam," she whispers. "God. What happened to you?"

Life tried to kill me, but I didn't die.

I only wish I did.

She'll need some kind of explanation to satisfy her curiosity, but I'll be damned if I'll share all my ugly stories of how I got from point A to point B. It would make her sick. And it would take too long, anyway. And it doesn't really matter.

I am what I am, no matter how I got this way.

My voice comes out flat. "Don't feel sorry for me."

"Oh, believe me, what I'm feeling for you right now isn't pity."

Her voice has an edge to it. When I glance at her, she skewers me with a look.

She says, "You were just inside me. That means I get to ask questions, and you get to answer them. What you don't get to do is shut me out and act like I'm irritating you with my concern."

I've never met a woman such equal parts salty and sweet.

I spend a brief moment wondering if a wolf and a lion could be happy as mates, but quash that ridiculous thought as quickly as it came.

"If I don't answer a question of yours, it's because knowing the answer would make you less safe. Add that together with the fact that I won't lie to you just to make you feel better, and you have me staying silent more than you'll like."

We stare at each other. I can tell she's not happy with that explanation, but she'll accept it. Grudgingly.

If my erection gets any harder, it will split a seam in my pants.

Holding her gaze, I say softly, "Now lie down and spread your legs."

There's a long, crackling moment as she decides whether or not she's going to obey my command. Our held gazes burn like a lit fuse. Impatience claws at me.

"If you don't do as I tell you, I'll put you over my knee and spank your ass until it's red."

Her eyes flare in outrage. "You wouldn't dare."

"Try me."

Now she's even angrier, but she's turned on, too. She likes the idea.

She likes it as much as she hates me for suggesting it.

When she licks her lips, I almost snap and lunge at her. But I hold myself in check and wait, gritting my teeth against the urge.

I'm right at the edge of my self-control when she lies back against the mattress in one fluid motion and stretches her arms out over her head.

I look at her, breathing shallowly and watching me with wary eyes, her knees pulled up and squeezed together, her hair spilling all over the silk duvet cover, her bare skin smooth and gleaming, and I feel a jolt of possessiveness far darker and more powerful than anything I've felt for her before.

She's my match.

The yin to my yang. The light to my darkness.

She's what I didn't know I'd been missing all these years: a soft place to fall.

"You're beautiful."

My voice is a harsh rasp in the quiet room. My blood rushes through my veins like wildfire. Heat must be curling off my skin like smoke.

She looks at my face and sees everything, like she always has. In a soft, teasing voice, she says, "I like you, too, wolfie. Take off your pants."

I rise and stand at the edge of the bed, looking down at her. "You're not in charge here."

"No? Hmm." Her gaze drops to the bulge behind my zipper. "You could've fooled me."

Suppressing a grin, I grasp my hard dick through the fabric of my slacks. "You want to play a game? It's called 'See Who Breaks First.' Spoiler alert: you'll lose."

Her voice stays calm, but I see the excitement in her eyes. "You're awfully confident. Overconfident, I think."

She parts her knees, opening her legs so she's exposed, pink, wet, and ready.

I stare down at her. Lust crashes over me like an ocean wave. A needy growl builds in the back of my throat.

She whispers, "That's what I thought."

I rip off the rest of my clothing before she could count to three, then settle myself between her spread thighs. I don't enter her, though. I just press our bodies together, balance my weight on my elbows, and frame her head in my hands.

"I'm not the only overconfident one here," I murmur, nuzzling her throat. When a little involuntary shudder passes through her body, I hide my grin in her neck.

She slides her hands down my back, gently exploring, then slides them up again and sinks her fingers into my hair. She gazes up at me with hot eyes and a half smile.

With a slight roll of her hips, she says, "So this game of yours. See Who Breaks First. How does it work?"

Her heat and wetness slide against my hard cock, making it throb. Amazed by her, I shake my head. "I think you know already."

She pretends innocence as she shifts her upper body so her hard nipples graze my chest. "I don't. I really have no idea."

She smiles.

I hungrily kiss that smile from her mouth, parting her lips with my tongue and delving deep.

She does the melting thing she does every time I kiss her, sighing into my mouth, her limbs automatically relaxing. Her fingers tighten in my hair.

I flex my hips so my hard cock rubs against the swollen little nub of her clit. She gasps but tries to stifle it.

Bending my head to her breast, I whisper, "No? No idea at all?"

I suck her nipple into my mouth, feeling a savage rush of satisfaction when she moans and arches into me. When I test that nipple with my teeth, she exhales with a shudder and rocks her pelvis into mine.

"So perfect," I whisper, squeezing the lush fullness of her breast as I lap at her nipple. "You're so fucking perfect, baby. I love how you respond to me."

She says my name, the barest whisper of need. It makes me want to let rip a Tarzan yell and beat my fists on my chest.

Then we start to play.

Fingers lazily stroking. Tongues gently lapping. The sound of rushing heartbeats and quickening breaths. My skin mists with sweat as need and hunger grow, but I hold myself back, resisting the drumbeat in my blood growing louder and more insistent with every teasing roll of her hips against mine.

She's warm and plush underneath me, soft everywhere I'm hard. The sensation of her thighs wrapped around my waist and her bare breasts pressed against my chest makes me feel like a mindless animal.

I want to shove my dick deep into her wet heat and start pounding, but instead I dig my fingers into her ass and start to talk to her, whispering everything I feel.

How much I crave her.

How crazy she makes me.

How not seeing her is torture, and how desperate I get at the thought of letting her go.

Only I say it all in Gaelic, so she can't understand.

She reaches down between our bodies and curls her fingers around my cock. Rubbing the crown up and down through her wet folds, she whispers into my ear, "How you doing, wolfie?"

"I could do this all day." I flex my hips. When the engorged head of my cock slips inside her, I stop and give her a deep, lingering kiss.

When we come up for air, she's panting. "Me too."

She looks a little dazed, her cheeks flushed and her eyes hazy. She's starting to shake.

I shift my weight to one elbow and lean down to suck her nipple, gently massaging her ass as I take a mouthful of her flesh.

Her moan is soft and broken. It takes every ounce of self-control I have not to throw her ankles over my shoulders and fuck her until she's screaming my name.

Then she levels the playing field by reaching down and stroking the throbbing shaft of my dick. When she gently fondles my balls, I exhale a ragged breath.

I reach down and press my thumb against her swollen clit.

She sucks in a breath, jerking. The movement drives me inside her another inch, and we both groan in pleasure.

"Wolfie." She whimpers, rocking her hips, trying to work me deeper inside her but failing. "Oh god. Will you...oh..."

"What, baby?" *Please say fuck me. Please. If this goes on any longer, I'll have a heart attack.*

She exhales. It sounds close to a sob. "Will you remind me to text Carla later and thank her and Dave for coming to dinner?"

I can't help it: I laugh. "Definitely."

"Thank you."

"You're so welcome."

Very carefully, I ease my hips forward, sinking my cock another inch inside her drenched pussy. She pulls on my hair and bites her lower lip, but doesn't break and beg.

So I stroke my thumb up and down and around and around that sensitive little nub of hers and watch as she starts to fall apart.

Quivering, she arches against me, tipping her head back on a helpless moan. Her hips rock in time with the motion of my thumb. Her thighs shake.

"Do you want all of me, baby, or are you gonna come with only a little bit?"

Teeth gritted, she says, "I'm not going to come. Oh—*god*—I'm not."

The hell you're not.

I say gruffly into her ear, "Do you want me to lick your sweet pussy again? You want my tongue and fingers inside you instead?"

Her groan is faint. She writhes against me, starting to buck.

"No, no. You have to tell me what you want. You have to ask for it."

She squeezes the base of my cock, stroking faster on the part of the shaft that isn't already inside her.

Her fingers are covered with her own wetness. She fondles my balls again, spreading all that delicious wetness around so everything is slick and hot.

All it would take is one hard shove and I'd be buried to the hilt inside her.

I want it so much I'm grunting with the effort to hold back.

"You're so hard," she whispers, eyes closed. "So big and hard and god I love how you feel. Liam. Liam, I love it so much..."

She trails off, breathless.

Watching her lost in the pleasure I'm giving her, about to tip over the edge, I feel something in the center of my chest unlock. A black door that has been bolted shut forever groans open on rusted hinges, letting a sliver of light shine in.

Immediately after that, I feel something I thought I could no longer feel. Something I haven't felt since I lost everything so long ago.

Fear.

No. Fuck. No. You can't—don't let yourself—

"Tru."

Her name slips past my lips before I can stop it. It's a plea, raw and hopeless.

Hearing it, she opens her eyes and gazes dreamily up into my face. "I have an idea," she murmurs. "Let's call this game Break Together so it can be a win-win."

Then she kisses me, flexing her hips so I sink the rest of the way inside her. She grabs my ass to grind me in deep.

I give up the fight with a sense of overwhelming relief, as if I'm giving up my last breath.

We kiss deeply as our bodies rock together, finding a rhythm. Her thighs tighten around my waist. Her breasts bounce against my chest. She makes soft noises deep in her throat, little mews of pleasure as I slide slowly in and out of her tight heat. Pleasure coils into a white hot ball at the base of my spine.

Her entire body flexes, arching against mine. She cries out my name.

Then she comes, jerking and moaning, clenching around my cock. The contractions are so hard it feels like a fist milking me.

I lose myself.

I start to buck, driving hard into her as helpless groans work from my throat.

She digs her fingers into my ass, moaning *yes yes yes* as I fuck her. I feel a spreading heat in my pelvis. My thigh muscles bunch. I can't catch my breath. My body is on fire.

I erupt with a sudden, violent jerk.

I groan and pull out of her, spilling myself onto her belly. My cock throbs with a pleasure so intense it's almost pain. Beneath me, Tru is shaking and panting. Her chest is flushed, gleaming with my sweat.

I drop my cheek to her breasts and give her my weight, my arms no longer able to support me.

When her arms slide around my shoulders and she gives me a squeeze, I roll to my back, taking her with me.

She makes a noise of surprise, but soon settles on top of me. My cock is trapped between us, still twitching.

We lie like that in silence for a long time, listening to the distant sounds of the city drifting up from far below as our breathing slows and our pulses return to normal, the sweat cooling on our skin.

Eventually, she stirs. Her cheek resting on my chest, she says sleepily, "Not to harsh the afterglow, but will your driver take me home or should I call a cab?"

I prop an arm under my head so I can better see her face. "You're already home."

Her lips part. Her eyes widen. I see it the moment she understands what I'm saying, but just to make sure there's no mistake, I clarify.

"At least for the next twenty-eight days."

18

TRU

I stare in disbelief at his handsome, serious face. "You... you're not saying...you're not telling me you think you're going to *keep* me here."

"Aye. That's exactly what I'm telling you."

I try to pull away from him, to jerk out of his arms, but he's too strong. He simply tightens his arms around me.

"Liam! No!"

"Yes, my beautiful queen bee. You're all mine for the next month, whether you like it or not."

"You can't keep me here against my will. That's kidnapping!"

His eyes take on that faraway look they sometimes get. That look like he's going for a long swim in his ocean of dark memories.

"Kidnapping is the least of my sins. And I can keep you here with your agreement or without it. There's no one who can stop me."

Watching me closely with his dark eyes, he lets that last part sink in.

I resist the urge to poke my fingers into his eyeballs and glare at him instead. "I want you to take me back to my apartment now."

"No."

My heart is a racehorse galloping inside my chest. "Liam. I'm not kidding."

He traces the rise of my cheekbone with his thumb and says gently, "I know, lass. But it's not up to you."

I can't recall ever feeling as angry or as helpless in my life.

Desperate to get through to him, I try a different tactic. Maybe logic will work. "I don't have any of my things here."

His gaze drifts lazily over my face. "Things?"

"Clothes. Toiletries. All the books and study materials I need to prepare for the bar."

"What makes you think they're not here?"

From one second to the next, it becomes impossible to breathe.

Seeing the expression of horror on my face, Liam says calmly, "Two things you should know about me: one, I always get what I want. And two, I always plan ten steps ahead to get it."

My mind is the vortex of a tornado, with shrieking winds and flying debris, spinning wildly out of control.

He moved my things here. My clothes...my books...

When? While I was at dinner?

It doesn't matter when, idiot! What matters is that he kidnapped you!

Oh god—I just had sex with my kidnapper.

My kidnapper just made me come.

Teetering on the edge of hysteria, I whisper, "Let me go. Let me go right now."

"Of course."

He opens his arms and puts his hands behind his head, propping it up to gaze at me as I scramble off him and back away from the bed.

I look wildly around the room for something to cover myself with. I can't run out into the street naked.

"Closet." Liam casually points toward a closed door on the other side of the room.

I whirl and run to it, bursting inside an enormous walk-in closet. The automatic lights flicker on, but I wish they hadn't.

Because my clothes—all of them—are hanging in rows on one side of the huge room, along with all my shoes arranged neatly on the floor beneath.

On the other side of the room hangs row after row of identical black suits and white dress shirts.

When I scream in frustration, I hear a low chuckle from the bedroom.

I stand in the middle of the closet nude and shaking, incandescent with fury.

That bastard is laughing at me.

Laughing.

I stride over to his side of the closet, tear one of his white dress shirts from its hanger, and wipe my stomach with it, tossing it into a corner with grim satisfaction when I'm through. Then I go to the row of my shoes, pick up a pair, and stride out of the closet and into the bedroom. Liam is still lying on the bed where I left him, naked and serene.

I chuck a shoe across the room at him.

It flies through the air, landing with an impotent thud on the carpet three feet away from the foot of the bed.

Liam is unmoving, except for a lifted eyebrow. "Not much of a throw, lass. You'll never make it in the big leagues."

Blood scorches my cheeks. Fire billows from my nostrils. I stalk a few feet closer to the bed, then take aim again and throw.

This time, my aim is more accurate. Liam has to roll aside to miss being impaled with the heel of my favorite pair of pumps.

"Better," he says, unfazed, rolling back to his original position.

"But if you really want to draw blood, there's a gun in the drawer of that nightstand."

He glances at the nightstand on the opposite side of the bed from him, then looks back at me.

"You said you hated guns."

"I do. Doesn't mean I don't own them."

Watching as I wrestle with myself, debating whether or not to head over to that nightstand, he smiles.

"You smug son of a bitch," I say, seething. "Don't think I won't shoot you, because I might."

"Maybe you could let me give you a few more orgasms first, though. Just a thought."

I want to scream again, but suspect that would only amuse him. So I clench my hands to fists and transmit a terrorist threat to him with my eyes. "This isn't funny, Liam. This isn't a joke."

He shrugs. "Who's joking? Not me."

I send a longing gaze to the nightstand, picturing his skull exploding when my bullet hits his forehead.

He mutters hotly, "Jesus, fuck, you're gorgeous when you're mad."

"Yeah? Well, by the time tonight's over, you're gonna think I'm a friggin' supermodel."

I whirl around and head back into the closet. I pull a shirt off a hanger and put it on, then drag on a pair of my jeans, not bothering with underwear. Then I shove my feet into a pair of sneakers, grab a jacket, and head out, heart thudding.

As I'm storming out of the bedroom, Liam calls after me, "What do you want for breakfast?"

"Your head on a platter!"

I jog through the vast, echoing apartment, trying to keep my rising panic under control. When I get to the living room, I head to the elevator doors discreetly tucked into an alcove behind a stand of potted palms. I stab my finger onto the call button, then impatiently do it again.

The button lights up. I wait, pacing, until the elevator doors open, then I run inside, expecting Liam to follow me.

He doesn't. I hit the L button, which I assume stands for "Lobby," and chew my thumbnail while enjoying a mental breakdown during the ride.

When the elevator doors slide open, they reveal four hulking bodyguards in black suits standing in a row, staring at me. Judging by their expressions, they knew I was coming.

Behind them is the parking garage where Liam and I came in earlier.

I grit my teeth and jab at another button on the console, this one labeled with the number one. When the elevator doors open on the first floor, I burst out, only to find myself in an empty space.

No people, no furniture, not so much as a houseplant interrupts the nothingness. It's just unfinished, open space, thousands of square feet of it. All around, floor to ceiling windows showcase the city at night beyond, but inside it's totally empty.

There isn't even carpet on the bare cement floor.

Unnerved, I get back into the elevator and hit the button for floor number two.

It's the same. Empty. Echoing. Not a single sign of life.

By the time I've visited the fifth floor, I know what I'll find on the sixth, seventh, and eighth. And every floor after that.

Except for the penthouse, the entire building is empty.

Liam owns a fucking skyscraper all to himself.

Glaring at the console forested with useless buttons, I mutter, "Smug. Arrogant. Infuriating. Pretentious—"

"Easy, now." A voice crackles through a speaker in the ceiling. "Pretentious is going a little far, don't you think?"

I'm so mad I resort to ridiculousness to express my fury and stamp my foot. Looking up at the ceiling, I shout, "You're spying on me, too? Kidnapping wasn't good enough, now you have to *spy*?"

Liam's voice warms. "I love looking at you, lass. Can't help myself."

I dig my hands into my hair, close my eyes, and huff out an angry breath between clenched teeth.

"If you need a nice massage to release some of that stress, I'll be happy to give you one."

"And I'll be happy to punch you in the nose!"

"So violent." He chuckles. "I knew we were a good match."

Beyond frustrated, I kick the elevator doors. The only thing it accomplishes is bruising my big toe. I jump back, hopping and cursing, and flip off the ceiling.

Wherever the camera is hidden, I know Liam sees the gesture, because he chuckles again.

"You have to go to sleep at some point, you cocky bastard! And when you do, I'll be there, hovering over your sleeping body with an icepick!"

Ignoring my threat, he muses, "Cocky? I don't know about that. Self-confident is more apropos, don't you think?"

"I'm going to light this building on fire and burn it to the ground is what I think," I mutter under my breath, stabbing my finger on a button marked P1 on the console. It's one button below the L, so maybe there's a way out there.

Liam is still talking through the speaker. "And would an icepick really do the trick? I think you'd need excellent aim, which you don't seem to have." He pauses. "Or make it up with sheer volume."

I snap, "That's exactly my plan, Mr. Black. All those big muscles of yours are soon going to be more holey than swiss cheese."

I ride for a moment in silence, the elevator creaking, until Liam says, "All those big muscles? Are you saying you're impressed with my body?"

I give up. I collapse against the elevator door and gently bang my forehead on it.

"Because I have to admit, I love it when you give me compliments. Like when you told me in the hospital that I was beautiful. Do you remember that?" He sighs wistfully. "It was really touching. No one's ever said anything remotely like it to me before."

Without removing my forehead from the metal door, I say flatly, "I was on drugs."

Through the speaker, his voice comes stroking soft. "I loved it. I want you to tell me that again. When I'm inside you."

"Ha! As if! You'll *never* be inside me again, pal!"

His voice drops an octave. "You want to bet?"

I start to shake with rage. My hands clenched to fists, I pull away from the door and direct my burning stare at it. If the camera is above my head, I won't give him the satisfaction of seeing my face.

"I'm not talking to you anymore."

"Have it your way."

Another crackle and he's gone.

The doors slide open on P1, but I'm right back where I was before, on the level where Liam and I first came in, the four goons staring back at me with blank expressions.

Unfuckingbelievable.

I shove my hand against the door to keep it from closing. "Where's Declan?"

The goons look at each other. No one speaks. One of them shrugs, like, *huh*?

"I know you speak English. Call Declan and tell him to get his ass over here right now."

Three of the goons look at the fourth one, who must be in charge. He's frowning down his nose at me, but I'm so far beyond scared it must show on my face. He purses his lips, removes a cell phone from a pocket inside his suit, and hits a button. He lifts it to his ear, listens for a moment, then says something in Gaelic to whoever answered on the other end.

He nods and clicks off.

Then he slips the phone back into his pocket and stares at me.

"So? Is he coming?"

He doesn't bat an eyelash. It's like talking to a brick wall.

But my question is answered within moments when Declan strolls out of the shadows around a corner where a row of Escalades are parked.

He's smoking a cigarette. Walking unhurriedly. Gazing at me with those arctic blue eyes.

The goon squad parts, making way for him as he approaches. He stops in front of me, takes a drag on his cigarette, and blows out a plume of smoke right into my face. "You rang?"

His tone is bone dry. I can't tell if he thinks this is funny or if he's about to snap into a rage, because his face is as unreadable as his icy eyes.

Waving a hand in front of my face, I say, "I need you to take me home."

He lifts his eyebrows. "I thought you were smarter than that."

"What are you, his slave?"

A ripple of tension goes through the bodyguards, but Declan remains unmoved, calmly smoking as he looks me up and down.

"More like his brother. And watch your mouth. Liam might enjoy that tart tongue of yours, but I like my women more respectful."

"It's a good thing I'm not yours then, isn't it?"

He tilts his head and runs a hand thoughtfully over his jaw. Then, unexpectedly, he laughs. "Aye. Your ass would be so sore from my hand paddling it, you wouldn't be able to walk."

As the goons share a chuckle, blood rises in my cheeks. "I'm glad you think this is so funny. Kidnapped many women for him, have you?"

Declan's smile fades. Tension grips his shoulders. He jerks his chin at the goons, and they melt away into the parking garage without another word.

When we're alone, he takes a step closer to me.

"No," he says, gazing steadily into my eyes. "I've never kidnapped a woman for him before. In fact, I've never seen him like this over a woman before, and I've known him more than twenty years."

I swallow, surprised by that, and unsure what to say in response.

Declan takes another drag on his cigarette. "What, no smart comeback?"

I fold my arms over my chest and shake my head.

"Huh. She does know how to bite her tongue."

He walks a slow circle around me, looking me up and down as he calmly smokes. When he stops in front of me again, he flicks the cigarette away, spitting out a stray piece of tobacco.

"How'd you know my name? Liam tell you?"

"No. I guessed."

His brows shoot up.

"I overheard him on a phone call with you when I was at the hospital. Then you drove us to my place, and here, tonight. I just assumed that was you."

His gaze is sharp and assessing. "That's some jump."

"But I was right."

He narrows his eyes at me, then nods slowly. "Aye. You were." He seems disturbed by that.

He reaches inside his black leather jacket, takes out a package of Marlboros, and shakes one out, sticking it between his lips. Then he holds the pack out to me.

"I don't smoke."

He puts the cigarettes away, pulls a Zippo from the front pocket of his jeans, lights his smoke, then snaps the lighter shut with a flourish. He takes a long drag, then exhales and says, "All right. You got questions. Ask 'em. I'll answer if I can."

That's so unexpected I simply stare at him for a moment in surprise.

He makes an impatient gesture with his hand. "For fuck's sake, lass. Get on with it."

I scramble to think of the important stuff. "So Liam is Boston's mafia boss?"

Declan snorts. "Incorrect. Liam is head of the Irish mafia. Full stop."

When I only stare at him, not understanding, he sighs. "Okay. You've seen *The Godfather*, right?"

I nod.

"Good. You know how Pacino was the boss of all the Italian families in New York?"

I picture a bunch of gangsters in suits bending to kiss Pacino's ring at the end of the movie when he was installed as the mob boss after his father died. "Yes."

"And you know how Brando was Pacino's father and the head of the entire Corleone family, both in New York and Italy?"

"Yes?"

"Take that up a hundred notches and you've got Liam."

I swallow. "I'm starting to get a really bad feeling about this."

Declan nods. "Liam oversees everyone, lass. All the families. All the operations. On both sides of the pond and all around the world. Think of it this way: the Catholic church has tens of thousands of churches, thousands of priests and bishops, a couple dozen archbishops, on top of those the cardinals, getting more and more important as you go up the ladder. And at the tippy top of that hierarchy is the pope, sitting on his golden throne."

He pauses meaningfully.

"You're saying Liam is the pope."

"Aye. Minus the funny hats."

I've been abducted by the mafia pope. I don't know whether to laugh or cry.

After a while when I don't say anything, Declan looks offended. "He won't hurt you, if that's what you're worried about."

"The only thing I'm worried about is getting home and getting back to my life."

I watch him smoke, thinking it might be nice to take up the habit. It gives you a great way to buy time during awkward conversations.

"What's so important for you to get back to, lass? Your job at Buddy's Diner?"

I bristle at the mockery in his tone. "Waitressing is honest work, which is more than you and Liam can say about what you do."

He snaps back, his voice cutting. "You have no idea what we do."

"I guess we have different definitions of the word honest."

He looks at me for a long, tense moment, then says softly, "They're closer than you think."

Understanding there's a hidden meaning there, and also that he immediately regretted what he said, I say, "Are you going to explain that?"

He shakes his head.

"Okay, then. I'll cut to the chase: how can I get out of here?"

"You can't, unless he decides to let you go."

He takes one long, last drag on his cigarette, then drops it to the cement and grinds it out under his heel. "But here's some free advice that'll help you in the meantime. Don't lie to him, because he'll know if you do. Don't betray him, because *I'll* know if you do." His eyes glitter. "And you won't like the consequences."

I will myself not to blink or swallow. "Is that it?"

He walks past me to the elevator and presses the call button. He's silent for a moment, waiting for it to arrive, then turns and gazes at me thoughtfully.

"Don't treat him like a king, like everyone else does. What you give him—that lip, that honesty—he needs it. You're real. For a man like him, that's priceless."

The elevator dings. The doors slide open. Declan steps back, gesturing for me to enter.

I walk slowly to the elevator and get inside. He hits the button for the penthouse, then stands outside the open doors with his arms folded over his chest, gazing at me.

I say, "What about me? What about what *I* need? Why is this all about him?"

"Because you're gonna be fine, lass. You're tough as any mob boss I've ever met. When this is all over, you're gonna have a long, happy life."

A chill runs over my skin. "You say that like he's not."

His eyes darken. "Word to the wise? Don't get too attached. Sooner or later, men who live their lives with one foot in the grave fall all the way in."

The elevator doors slide shut and Declan's gone.

19

TRU

*W*hen the elevator doors open on the penthouse level, Liam's standing there waiting for me, shirtless and barefoot, wearing only a pair of black boxer briefs.

His body is beautiful. Masculine architecture at its finest, sleek and strong. His shoulders are wide and his waist is tapered, and he's got a set of abs that could make angels weep. Add in all the tattoos, and he's magnificent.

The bastard.

"I want you to take me home now."

"So you've said."

He closes the few steps between us with his long stride and picks me up.

As he's turning around to head out, I snap, "I'm perfectly able to walk."

"Aye, but it's my privilege to carry you."

I glare at his profile, furious that he could be so calm and courtly at a time like this.

"Go ahead and pick a fight," he says. "I like it when you quarrel with me."

"Only because you're bored with everyone else kissing your ass."

"I admit it gets tedious."

"If you're taking me back to your bedroom, don't bother. I'm not sleeping with you."

"You're adorable."

His smile is indulgent. I'd like to smack him over the head.

"Seriously, Liam—"

"Shush," he says firmly. "It won't make a difference. You won't change my mind."

We enter the bedroom. He carries me to the bed and sets me down on the edge. When I stand up, he pushes me back down.

I close my eyes and sit there, rigid, taking deep breaths through my nose, until he says, "Get undressed."

I open my eyes and stare angrily at him. "You're joking."

"You need sleep."

"I need a hatchet and for you to stand still while I swing it at your head."

He cups my jaw in his hand and gazes down at me, his eyes dark and beautiful and sad. He murmurs, "You don't mean that."

I feel a twinge of guilt and hate myself for it. Sighing, I close my eyes again. "No. I don't."

He crawls onto the bed and drags me on top of him, arranging my limbs so I'm using his body like my own mattress. I admit, he's a very comfortable mattress. Comfortable and good smelling. I have to consciously resist the urge to snuggle into his broad chest.

I groan. "Why are you doing this?"

"Because I want to. And I can. And you want it, too, only you're stubborn as hell and won't give me the satisfaction of admitting it."

"I said no to your insane cohabitation proposal."

"You considered it."

"But *I said no*."

He strokes a hand over my hair. His chest rises and falls with his heavy exhalation. "Tru. It's done. You're mine for twenty-eight days. You can hate me for the rest of your life after that if you want, but for now, let's enjoy it."

"You say that like I'm being unreasonable!"

His voice hardens. "Squawk all you want, it's done."

I take a moment to enjoy a visual of him howling in pain as I bite off his nipple. A yawn distracts me from the impulse to disfigure him.

Liam kisses my forehead, wrapping his arms around my back. He starts to rub a gentle circle over my spine with his palm. "What's your favorite color?"

"Oh, I'm sorry, is this a new personality I'm talking to now?"

"I need to know your favorite gem stone, too."

Gritting my teeth, I drum my fingers impatiently on his chest. "And your ring size."

Ring size? I feel all the blood drain out of my face. I'm frozen. I can't even swallow.

A pleased chuckle rumbles through his chest. "That got her attention."

After a moment, I say carefully, "I feel like I might have fallen through a hole into another dimension."

He rolls me onto my back and settles his weight on top of me. His eyes blaze as he stares down at me, fiercely intense.

He growls, "I'm not going to force you to marry me, if that's what you're thinking."

My throat muscles relax enough for me to exhale a ragged breath. Until he says thoughtfully, "Though I could," and they freeze right up again.

When a slow smile spreads over his face, I realize he's teasing me.

Horrified, I breathe, "You...you...*psychopath.*"

He looks unimpressed. "I've been called worse."

I shove at his chest. "Get off me."

He sighs and mutters, "Here we go."

"Get off—"

He silences me with a kiss.

I break away as soon as I can. Which isn't soon enough, because I like the way he tastes just as much as the way he kisses, and what it does to my body when he kisses me.

I'm going to need so much therapy when this is through.

He says, "We're going to sleep now. I'm a light sleeper, so forget about trying to sneak off."

He rolls over, flips the covers off one side of the bed, and grabs me, pulling my arm so I tumble over his body. Lying on his back, he tucks me into his side and flips the covers back over us, then settles in with a satisfied sigh.

"Liam."

"Aye, baby?"

"I still have my shoes on."

"You're the one who didn't want to get undressed."

"So you're listening to what *I* want now? That's a nice change of pace."

My hair stirs, and I realize he's silently laughing into it.

"Glad I amuse you."

He whispers, "You have no idea."

I stare in disbelief at the ceiling. *This can't really be happening. This can't be my life.*

"You can holler at me some more in the morning," he says, sounding relaxed. "For now, just go to sleep."

"It's not like I have a choice."

A tinge of warmth sneaks into his voice. "You might discover you enjoy having all your decisions made for you."

"Sorry, but this isn't the middle ages. Women have the right to vote now, did you hear?"

"I did. Terrible development, if you ask me. Everything has gone straight downhill since."

He's teasing me again. Who is this jolly new Liam, this smiling, joking version of my glowering, smoldering wolf? He can't really be that happy that he kidnapped me and we're going to be spending the next month together full-time...can he?

And if he is, how awful was his life before that it takes something like this to make him smile?

Don't you dare start empathizing with him! He's a mafia king! He's a kidnapper! This isn't the guy you feel sorry for!

I shout at myself mentally for a few minutes, until Liam nuzzles my ear, murmuring sleepily, "Go to sleep soon or I'll think you're waiting for me to rip off all your clothes and fuck you until you're limp."

Exasperated, I roll onto my side and bury my face in the pillow.

He follows me, throwing an arm and a leg over my body and pulling me close. He presses a kiss to the nape of my neck. After a few minutes when we remain unmoving, the lights dim, then fade to darkness.

I'm left alone with my racing thoughts as Liam holds me fast, even after he falls asleep.

I wake up sometime later with no idea where I am.

For a moment, my mind is blank. Lying on my side, I let my gaze drift around the unfamiliar room. It's quiet and still. Light peeks all around the edges of heavy gray curtains along one wall, so I know it's morning.

Then I hear slow, heavy breathing coming from behind me, feel the weight of a big male arm wrapped around my waist, and it all comes back in a rush.

I'm a captive.

I wait for the outrage and anger to kick in, but all I feel is a pale sort of irritation, quickly followed by the urge to turn over and burrow into all that delicious warmth heating my backside.

Apparently, Stockholm Syndrome sets in fast.

"Good morning."

Liam's voice is thick with sleep. He stretches his legs, inhales deeply against the back of my neck, then pulls me tighter against his body.

Feeling his erection pressed against my ass, my face heats. *Good morning wood, you mean.* I clear my throat. "Hi."

"You didn't run away."

"I figured you'd tie me to the bed if I tried."

"You figured right." Gripping my hip, he rocks his pelvis into my bottom and exhales. "Remind me again why you're dressed?"

"Because I'm mad at you. Kidnapping, remember? Abduction? Any of this ringing a bell?"

"Hmm. Right." He slides his other arm under my body and squeezes me, nuzzling my neck. He murmurs, "My beautiful captive. I need to come inside you. How do you feel about anal sex?"

My eyes pop wide open and my heart starts to pound. "I'm very opposed to it. *Very*, with a capital V. Especially with the mafia pope who stole me away from my celebration dinner and locked me up in his skyscraper."

There's a thoughtful pause. "Mafia pope?"

"Never mind. I'm getting angry again."

He slides his hand to my breast and squeezes. In a husky whisper, he says, "Let me make you come. You'll feel better."

About ninety percent of my cells are on board with that idea, screaming with glee, while the other ten percent set about trying to club them into submission.

Screw that stupid ninety percent. I'm in charge here, not my crazy hormones.

Deliberately, so there can be no misunderstanding, I say, "No."

"Okay. You're the boss."

I lift my brows. "Really? Since when?"

He chuckles. "Since never. I was only trying to placate you."

"Gotcha. Just out of curiosity, is there a gun on the nightstand on this side of the bed, too?"

His chuckle turns into full-on laughter. He flips me over so I'm flat on my back on the other side of him, then—as he seems to love to do—he throws his leg over me, pinning me down.

Gazing down at me with soft eyes and a sleepy smile, he says, "There you are."

Jesus. Why does he have to be so damn beautiful? It makes everything so much worse.

"Are you always this happy after you abduct an unsuspecting victim?"

"No," he says softly. "I'm happy because I'm waking up to you."

Shit. He's in charming mode. Wary, I narrow my eyes at him.

"Don't look so suspicious, it's true."

"When I don't come home, Ellie will call the police."

He trails his nose along my jawline, tickling my skin with his beard. "Ellie knows you're staying with me. She thinks it's a great idea."

The traitor!

"And your boss knows you won't be in for a while. He told me to tell you hello."

I glare at him. "How long have you had this planned?"

"You're wasting time with all this unnecessary outrage. Let's move on to something more important: how long are you going to be mad at me? My dick is aching for you, and I need to hear you scream my name again. Like within the next five minutes."

"Get used to disappointment."

He raises his head and stares deep into my eyes. "You could never disappoint me. Even if you don't let me touch you again for the next month, it will still be the best month of my life, because we'll be spending it together."

I stare at him in slack-jawed disbelief. "Come on!"

He drops his gaze to my mouth. His eyes heat. He licks his lips.

"No, Liam. This isn't how it works. You don't get to ignore my wishes and trample all over my free will and then expect me to happily spread my legs for you."

"God," he says hotly, "keep talking. Spread your legs? Go on."

Useless, all of it. I might as well be arguing with a block of cement for all the good it will do me. "Forget it."

He takes my hand and curls it around his massive erection.

Into my ear, he whispers, "I want you. I've wanted you since the first time I saw you, but I want you even more now that I know how you sound when you come. Now that I know how that beautiful mouth feels around my cock. The way you claw my back and scream my name when I fuck you. The way you never hold anything back.

"But even more than all that, I want you to feel safe with me, and to trust me, and to know that there's nothing I wouldn't do to make you happy, including putting a bullet in someone's head."

When he pauses, I open my eyes and look at him. His voice turns dark.

"And if it's going to make you happy to keep that delicious wet pussy to yourself, so be it. I might force you to stay with me, but I'd *never* force you to fuck me. I won't ask again."

He releases me abruptly, rolling away to stand at the edge of the bed and drag his hands through his hair. Then he stalks off to the bathroom and slams the door shut behind him.

The shower goes on.

Wait—*he's* mad at *me*?

Disoriented, I listen to the water run for a while until it goes off. After a few minutes, Liam reappears from the bathroom, nude. Without sparing me a glance, he goes to the closet.

He emerges moments later fully dressed. Black suit, black tie, white dress shirt, black leather shoes. He's the wolf again, dark and dangerous, his expression closed off and his eyes unreadable.

On his way out the bedroom door, he says over his shoulder, "Your books are in the library. Enjoy your studies."

He leaves without a backward glance.

20

TRU

*I*t takes me a while to gather the presence of mind to decide I should shower, too, get into clean clothes, and find something to eat.

First things first. I'll work on the bigger problems later.

The shower in the master bathroom turns out to be amazing. It has one of those rainfall showerheads in the middle of the ceiling that make you feel like you're bathing outdoors on a tropical island during a summer storm, along with half a dozen strategically placed jets on the walls that spray pulsing water at your body from all sides.

My toiletries are lined up neatly along the counter behind one of the two marble sinks. I comb out my wet hair, brush my teeth, and put on deodorant, using all my own stuff, pilfered from my apartment.

Half of me marvels at the trouble Liam went through to get me here, the other half of me wants to kick in his front teeth.

Another part—a small, hidden part that I'm actively ignoring —tells me I like this crazy plan and should stop whining and get on board with it.

After all, I won't have to listen to Ellie and Tyler scream in conjugal ecstasy for weeks. I can study for the bar in peace and quiet. And considering I'm an introvert whose idea of a perfect date is sitting on opposite ends of a sofa reading in silence, being trapped indoors for weeks on end with a sex bomb of a man who doesn't talk much could be nirvana.

It could also be living hell.

Unfortunately, I suspect that if I somehow managed to get out, I'd be right back here within hours. I'd have to smuggle myself out of the country in someone's suitcase to escape from the reaches of Liam Black.

I dress in clean jeans and a T-shirt, then pad barefoot through the apartment, wandering from room to gargantuan room.

The main living areas are designed in an open format. The kitchen gleams with stainless steel and black granite. The living room and dining room are separated by a thick sheet of tinted glass suspended from the ceiling. A media room sports a giant flat screen TV and triple rows of comfy lounge chairs, like a theater. The library is on the opposite end of the apartment from the master suite, and is almost as large.

Next to the library is an office.

Liam's office.

I stand at the open door with my hand on the knob and my heart starting to pound, staring at his desk.

It's big and black, because of course it would be. It has all the usual things a business desk would have: blotter, cup of pens, computer with a big screen. The only thing I don't see is a phone. There weren't any in the other rooms of the apartment, either.

I spend a few minutes debating with myself about whether or not to head over to that computer and turn it on, but end up deciding that Liam would undoubtedly have a password.

And if there's a camera in the elevator, there are probably cameras in here, too.

So I go back into the library for a look around.

All my study materials, school books, and test prep aids have been placed neatly in piles on a large wooden table near the unlit marble fireplace at one end of the room. My laptop is there, too. There's no television in here, but there are rows upon rows of books in bookcases, lined up all the way to the ceiling. A rolling ladder rests against one of the cases, waiting for someone to climb.

I walk in slowly, trailing my fingers over the back of a big leather sofa the color of coal, marveling at the atmosphere of understated luxury and reveling in the smell of old books.

The room is a bibliophile's dream.

I spend a while browsing through the bookcases, growing more and more impressed. First editions of Proust seem to be Liam's weakness, but his philosophy collection impresses me the most. He's got everything from Aristotle to Nietzsche, Descartes to Kant. From a shelf, I select a battered copy of *Meditations* by the ancient Roman emperor Marcus Aurelius, open to a dog-eared page, and read a highlighted passage aloud.

"Do not act as if you were going to live ten thousand years. Death hangs over you. While you live, while it is in your power, do good."

I stare at the words, perplexed. A man in charge of an international criminal empire is highlighting quotes about doing good? Maybe this book originally belonged to someone else.

I flip to the front. There's an inscription in looping feminine handwriting on the title page.

My love,

Some words of wisdom from a wise man, because you enjoy that sort of thing.

Happy birthday.

Julia

It's dated August tenth, eighteen years ago.

I stare at the note with a dry mouth and the fine hairs on the back of my neck standing on end. Then I snap it shut and slide it back into its place on the bookshelf, feeling skittish, unnerved, and vaguely guilty, as if I've seen something I shouldn't have.

Like I've looked through a keyhole into a locked room and spied a ghost.

I shake the feeling off, telling myself that I'm being silly.

Whomever Julia is or was, there's no evidence that book was a gift to Liam. She didn't write his name, after all, just a non-specific "my love." Liam could've bought that copy of *Meditations* at a used book store. It could have belonged to quite a few people before it made its way into his hands.

Besides, eighteen years ago, he was very young. Younger than I am now. I don't know the exact amount of years we are apart in age, because he refused to tell me, but anyone called "my love" by a woman named Julia would probably be older than Liam was then. It all sounded very sophisticated.

Maybe it was his father's book? Maybe Julia was Liam's mother?

Another mystery to add to the list.

I head back to the long wooden table and pull out a chair. I settle in, gathering my study schedule and laptop, and try to login to the bar exam prep site I paid two month's wages for. I've already been working on the multiple-choice question portion of the exam for weeks, between school and work, but now I realize with a sinking feeling in the pit of my stomach that I might not be able to study online at all anymore.

I don't know Liam's Wi-Fi password.

Shit.

It's possible to study offline, but the online course has on-demand and live streaming lectures, plus Q&As with professional attorneys, access to a database of sample test questions and essay answers, and a bunch of other great tools I'd miss out on if I simply studied the old fashioned way: from books.

This isn't the worst development. I'm good at working alone and have no problem self-motivating. I won't miss the camaraderie of my study team, because I mostly ignored them anyway. But I will miss those lectures and the database, which is primarily what I paid for in the first place.

Which means I'm going to have to ask Liam for the password.

Which means I'm going to have to talk to him.

I tell the computer screen, "How much do you want to bet he'll say no? I mean, if I get the Wi-Fi password, that means I can access my email, too. Which means I could send a message to the Boston police department letting them know I've been kidnapped." I think for a moment. "Or does the FBI handle kidnappings?"

The computer screen stares back at me dispassionately.

"You're right. Who am I kidding? The FBI is probably on his payroll, too. He's probably got the President on speed dial, now that you mention it. Everybody knows politicians are a bunch of crooks."

I allow for a moment of self pity, then I crack open my study guide and get to work.

If I'm going to be stuck in this sky mansion for a month, I might as well make the most of it. I'm nothing if not practical.

Four hours later, I break for lunch.

I only know what time it is because there's a clock on the mantle above the fireplace. I don't have my purse, so I don't have my phone, and that feels like I'm missing a limb.

One more thing I'll have to ask the lord of the manor for.

In the colossal stainless steel refrigerator in the kitchen, I find a curious selection of elegant black glass containers of all sizes stacked on the shelves. I open one and find filet mignon with garlic mashed potatoes. Another holds miso glazed salmon with buttery asparagus. Still another reveals decadent-looking meat lasagna topped with shavings of black truffle.

My mouth watering, I select the lasagna and pop the container into the microwave. As it cooks, I rummage around in drawers for silverware. Everything is laid out with anal-retentive precision, from the cutlery to the salad tongs. Unlike in my apartment, the drawers have those soft close hinges, so no matter how hard you slam them shut, they glide closed on a whisper of air.

Very inconvenient for when you're in an argument in the kitchen and want to make a point, if you ask me. When we're irritated with each other, Ellie and I can turn cabinet and drawer slamming into an art.

I wolf down the lasagna standing at the granite kitchen island, then rinse the container and fork and put them into one of the dual dish washers. Then I head back to the library, trying not to wonder where Liam went.

I study until it's dark outside and the city lights are winking up at me through the glass wall. I'm about to stand and stretch when a hand reaches out and sets a glass of red wine on the table beside me.

I glance up to see Liam gazing down at me.

I didn't hear him come in.

He's still in his suit and tie. In his right hand, he holds a snifter of brandy.

Without a word, he turns and crosses to the big black sofa on the other side of the room. He sets his brandy on the glass coffee table in front of the sofa, loosens his tie, then sits and leans his head against the back of the sofa. Exhaling heavily, he closes his eyes.

The urge to go sit in his lap and curl into him is infuriatingly strong.

I take a sip of the wine. It's excellent, bold and dry with a hint of spice and chocolate. After a while when it becomes clear Liam isn't going to speak to me, I decide to go first.

"How was your day, dear?"

He doesn't move or open his eyes, but my sarcasm makes a ghost of a smile lift the corners of his lips. "Total shit." Then, after a pause, his voice drops lower. "But it's better now."

I take another sip of wine, wishing my hands would stop trembling.

"You?"

"It was..." I search for the right word to encapsulate my experience of the day, finally settling on one that surprises me. "Productive."

He lifts his head and moistens his lips. Gazing at his glass of brandy on the coffee table, he pulls his loosened tie over his head, discards it to the sofa beside him, and opens a few buttons on the collar of his dress shirt. Then he leans forward and picks up the brandy. He swirls the glass under his nose for a moment in thoughtful silence, his elbows propped on his knees.

He's so handsome in profile. Handsome, mysterious, and very far away.

"Liam?"

"Aye, lass?"

"How old are you?"

He answers without hesitation, his gaze on the glass in his hand. "Thirty-nine."

He's fifteen years older than me. Eighteen years ago, he would've been twenty-one.

Is twenty-one old enough to have a woman named Julia calling you "my love?"

Even before I've finished asking myself the question, I already know the answer is yes.

When I don't say anything more, he murmurs, "Does that bother you?"

I answer without thinking. "No. I like it."

He turns his head and looks at me. His gaze is blazingly intense.

Flustered, I look down at the glass of wine in my hand. "I need to get the Wi-Fi password."

"Of course. Anything you want, just ask me for."

Surprised, I glance up at him. He's still staring at me with that dark fire in his eyes. "You don't mind?"

"Why would I mind?"

"Because, I mean...what if I tried to send somebody an email?"

When his brows quirk together in a confused frown, I add, "Like an SOS."

He has me trapped in his eyes. I want to look away, but can't.

His voice low and his gaze locked with mine, he says, "I know you're not going to do that."

My heart is a frantic bird, its wings beating against the cage of my chest. "How do you know?"

"Because you want to stay with me. Because nothing has changed from the time you said you trusted me." His voice drops even lower. "Because you know I'll keep my promise to let you go back to your life at the end of twenty-eight days, even though neither of us will want that to happen."

A wave of heat flashes over me, flushing my skin. It seems I can feel every one of my nerve endings.

I tear my gaze from his and fidget in my chair. For lack of anything better to do, I take another swig of the wine, feeling Liam's gaze on me the whole time.

"Have you eaten?"

"I had lunch around one, some stuff from the fridge. Lasagna. It was good."

Calm down. Keep it together. Why are you so emotional? He's only asking you about food.

"Would you like to go to dinner?"

I whip my head around and stare at him. "You mean...*out* to dinner?"

He inhales slowly. A muscle flexes in his jaw. When he speaks, he sounds as if it's through gritted teeth. "Aye."

After a moment, I realize I've insulted him.

That confuses me so much I have to sit in silence for a while, readjusting my mental compass. "I didn't mean to offend you. I'm just not sure what the rules are. I've never been kidnapped before."

He examines my expression for a moment. His own is tense and dark. Then he turns his attention to the glass of brandy in his hand. He lifts it to his lips and drinks until all the amber liquid is gone.

"There are no rules," he says, his voice husky. "Except that you live here with me for the next few weeks."

Why is he so melancholy? And why do I care? More importantly, what am I missing?

"I'm curious about something."

He waits silently, gazing at the empty glass in his hand.

"What is it about me that you think you need?"

I feel his surprise, though he makes no outward reaction. He doesn't move even an inch. But I'm attuned to him now, to his moods and the small inflections of his voice and expression. To the way he speaks volumes if you watch closely enough, if you take in all the silent signs.

He answers after a long time in a voice that's so sad it could break my heart.

"You make me feel human."

Emotion wells in me, tightening my chest and forming a lump in my throat. It might be stupid, it might even be insane, but the empathy I feel for this dangerous, enigmatic man is so powerful I'm breathless from it.

He's suffered more than most people could endure and go on living, of that I'm certain.

On impulse, I whisper, "I'm glad."

He looks up at me with dark, empty eyes.

Shit. This is all kinds of wrong. Don't say it. Don't say it. Don't —"How about Italian for dinner?"

He gazes at me for a moment, then murmurs, "You had Italian for lunch."

"I never get tired of my favorite things."

"Me neither."

I have a feeling he's not talking about food, but I don't have time to think about it, because he stands, crosses to me, and gives me a gentle kiss before leaving the room.

21

TRU

*A*fter I change into a dress and the pumps I threw at him, Liam takes me to dinner.

It's a charming Italian place, designed like an old Tuscan villa, with two floors surrounding a central courtyard. The structure is made of terracotta bricks draped with hanging ivy. A thousand white lights twinkle in the olive trees on the patios and courtyard and around the edge of the roof.

It's magical, romantic, and completely unexpected.

It's also empty. Aside from the waiter who seated us, there isn't another soul in sight.

Liam sees me glancing around in confusion. "I own it." He flicks open a white linen napkin and drapes it across his lap.

"Oh. It's not open to the public?"

A hint of a smile crosses his face. "Not tonight, it isn't."

I take it that means he closed the place down so we could dine in private. I can't decide if that's romantic or controlling. Then I recall all the glass containers of food in his refrigerator and another thought crosses my mind: maybe he did it for safety.

Maybe the mafia pope can't eat in public because it's too dangerous for him.

Or for me.

Or he thinks I'd scream for help in a crowd.

I'm busy mulling it over, toying with a gleaming salad spoon, when Liam says, "Considering you're so shy and awkward around strangers, I thought you'd feel more comfortable if we were alone."

My fingers fall still. I glance up at him. He's trying to suppress a smile.

"So you remember that conversation."

"I remember everything."

He conveniently forgot the part where I said I wouldn't move in with him.

I place my napkin in my lap and take a sip from my water glass to buy time, thinking of that kiss he gave me before we came here. It was gentle and quick, nothing like his usual ravenous plundering. It seemed like he was deliberately restraining himself. Like he didn't want to spook me.

I really hate it that he can be so considerate and gentlemanly one moment, but then, when it suits him, he can turn around and throw all his manners out the door.

He demands, "What?"

I also hate it that he can read my damn mind.

"I was just thinking you're a very complicated person."

"I hate to disappoint you, but I'm the least complicated person you'll ever meet."

When I look at him with a wry twist to my lips, he adds softly, "You just don't know me well enough."

Something in his tone makes my blood quicken. "Will I get to know you? Will I ever find out all your secrets?"

His gaze on mine is steady, revealing nothing. "If you do, something will have gone very wrong."

I blurt, "I wish I knew everything there is to know about you."

I've surprised us both. A muscle slides in his jaw. His Adam's apple bobs as he swallows. I see him debate with himself whether or not to pursue this line of conversation, until curiosity gets the better of him.

"Why?"

I don't have the guts to answer him while looking into his guarded eyes, so I look down at the tablecloth instead. I chew the inside of my lip, then take a breath and admit it.

"Because you fascinate me. You're unlike anyone I've ever met. You have all these sharp edges that scratch, and you're obviously accustomed to violence, but you're also...tender. Under that intimidating surface, you're sensitive. And, I think, very sad. It's a compelling combination."

The following silence is blistering. I don't dare look at him.

"I thought you were angry with me."

Flustered, I exhale in a gust. "I am. Very. But I'm also giving myself whiplash with all the back and forth I'm going through." My voice drops. "I still want you."

There's another crackling silence, then Liam murmurs, "Look at me."

I glance up at him, my heart pounding. He's looking back at me with shining eyes and an expression of unspeakable pain.

He says, "Thank you."

"For what?"

"Being honest. Being you."

"You're welcome." We stare at each other. I feel like my heart is beating outside my chest.

The waiter arrives at our tableside. "*Buonasera signore.*" He bows to Liam. To me, he sends a respectful nod of his head. "*Signorina.*"

"*Buonasera,*" replies Liam. "*La lista dei vini, per favore.*"

When I laugh in disbelief, the waiter sends me a quizzical look.

"Sorry. Ignore me, I've got low blood sugar. Haven't eaten anything since lunch."

Liam says something else in Italian to the waiter, who smiles. He retreats, whistling, and disappears around a corner.

"So you speak Italian, too."

Liam shrugs.

"Along with Gaelic, Spanish, and French. Any others?"

"A few."

"Did you study languages in school?"

"It was more like on the job training."

I sit back in my chair and gaze at the Mona Lisa smile on his face. "Oh, look, we're being vague and inscrutable again. Was that part of your training, too?"

"As a matter of fact, it was. Have some bread."

He passes me the bread basket from the middle of the table. It's covered in a white linen cloth. I pull the cloth back to reveal a beautiful selection of fresh ciabatta rolls baked with olive oil, salt, and rosemary. They smell like heaven.

I take one, put it on my bread plate, hand the basket back to Liam, then slather the roll with butter from a small round butter dish near my water glass. Then I tear off a hunk and pop it into my mouth, moaning when the taste explodes on my tongue.

"I'm glad to see you're not on the low carb bandwagon."

"If carbs are good enough for Sophia Loren, they're good enough for me."

That earns me a laugh. "She's a little before your time, isn't she?"

"I saw a picture of her in a bikini once along with a quote about how she owed her figure to spaghetti. I thought it was cute. I feel sorry for women who don't love food. It's almost better than sex."

Liam's eyes go hot, and his voice turns husky. "It's not even a close second."

"You haven't tried the bread yet."

He chuckles, shaking his head.

The waiter returns with a wine list as thick as my arm. Liam scans through it, flipping pages, then says something in Italian. The waiter bows again, then retreats.

We're quiet for a moment, then Liam says suddenly, "If you could go anywhere in the world, where would it be?"

It's a strange turn in the conversation, but I consider it. I tear off more of the ciabatta roll and chew on it while I think. "Probably Argentina."

"Interesting choice. Have you been?"

"I've never been anywhere. But there was this woman named Valentina who lived in the town I grew up in who was from Buenos Aires. She had to be at least seventy years old, but she was beautiful in that way certain older women are. Sexy, too. She had lovers half her age. I'd see her sometimes, riding through town on this big black horse with red ribbons braided in its mane. She was always singing to herself. Singing and smiling, like she had a delicious secret she was thinking about.

"My mother thought she was crazy, but I thought she was so glamorous. You could tell just by looking at her that she'd led an interesting life. A big life. That's what I wanted, too."

He studies me with such intensity I start to feel self-conscious.

"Is that why you moved to Boston? To live a big life?"

My laugh is small and dry. "I moved here because my boyfriend at the time was starting medical school at BUSM."

Liam's scrutiny grows sharper. I can tell he wants to ask more, but doesn't. And because he doesn't pry, I tell him.

"He cheated on me a few months after we got here. With the dean of the university, if you can believe it. I always knew he was ambitious, but that really took the cake."

"He's a damn idiot."

"Thank you."

"Would you like me to break his legs?"

He looks serious. I take a moment to consider it, then shake my head. "He's not worth the trouble. Besides, I already got my revenge."

Liam sits forward in his chair, folding his arms on the tabletop and pinning me with a razor sharp look. "How?"

"I dumped all his clothes into the street and lit them on fire." A little embarrassed by the admission, I add, "It might be petty, but it made me feel better."

Liam stares at me. He says softly, "Oh, I know. Revenge is good medicine."

He's my wolf again, all glittering eyes and ferocious energy. A shiver goes through me, but it isn't fear.

"Were you in love with him?"

"I thought I was."

"That sounds like a no."

"I moved on too easily for it to be true love. My ego was bruised more than my heart."

The waiter returns at that moment, carrying a bottle of wine and two glasses. Liam and I are silent as we watch him uncork the bottle and pour a small measure into a glass, but I feel every bit of his attention. It's bright and burning hot, like sitting under the summer sun.

He samples the wine. He swirls, sniffs, sips, rolls it over his tongue. Then he nods at the waiter, who appears incredibly relieved.

He pours me a glass, refills Liam's, then retreats again.

Liam lifts his glass and holds it out. "A toast."

I pick up my own glass, matching his gesture. "To?"

He licks his lips, staring hungrily at me. "To lighting things on fire."

We touch glasses, our gazes locked. When we drink and set our glasses back down, it feels final, as if something has been decided.

Perhaps what's been decided is that I'm certifiably insane. I'm toasting my kidnapper? Next I'll be having a heartfelt conversation with my grandfather's ghost.

"So."

"So."

"You own a skyscraper."

"Technically, I lease it through one of my corporations."

"*One* of your corporations. Must be nice to be a bazillionaire."

"Mostly, it's just exhausting."

That admission surprises me. He sees it on my face.

"After a certain amount, money is a burden."

"I'm dubious."

"You'll have to trust me on this one."

"So you'd rather go back to being poor like you grew up?"

He's surprised again. "You remember I said that."

"I remember everything."

When his eyes sharpen, I avert my gaze and sip more of my wine.

Drumming his fingers on the tabletop, he watches me closely for a moment, his head tilted to one side. Then he switches the subject. "Why a criminal defense attorney?"

My heart skips a beat.

This isn't a topic I want to discuss. There are too many emotional minefields. I drop my gaze to the bread basket and carefully set down my glass of wine. "It's a long story."

"I'd like to hear it."

When I don't say anything, he prompts, "Are you planning on representing celebrities?"

My gaze snaps back to his. A flash of irritation tightens my stomach. "What would make you say that?"

"Law school is expensive. Low six figures, at least."

His stare is challenging. He's right, so I look away, even more irritated than before.

He says, "And there's no money in criminal defense, unless your clients are very wealthy."

"I don't care about the money."

"Then you're one of the few people who don't."

"You just said yourself that money is a burden."

"Don't avoid the question."

Aggravated now, I look away and huff out a breath. "Fine. I chose criminal defense because I know firsthand how shitty the justice system is for people who can't afford a good lawyer. If you're poor and you've been accused of a crime, you're fucked, regardless of your guilt or innocence. There are no country club prisons for poor folks, only politicians, hedge fund managers, and millionaires."

There's a pause, then Liam murmurs, "Freedom for the wolves has often meant death to the sheep."

When I look at him askance, he says, "It's a quote from Isaiah Berlin."

"It's morbid."

"It's the truth. There are only two kinds of people in the world: predator or prey. The poor are always prey. Poverty is helplessness. Which apparently you know."

We stare at each other, unblinking.

The waiter—who, as it turns out, has impeccable timing—returns holding two plates. He sets them down in front of us with a flourish and explains what he's serving. In Italian, so I'm stumped.

When he leaves, Liam says, "I asked the chef to do a tasting menu for us. That way you can try little bites of all the best items on the menu. I hope that's all right."

I wrestle with my irritation for a moment, before replying, "It's wonderful. Thank you."

Liam observes me eat, all clattering cutlery and scowls, until he says, "You're angry with me again."

I collapse against the back of my chair, sighing. "It's just that digging in graveyards is dangerous. Sooner or later, you're going to uncover something bad."

He looks at me like I'm the most interesting creature on earth. "I couldn't agree more."

That's a loaded statement if I've ever heard one. But he

doesn't give me a chance to dwell on it before going in another direction with the Random Question Interrogation.

"Do you take after your mother or your father?"

"My mother, for sure. My dad's helpless. Leave him alone for ten minutes and something will either be burning, exploding, or flooded. He's a walking danger zone. Without my mother keeping an eye on him, he'd have accidentally killed himself years ago."

Thinking of him, I can't help but smile. "It was a lot of fun growing up with a father like that, though. He was like another one of the kids, always inventing new games for us to play. He has the best imagination. And he's the only person I've ever met who lives fully in the present. He never looks back, not for a second. He's kind of this big, goofy, cowboy Zen master, bumbling around causing trouble while at the same time happily eating life with both hands."

Realizing I'm babbling, I stop talking abruptly and take another swallow of wine.

If Liam examines me any more closely, he'll be peering inside the atoms that make up my bones.

"Your cheeks are red."

"That's just from all the blood pulsing in them. Stop looking at me like that and it will go away."

"I don't want it to go away. I love it when you blush for me." When I move restlessly in my chair, his voice drops. "And when you squirm."

I prop an elbow on the table and cover my eyes with a hand. "I wish you didn't see me so clearly."

He reaches across the table and takes my wrist, moving my hand away from my face so I can see his expression, all flashing eyes and need.

"No, you don't. You love it."

His fingers are on the pulse point on my wrist, so I know he can feel how my heartbeat ticks up. How wildly it starts to beat, stirred by the look in his eyes, the tone of his voice, and the heat scorching the air between us.

"You're right. I do love it." I take a breath. "And you love it that I see you, too."

His fingers tighten around my wrist. He says nothing, but his eyes are on fire.

The waiter comes back, bearing more plates. Liam shoots him a threatening look, and he turns around and goes back from where he came.

When he's gone, Liam says, "I meant what I said. I won't pressure you to sleep with me."

The heat in my cheeks flames hotter.

"But you will be *sleeping* with me. In my bed. Understood?"

I exhale a shaky breath. "Why?"

"Because I need you," comes the hard response. "And if I can't have you one way, I'm damn sure going to have you the other."

"What about what I need?"

"What is it you think you need?"

"My freedom of choice, for one thing."

He looks at me for a beat, then releases my wrist. He relaxes back into his chair and folds his hands in his lap. "Why don't you go to the ladies' room. It's right around that corner."

Mystified, I look in the direction he's pointing. When I look back at him, he's gazing calmly at me, as if his suggestion made sense.

"I don't need to use the restroom."

"Don't you?"

What. The. Hell. "No, Liam, I don't."

"I think you do."

His eyes glitter. There's something behind them I don't understand, but I do know that he's got a reason for wanting me to go to the restroom.

I debate with myself for a moment, then push back my chair.

I cross the courtyard and turn in the direction he pointed. As soon as I'm out of his sight, I pause for a moment, resting my hand on the rough brick wall to give my heart a chance to recover. When it slows to a more normal beat, I continue down the walkway, passing the men's room. There's an arrow on the wall indicating the women's toilet is around another corner to the right.

I turn the corner and stop dead, staring.

The ladies' room door is there, as the sign said it would be. But ten feet beyond it is a break in the building where there's no wall or doorway, just an open arch leading to the street outside.

My heart starts to pound.

I could walk right out that arch and be gone. Which, obviously, he knows.

He's giving me a choice.

I stand there thinking for what seems like a long time, but might only be seconds.

Then I exhale the pent-up breath I've been holding, push open the ladies' room door, and go inside.

22

TRU

*W*hen I return to the table, new food has appeared and the old plates have been cleared. Liam is finishing his glass of wine.

I sit. We eat in silence only interrupted by the reappearance of the waiter to clear plates and bring new dishes. I drink two glasses of wine in quick succession, not bothering to try to figure out what it means that I didn't run away.

I don't need to wonder. I already know.

This is an absolute disaster in the making.

When all the dinner plates have been cleared and we're sipping cappuccinos, Liam says, "You left your handbag in the car last night. I asked Declan to bring it into the library."

The handbag with my phone in it, he means. The phone I'm not going to use to make an emergency call to the police, or anyone else, to come and rescue me.

"Why are you shaking your head?"

"Because I keep surprising myself."

"Now you know how I feel."

I lift my gaze from the creamy foam of the cappuccino cup in my hand and look at him. "You always seem to know exactly what I'm going to do."

His enigmatic smile makes a reappearance. "Do I?"

When I don't return the smile, it fades. Looking frustrated, he leans closer. "Tell me what you're thinking."

"I can't believe you don't know."

"I'd like to hear you say it."

"So you *do* know what I'm thinking."

"You look disturbed by that."

"Can you blame me?"

"If it makes you feel any better, I'd never use it against you."

I set down the cup and rub my forehead, sighing.

"Am I giving you a headache?"

"No. I'm just...this is very..."

His voice turns husky. "It's not complicated at all, Tru."

I say drily, "It would be helpful if you'd stop reading my mind."

"I can't help it. You're an open book."

"Could you at least pretend?"

"I told you I'd never lie to you just to make you feel better."

"Wait—I thought you said I was unpredictable?"

"No, I said I kept underestimating you."

I think for a minute. "I'm not sure I get the difference."

Eyes burning, he growls, "Have I told you how beautiful you are when you come?"

I laugh. "Whoa! Give me a minute to recover. Where's a neck brace when you need one?"

"Because you are. My dick gets hard if I think about it."

Exasperated, I stare at him. "You said you wouldn't pressure me."

He considers me with heated eyes, then apparently decides he's pushed me too far, because he sits back in his chair and casually crosses one leg over the other. "Fair enough. Would you like anything else to eat?"

My god, this man could test the patience of Mother Teresa. "No," I say coolly. "Thank you for dinner. It was lovely."

"You're welcome."

I get the sense he's trying hard not to show any of the amusement he feels. That only makes me angrier. "Liam?"

"Aye, lass?"

"You're bad for my blood pressure."

His dark eyes dance with mirth. He stands, drops his napkin on the tabletop, and holds out a hand to me. "Come on. You can throw more shoes at me when we get home."

I look at his hand, tempted to snap at his fingers like a turtle.

But in the end, I take his hand and let him lead me out to the car and take me back to his skyscraper.

There's nowhere else I'd rather be, anyway.

When we get back to the apartment, the first thing Liam does is turn on music.

"What is that?" I follow him into the living room where he's fiddling with a remote control.

"Gotan Project. They're based in Paris, but the music is Argentinian electrotango."

"Electrotango? I didn't know there was such a thing."

"It's a hybrid of electronic dance music and traditional tango." He sets down the remote on a coffee table and watches me as I listen, intrigued by the sultry, thumping beat.

"It's sexy," I pronounce, which makes him smile.

"It is. And the music isn't the only sexy thing about Argentina."

I quirk my lips. "You're talking about the women."

"I'm talking about the atmosphere. The culture. The weather. The way Argentinian's live their lives. They're very passionate people."

"You've spent time there?"

He lets his gaze linger on me, drifting down from my face to my hips. "Aye. And you're right to want to go. It's the kind of place you could lose yourself in and be grateful to get lost."

He lifts his lashes. Our gazes lock. I can tell he knows something about getting lost.

Looking into his eyes, I'm beginning to think I do, too.

Emotion rushes through my body like an incoming tide. I feel hot, then cold, then panicked, unsure if I should stand still or bolt.

"I think I'll go study for a while longer."

He nods and turns away, his eyes shuttering. Then he heads down the hallway toward the master bedroom, loosening his tie as he rounds a corner and disappears.

When he's gone, I exhale a shaky breath. I'm far out to sea in a leaky boat with a storm coming in, and I know it.

Actually, the storm has already arrived. Now it's just a matter of seeing if I'll sink or swim.

In the library, I find my handbag lying on the table beside my laptop. I dig my phone from the bag and unlock it, sighing when I see I've got fifteen missed calls from Diego, along with several panicked texts. The last one is in all caps.

PLEASE LET ME KNOW YOU'RE OKAY!!!

I dial his number, worried he'll do something stupid if he doesn't hear from me.

"Tru!" he shouts the second he picks up. "Thank god! Are you all right?"

"I'm fine, I promise. Everything is okay."

There's a pause, then he exhales a heavy breath. "Jesus. I've been totally freaking out."

"I'm sorry about last night. I had no idea he would—"

"Don't fucking apologize for him!"

When I'm silent, startled by the viciousness of his tone, he turns sheepish. "Shit. Sorry. I didn't mean to yell at you. I've just been so worried. Then you didn't come into work tonight, and I thought..." He's quiet for a moment, then his voice drops. "I thought he might have hurt you."

I say with conviction, "He'd never hurt me."

"Tru," he replies softly, "don't be naïve. We're talking about a man who's ordered the execution of dozens of his enemies. He hurts people because he likes to."

Or maybe because they deserve it.

I'm so surprised by that thought, I remain silent. I don't want to consider what it means, much less let it come out of my mouth.

"Listen, I know you don't know much about him—"

"I know enough."

It's Diego's turn to be surprised into silence. After a moment, he says, "So you know he's the head of the Irish mafia?"

"I do now."

"But you didn't before last night?"

"No."

"So, basically he was lying to you about who he was."

"He was trying to protect me."

Diego's laugh is hard and disbelieving. "You're too smart to believe that."

Anger slowly unfurls in my stomach, like a snake with its coils. "Did he hurt you?"

A grudging pause, then: "No."

"Do you know why?"

Through gritted teeth: "Because you asked him not to."

"Correct. And if you think I'm a helpless victim here, you're wrong."

"You might not be helpless, but you're still his victim."

Heat crawls up my neck, making my ears glow, setting my face on fire. "I've never been a victim in my whole life, and I'm definitely not one now."

There's a long, tense silence. "He's listening, isn't he? He's standing right there with a gun to your head, telling you what to say."

Slowly, clearly, I say, "No. He's not listening. There's no gun. And he'd never presume to tell me what to say. He doesn't treat me like that."

"I don't believe you."

"I can't help that, but it's the truth."

His voice rises. "Do you hear yourself? You're defending him! He's a gangster, Tru! He's a thug!"

I keep my voice even, though my hands are shaking and my stomach is in knots. "As I recall, you told me *you* were once a thug."

"Who I was ten years ago is a very different fucking thing than who Liam Black is right now!"

"I'm going to need you to stop shouting at me, or this conversation is over."

I hear his breathing over the line, hard and irregular, and know he's infuriated.

"So you're his girlfriend now or something?"

Or something. A faint smile lifts my lips.

I wonder who I'm becoming. This woman who finds humor in her own demise. This person who can hold such vastly opposing ideas in mind and still function.

Idea one: Liam is a criminal.

Idea two: Liam is a good man.

I don't know how, or why, or when I became someone who could excuse the worst in a man for something I sense, but don't know, might be a greater good. All I know is that I believe in Liam—in all his darkness and beautiful light—and it feels like something sacred to me, even though it might just be insanity.

"Look, I just called to let you know I'm fine and to check in."

He huffs. "You could've called earlier to find out if *I* was fine. You saw the way he had that guy throw me out of the restaurant. I could've been lying in an alley somewhere with a bullet in my head!"

"I know you won't understand this, and you probably won't believe it, either, but when he told me he wouldn't hurt you, that was a promise."

He snaps, "And when I told you I didn't need you to ask him for protection, *that* was a promise, too."

I frown. "What's that supposed to mean?"

"It means I've got my own ways of protecting myself. Liam Black isn't the only one with connections. And he sure as hell isn't the only one who knows how to make people disappear."

That makes all the hair on my arms stand on end. "Diego, please don't do anything stupid. There's no need to escalate this situation. Nobody got hurt—"

"Not yet, they haven't," he says darkly. "But you're lying to yourself if you think getting involved with a man like that ends any other way than with blood."

He disconnects.

I stare at the phone in my hand, so unsettled I can't think straight. Then I turn around and walk out of the library, down the long, echoing hallway and into the master bedroom.

Liam is lying on his back on the king-size bed staring at the ceiling with his feet crossed at the ankle and his arms crossed behind his head. He's bare chested and barefoot, wearing only a pair of black jeans.

I say, "How does almost everyone in this town seem to know who you are, but I can't find out a single thing about you on the internet?"

His tone is quiet and calm. Unlike mine, which is high and bordering on hysterical.

"I employ people to keep my name off the internet, but word of mouth is unstoppable. Why are you upset?"

Agitated, I shift my weight from foot to foot. "I just talked to Diego."

His gaze slices from the ceiling over to me. He waits.

"He thinks I'm your victim."

"Then he doesn't know you at all."

"You did kidnap me."

His eyes glitter. His voice drops. "But you still don't feel like a victim, do you?"

I think of the open passageway to the street at the Italian restaurant. "No."

When his eyes warm, I add, "I could be deluding myself. My hormones might have staged a coup on my brain."

His strong chest rises and falls with his heavy breath. He returns his gaze to the ceiling. "I'm really starting to dislike that kid."

Though his tone is dry, I know it's not a threat. "He didn't tell me that. I came up with that one on my own."

Liam remains silent.

After thinking it through, I say softly, "Okay, I'm not deluding myself."

His head doesn't move, but his eyeballs slide toward me again.

"I mean, yes, my hormones are a circus lately. But I think, overall, I think I'm just..." I take a deep breath and decide to be totally honest. "It's going to take me a minute to mentally adjust to the situation."

"Understandable," he murmurs.

I look at him, that body, that face, all those muscles and tattoos, that aggressive sexual energy he's holding in check by sheer force of will, and I feel a pang of desire so strong it frightens me.

To combat it, I say, "So you've killed dozens of your enemies?"

His tone is tranquil. "More than that."

My voice comes out faint. "Oh." I clear my throat. "Well. I appreciate the honesty." I laugh softly. "I guess."

After examining my expression for a moment, he says, "Ambivalence is a real bitch, isn't it?"

The question is rhetorical, so I bypass it. "I think Diego is going to be a problem."

Liam lifts his brows. "For whom?"

"For you."

His look sours. "How little you must think of me."

"Goliath underestimated David. Look where that got him."

He draws his brows together, squinting his eyes and peering at me from across the room like he's gazing into a crystal ball, trying to discern the future. Then his look clears to one of understanding.

In a tone of wonder, he says, "You're worried about me."

I say stiffly, "Don't get all puffed up about it. I'm just trying to be practical."

His eyes are as soft as his voice. "I'll keep it in mind. Thank you."

"But I'm *not* saying I want you to try to scare him or even do anything about it, okay? And the don't-hurt-him directive still stands. I'm just giving you a head's up."

"Understood."

"Promise?"

"Pinky swear."

He smiles broadly. It's breathtaking. Our gazes hold for a moment before I turn around and head back to the library, my head screaming at me not to let myself have feelings for this stranger who's suddenly taken over my life while my heart warns that it's already too late for that.

I try to study for a while, but give up. I'm too distracted. I call Ellie, but it goes to voicemail. I leave a message telling her I'll be staying with Liam for a while, which I know she already knows, and for future reference, I'd appreciate it if she took my side once in a while.

I text Carla to thank her for coming to dinner, but don't get an answer.

As I'm sitting there looking at the phone in my hand, I

become overwhelmed by everything that's happened. The attack in the alley, finding out about Liam, Diego's bizarre reactions, graduating from school, being here...everything swamps me, battering me from all sides.

I lean over, rest my head on my arms on the tabletop, and close my eyes, trying not to cry.

I fall asleep that way, sitting in a chair, face down over a table. Which is how Liam finds me when he comes in sometime later.

Without a word, he picks me up in his arms and takes me back to bed.

23

TRU

I don't understand how a criminal mastermind who terrifies grown men by the mere mention of his name can also be such a snuggler.

We're back to front, spooning, his favorite position. His big body curves around mine like we were molded this way in a lab. He didn't bother trying to undress me, he simply laid me down on the bed and pulled the covers up over us, then turned me on my side and burrowed against me.

His warm breath tickles the fine hairs on the back of my neck.

In a drowsy voice, he says, "Are you comfortable?"

"Physically, very."

Knowing what I left out, he murmurs, "The hardest thing in the world is to be at odds with yourself."

"You make it sound like you have personal experience in that area."

"I do. I also have a recommendation."

"Which is?"

"Let it be. Accept that you have warring factions inside you. If you're living by your core values, all the second-guessing is just noise you can give yourself permission to ignore."

My philosophical wolf. I think about his words for a while, staring into the dark.

He prompts, "Let's hear them. I know you have a list."

That shouldn't surprise me, but I ask anyway. "How do you know?"

"Because I was once an idealist, too."

His voice is heavy with something that could be regret. Or maybe it's just weariness.

"Okay. Not in any special order, my top five core values are non-conformity, self-reliance, kindness, honesty, and courage."

"Top five of how many total?"

"Twelve."

I can't see his smile, but I can feel it. "Let's have the rest."

"Curiosity. Freedom. Persistence. Learning. Humor. Gratitude. Solitude."

After a while, he says softly, "It's a good list."

"Thank you."

"I'm curious, though. Solitude? Most people don't like to be lonely."

"Loneliness and solitude are two totally different things. All the times I've been loneliest have been in a crowd."

His silence is thoughtful, then he squeezes me tighter against him, sighing against my hair. I feel him struggling with himself, but I don't know why.

I whisper, "How did you get to be what you are, Liam?"

"What am I?"

"A man standing on top of a mountain of bones."

He exhales slowly, turning his forehead to the back of my neck. It's hot, as if he's running a fever. His voice thick, he says, "It was either climb to the top or be one of the skeletons."

"Are you happy?"

His laugh is cutting. "Are you joking?"

"No."

"Happiness is an illusion."

"I feel sad for you that you think that. Most people think happiness is basically the whole point of life."

His tone is laced faintly with disgust. "Which is exactly why most people are depressed. They value happiness over everything else. Over the more important things. But it's just an emotion. It hardly matters at all."

He's upset. I've touched a raw nerve, but he's touched so many of mine that I'm not backing down from this.

"What's more important than happiness?"

He answers without hesitation, his voice ringing with conviction. "Honor. Without his honor, a man might as well be dead."

It hangs there in the air, glinting and dangerous like an unsheathed sword, its sharpened edge gathering the light and my curiosity along with it.

Why would a mafia boss speak so vehemently of honor? He sounds more like a soldier, willing to give his life for god and country. A knight sworn in service to his king.

A man whose values don't match his life.

I recall Declan's odd comment about honesty in the parking garage and wonder if his talk of honesty and Liam's talk of honor are related.

For men who deal in power, violence, and human misery, what use is there in such things?

With a strange intuition buzzing along my nerve endings, I turn my face toward him in the dark. "Liam?"

"Aye?"

"I'm adding honor to my list."

His chest is pressed tightly against my shoulder blades, so there's no way he could deny how hard his heart starts to thump.

And that, more than any words he could say, makes me certain that I was right when I accused him of having more secrets than one.

I'm beginning to think Liam Black is a labyrinth of secrets.

A layer cake of lies.

I'm going to peel back the layers until I find true center of him, even if it kills me.

After that night, we fall into a pattern.

When I wake in the mornings, Liam is already up. We have breakfast together, then I head to the library to study, and he heads off for the day to do god only knows what. I don't ask. He doesn't offer. After dinner, evenings are spent together in front of the fireplace, reading, talking, or in complete silence.

It's strange to me that we can sit in each other's presence for hours at a time without feeling the need to speak. Strange and wonderful, and comforting in a way I think we both need.

I catch him watching me often. I'll look up from a book and his gaze will be on me, sometimes thoughtful, sometimes dark. Behind his eyes lurks a wild forest at nighttime, filled with dangerous creatures and hidden trap doors.

No matter how dark his gaze, it always burns with longing.

But he doesn't touch me after that first night.

He keeps his promise not to pressure me like a sacred vow. We sleep in the same bed, often touching, always with his erection making itself known sooner or later, but he acts as if he's unaware of it, keeping his hands and his dick to himself.

After a week of it, I'm dying.

It's an undisputed truth that the flames of desire are fanned by being thwarted. That what we want, but can't have, drives us mad. He warned, "I won't ask again," and by god, he makes good on that, until I'm climbing the walls with pent-up lust.

I don't know if that was his plan or if he's simply honoring his word, but lying next to his heat in the dark becomes a nightly torture.

On day eight, I break.

We're in the kitchen. I'm sitting on a stool at the big black granite island, watching him slice bananas into my cereal. It's a simple task, very domestic, but he's shirtless and gorgeous and his hair is mussed from bed, and the urge to grab onto that hair while he has his face buried between my legs is an arrow through my heart.

Toying with my spoon, I say casually, "We'll need condoms."

Banana in one hand, knife in the other, he freezes. His gaze flashes up to mine.

"There aren't any in the nightstands or the bathroom cabinets," I continue lightly, as if I haven't just been burned to cinders by his look. "I checked."

He licks his lips. It makes my nipples harden.

Then he simply nods and turns his attention back to the banana.

I, meanwhile, have to grip the edge of the countertop so I don't slide onto the floor in a puddle.

We eat our breakfast in silence so blistering hot I start to sweat. After he showers and dresses, he leaves the same way he has every day, with a kiss to my forehead at the door.

Right before he walks out, however, he lowers his head and says into my ear in a throaty voice, "You're going to have to say please."

He strolls away without a backward glance, leaving me equal parts steaming mad and just plain steaming.

I can't study. So instead I pace like a lunatic, up and down the length of the library, back and forth through the living room, round and round the kitchen island, wringing my hands.

By the time he returns late in the afternoon, I'm a wreck.

He finds me on the living room sofa, my legs curled up underneath me, drinking a glass of red wine. It's my second. The pleasant buzz it gives me also somehow makes him appear even sexier than usual, all hard jaw and hotness, his eyes burning coals.

He's carrying a small brown bag.

He doesn't greet me. I don't greet him. Instead, we stare at each other like we've got a bet on who'll blink first.

He sets the bag down on the coffee table, pushes it toward me, and straightens. He loosens his tie, watching me, waiting for me to say something.

Jesus. He's not going to make this easy.

I set my wine glass on the coffee table and stand. "Are you hungry?"

His eyes eat me up. He growls, "Fuck yes I am."

"I meant for dinner."

He pulls the tie over his head and drops it to the floor. "No. Say it."

My pulse goes haywire. He's in bossy mode. Wild, impatient mode. With a bushy tail and bared fangs, his fur bristling.

I nervously moisten my lips. Then I wipe my sweating palms on the front of my jeans. "Um..."

He shrugs out of his suit coat, letting it fall to the floor, then swiftly unbuttons his dress shirt, pulling the tucked ends from the waist of his slacks. The entire time, he stares at me, unblinking.

"I, um..."

He unbuckles his belt. My breasts feel heavy, and my nipples start to ache. It suddenly becomes hard to breathe.

"Liam."

He whips the belt through the loopholes. It makes a loud *zizz* that nearly makes me gasp.

His voice is a patient drawl, unlike his eyes, which are on fire. "Aye, lass?"

I know he won't call me baby until we're in bed. He only ever calls me that in bed.

"Will you...will you please..."

He makes a loop of the belt in his fists and snaps it.

I jump, blurting breathlessly, "Will you please make love to me."

It wasn't a question, but he doesn't care. Striding around the coffee table, he commands, "Get the bag." I barely have enough time to comply before he picks me up and throws me over his shoulder.

Holy shit. He just threw me over his shoulder.

I cling onto the bag with one hand and his shirt with the other, swaying upside down as he carries me into the bedroom, one big hand splayed over the backs of my thighs. I should probably feel ridiculous being carried this way, but instead I'm wide-eyed and thrilled, my heart banging like a drum.

The first time, we fucked.

The second time, we had sex.

This time, we make love, and that makes it so much better and so much worse.

And far, far more dangerous.

He lowers me to the bed, lowers himself on top of me, and kisses me deeply, his tongue searching my mouth and his hands dug into my hair. I've got my arms around his broad shoulders. My legs are bent on either side of his waist. I'm clutching the little brown bag like my life depends on it.

He rears up to his knees and whips off his shirt. I lie on the bed staring up at him, feeling electrified.

"Say it again." His voice is thick with desire.

I whisper, "Please make love to me."

"Put your arms over your head."

I comply instantly. He pulls off my jeans and panties, then pushes my T-shirt up over my breasts to my armpits so it's crumpled up under my chin. The closure on my bra is on the front. He flicks it open, then takes my breasts in his hands and feasts on them.

He sucks hard on a taut nipple, making me arch and moan, then moves to the other one and does the same. He goes back and forth, taking his time, enjoying himself, while I rock my hips into his, whimpering.

"Tell me what you want."

"Your mouth."

He gently bites down on a nipple. "You have my mouth, baby."

"No—down there."

He whispers teasingly, "On your toes?" and bites down harder.

My moan of pleasure is garbled. "Between my legs. Please."

"You like my mouth on your pussy?"

I'm delirious. His voice is so hot and dark, it's making me crazed. I start to babble. "Yes, please, I love it, I want it, please hurry, I want it *now*."

A rumble passes through his chest, an animal's territorial warning.

He slides down my body, gently biting my belly and hips as he goes. He bites one thigh, then noses down the seam where my thigh meets my sex, inhaling deeply with a sound of masculine need.

My face goes scarlet. I bite my lip, helplessly rocking my hips.

He opens me with his thumbs and presses the gentlest kiss to my throbbing clit.

I tear a hole in the brown paper bag with my fingernails.

"Look at this pretty pussy," he whispers, gently pinching my folds. He slides a finger inside me. "Ah, and you're soaked. Fucking *soaked*."

When he sucks on my clit, I sob, jerking.

He gently works his finger in and out while he licks me, reaching up with his other hand to fondle my breasts. I forget the bag and his instruction to keep my arms overhead and sink trembling fingers into his hair.

When I moan, long and low, he murmurs, "God, I love that sound. Almost as much as when you scream my name when you come."

I say breathlessly, "Please make me come. God yes please, Liam, I need to come."

"You know I will, baby. You know I'll take care of you."

He slides another thick finger inside me, then reapplies his mouth to my clit and sucks.

Panting, I rock my hips faster and faster. My skin is on fire. The room is too hot, too close.

Liam brings me right to the edge of orgasm, but before I fall over, he stops.

He stands, takes off the rest of his clothes, then commands, "Wrap me up."

Half delirious, I fumble around for the paper bag. Inside is a box of condoms that I tear open. The small foil package I rip open with my teeth. Then I scooch to the edge of the bed and, with shaking fingers, roll the condom down the length of Liam's rigid cock.

He watches me with dark, intense eyes, one hand fisted in my hair.

As soon as I'm finished, he pushes me back onto the mattress and pushes inside me.

"Needed you to come on my cock first," he growls into my ear. "I've been obsessing about it for a week."

He kisses me, giving me his weight. I sink into the mattress, rolling my hips in a rhythm to meet his.

Everything takes on a dreamlike quality. The air is soft and shadowed. The warm, clean smell of his skin and hair fills my nose. I'm stretched open by his girth, frantic for the friction, for every slide and thrust, for his deep-chested grunts, for the way I feel so small and safe underneath him.

For the way my heart feels like it's cracking open wide.

He breaks the kiss to moan my name into my ear. It's soft and desperate, tinged with a sadness I don't understand.

As I build toward orgasm, emotion builds inside me, too. I

fight it, not wanting to give into it because I'm afraid of how huge it feels. How overpowering.

He knows. Somehow, he knows.

Slowing the movement of his hips, he lifts his head and gazes down at me. In a husky voice, he says, "Don't you dare hold back on me, baby. If this is all we get, you better give me everything."

The hot prick of tears stings my eyes. I look away, my heart pounding, but he frames my face in his hands and forces me to meet his eyes.

"Come on," he says. "Give me all of you."

"I'm scared."

"I know. Do it anyway."

My throat closes. He stares down at me, trapping me in the dark depths of his gaze, fucking me slower but deeper.

It's a thrust like all the others, but it takes me and tears me apart.

I gasp, arching, staring wide-eyed up at Liam as contraction after contraction rocks me. My arms, thighs, and pussy all clench around him at the same time.

He breathes, "Fuck. Fuck yes. You're so beautiful, Tru. Look at me. Don't look away."

The smallest sob escapes my throat. The bed drops out from under me, and I have to cling to him so I don't fall along with it, tumbling down into the terrifying darkness waiting far below.

Whatever he sees in my eyes as I come makes him lose control of himself.

With a groan, he closes his eyes and kisses me. It's savage. Rough. He starts to buck, driving into me hard and wrapping a hand around the back of my thigh to push me open wider.

I'm still coming, drunk with pleasure, moaning into his mouth as he owns me.

When he comes, it's hard, with his head thrown back and a shout to the ceiling, every muscle in his big body clenched.

I feel him throbbing inside me and watch breathlessly as he

gives himself over to his own violent orgasm as my contractions begin to slow.

Then I'm boneless underneath him, spread open and panting, my fingernails sunk into the hard muscles of his back.

He collapses on top of me. His heart pounds hard against mine.

After a moment when he catches his breath, he rolls over, taking me with him. He positions my body on top of his—chest to chest, belly to belly, thighs to thighs—tucks my head into the crook of his neck, and holds me in a crushing embrace.

We lie like that in silence for what seems like a very long time. Listening to each other's ragged breathing and heartbeats as they begin to even, the nighttime sounds of the city drifting up faintly from the streets below, until Liam murmurs something in Gaelic.

I turn my head on his shoulder and look up at his face. He's gazing at the ceiling with an expression that looks eerily like anguish.

I whisper, "What is it?"

He closes his eyes. Swallows. Exhales a slow breath. When he answers, it's in a raspy voice. "I don't get close to people. Not ever. It's how I've lived for a very long time."

My heartbeat starts to tick up again. I watch him struggle for a moment, anxiety singing along my nerve endings.

He turns his head and meets my eyes. In his own, oceans of darkness are churning.

"I had it all under control," he whispers, caressing my cheek. "But I never expected you."

24

TRU

I don't know what to say. My throat has closed, anyway, so it's probably just as well that I'm speechless. I simply stare into Liam's eyes with a sinking feeling that this thing between us is going to get rapidly out of control.

If I'm being honest, it's out of control already.

I know because what I see reflected back at me in the dark depths of his eyes is the same craving I feel myself. The same powerful, burning need.

If it's this good now—this scorching, this satisfying, this raw —it can only get better from here. Better and more addicting.

Making it ultimately more painful when it ends.

For the first time since I've known him, fear sinks long, icy fingers into my heart.

I whisper urgently, "Promise me something."

"Anything," he says instantly. "Name it."

I swallow, working up my courage. My voice comes out small. "Don't let me fall in love with you."

His lips part. He gazes at me in silence while my heart pounds frantically, until he rolls me over onto my back and settles his weight on top of me. He throws a heavy leg over both of mine.

Propped up on an elbow, he cups my jaw in his big hand and stares at me with fevered eyes. He whispers, "Could you?"

Oh god. He wants it. He wants me to fall in love with him. He wants me to give him every single thing I've got to give, including my fragile heart.

I consider lying to him. I consider making a joke. I consider a hundred different safety nets that could catch me to soften my fall, discarding them all in an instant.

The truth is the only thing that might save me.

My voice shaking, I say, "I'm halfway there already."

He looks like I've just stabbed him in the gut.

His eyelids flutter closed. He exhales slowly, his dark brows drawn together, then gives me a gentle, lingering kiss.

I don't understand how this man—this powerful and violent man—can also be so incredibly tender. There's another side of him I glimpse at times like this, a raw, emotional side that wells to the surface, breaking through all his iron self-control. He wanted so badly to stay away from me, yet he kept coming back, inexorable as the moon-pulled tide.

And I kept welcoming his return into my orbit.

The attraction between us feels like that: irresistible as a gravitational force. We're two planets in motion held together by something much larger than our individual parts. Something fundamental and undeniable.

Something I sense will be incredibly destructive for us both.

But it's too late to walk it back now. I'm in the wolf's den, deep under his spell. There will be time soon enough for me to figure out how I got here.

And how I'm going to piece myself back together when he's gone.

∼

Hours later, I wake alone.

It's disorienting. Mainly because I don't like it.

I rise and use the toilet, then put on a pair of yoga pants and a T-shirt. Then I wander out of the bedroom and through the dark apartment, looking for Liam.

A seam of light glows under his office door. I head toward it, wondering if it would be a better idea for me to go back to bed and to sleep, but that idea gets tossed out when I hear Liam's voice coming from inside his office.

The door is cracked, so his voice is muffled, but still discernable.

"I don't care about the consequences. I want out."

He sounds agitated.

"That's bullshit, and you know it. No one's paid a higher price than me."

Curious, I tip-toe closer to his office door.

His voice rises. "Aye, I *know* we're close. You think I'm not aware of what's at stake?" There's a pause, then he growls, "Eighteen years is enough. It's a miracle I've lasted this long!"

I think of the inscription on the front page of the book I found in his library, dated eighteen years ago. The inscription from Julia, to her love.

Eighteen years of what is enough?

My heart thumping, I creep closer and closer. Liam is silent, listening to whomever is talking on the other end of the phone.

Then suddenly he roars, "Because it won't bring them back!"

I remember describing him as standing on top of a mountain of bones and get chills.

"Hold on a minute."

Footsteps pound over the floor. Before I can whirl around and run away, Liam yanks open the door and stands there staring at me. He's barefoot, wearing only his briefs.

I swallow, my pulse flying. "Sorry. Um. I was just coming to find you. I'll go back to bed."

Mortified at being caught, I turn to run away, but he catches my arm and pulls me inside. He says something curtly in Gaelic into the phone then hangs up.

Then he wraps his arms around me and pulls me into a bear hug.

We stand there like that for several long moments until Liam gets his breathing under control. Every so often, a fine tremor runs through his chest.

With my cheek resting over his hammering heartbeat, I whisper, "Are you okay?"

"I will be." His voice is gravelly. He exhales, then nuzzles my neck. "Why are you awake?"

"You were gone."

He stills, then pulls away. His eyes search my face.

I keep my tone light. "You're not the only light sleeper around here."

"Come on."

He releases me from the hug, takes my hand, and leads me back down the hall and into the bedroom. He sets his phone on the nightstand next to the bed, then turns back to me, gently pushing me down onto the mattress.

Within moments, we're spooning again. Only this time, both of us are wide awake.

After the automatic lights fade and it's dark again, I say, "You didn't carry me."

"You said you didn't like it."

I think about that. "No, I said I was capable of walking."

"So you *do* like it."

"Don't be smug. It's unflattering."

He exhales slowly. I feel some of the tension leave his body, but my curiosity is such that I risk him getting worked up again. "Who were you talking to?"

There's a long, tense pause. "My brother." Another pause. "There's a...business situation...that's causing some problems."

He told me the less I know the better, but I can't resist

pushing a little bit more. "Is your whole family in business together?"

"No. We're the only two left."

Left? I whisper, "Left as in working together?"

"Left as in alive."

My heart clenches to a fist. "Your parents, too?"

His sigh is heavy. "Aye."

He told me he was one of eight children. Including his parents, that's ten in his family. But now there are only two? How is that possible?

"Liam, I'm so sorry." I hesitate. "Was there an accident?"

His voice comes very low. "A fire."

I think of the scars on his back, and how he agreed when I told him digging in graveyards was dangerous, and want to throw up. "Oh god."

"Go to sleep."

He doesn't want to talk about it. I get it, but if he thinks I could sleep now, he's crazy.

I lie awake long after he falls asleep, lost in thought as I listen to him breathe in the dark.

In the morning, he's preoccupied. I don't ask if he slept well, because I know he didn't. He tossed and turned while I stared at the ceiling and wondered.

And speculated.

And brooded about Julia and the eighteen years.

"It won't bring them back," he shouted into the phone. I can't stop thinking about it, or of the fire that wiped out almost his entire family. The man has so many mysteries, I can't keep them all straight.

We have sex in the shower before he leaves, then again as soon as he walks in the door that night. He doesn't even remove his clothing that time, he simply walks into the library, kisses me passionately, then pushes me face down onto the table on top of my open books. He lifts my skirt and yanks down my panties, then fucks me from behind, one hand on my hip and the other gripped around the back of my neck, holding me down.

It's animalistic.

I love it.

After, he feeds me steak and mashed potatoes by hand. One forkful at a time as I sit on the edge of the island in the kitchen and he stands between my legs, watching with avid eyes as my lips close around the tines of the fork with every bite.

Stripped from the waist up, he's sexy as hell, all those bulging muscles and tattoos burning my eyes.

I'm wearing one of his white dress shirts and nothing else. Every so often, he fondles my breasts or hips, leaning in to kiss my neck and breathe me in. I'm pretty sure we're about to have sex on the kitchen island, too, but we're interrupted by the sound of my cell phone ringing. It's plugged into a recharger on the counter across from us.

Liam crosses to it and looks at the screen. Without a word, he unplugs the phone and hands it to me.

The screen reads, "#1 Dolly Fan."

Dear god. It's my mother.

When I glance up at Liam, he's smirking.

He pulls out one of the stools tucked into the overhang of the island, settles his bulk onto it, props his elbows on the counter-top, and rests his chin on his folded hands, making it clear he's eager to listen in on the conversation.

I debate with myself for a millisecond, not at all certain this is a good idea, but quickly realize my mother will call everyone I know if she can't get in touch with me. Might as well get this over with.

I hold the phone to my ear and pinch the bridge of my nose, bracing myself. "Hi, mama."

"Hi, honey! It's so good to hear your voice! How y'all doin'?"

As soon as I hear her Texas twang, I feel a rush of unexpected relief. "Right now? Feeling guilty that I don't call you more often."

She scoffs. "Don't be silly, Truvy. You've got a busy life up there in the big city. You know nothin' ever changes down here on the farm, anyway. Oh, except your daddy burned down the shed."

I blink in surprise, though it should never surprise me that my father has set fire to anything. "His taxidermy trophy shed?"

"The very same. Smelled to high heaven. Burnin' fur creates quite the stench."

Grimacing, I say, "I can imagine."

"Those poor little stuffed critters went up in a cloud of smoke so black and noxious the county health inspector himself showed up to see what was goin' on."

She clucks her tongue. "Your poor daddy was beside himself. You know it took him twenty years to hunt and stuff all those varmints. Now he'll have to start all over from scratch."

I can't help but laugh at the image of my father mourning a smoking pile of charred stuffed animal corpses, his precious collection. Each of them had a little gold plaque on the wooden stand they stood on with their name—yes, he named them all—and the date they were "immortalized."

It's a miracle I grew up halfway normal.

"How did it happen?"

My mother's voice turns dry. "He got himself a new Weber barbeque, didn't he? A big, ol' shiny gas one, with flames shootin' out of the grill like the exhaust on that rocket-powered ship Evil Knievel jumped the Grand Canyon in. And he had to put the blasted thing right next to the shed because he wanted to enjoy his two favorite hobbies at the same time, the big dummy."

I'm laughing so hard, my cheeks hurt. "Daddy burned down his taxidermy shed with his supercharged barbeque?"

"Mmhmm, he sure did. Ruined those nice T-bone steaks I got at the butcher's that very mornin', too. He's been sleepin' on the couch since last week."

I laugh until tears stream down my cheeks. Liam stares at me like this is the most fascinating conversation he's ever eavesdropped on.

My mother says drily, "I'm glad somebody thinks it's funny."

I take a few hitching breaths, wiping my eyes. "I'm sorry, but it really is."

She harrumphs. "Story of my life. Married a man who can't be trusted to change a light bulb without somehow causin' a blackout four counties wide."

"But this is why we love him."

Her voice turns warm. "We surely do. Lucky for him, he's got those dimples and that sweet Southern charm. Speakin' of love, you datin' anyone special, honey?"

My mind goes blank with panic. I force myself not to look at Liam and look at the ceiling instead. "Uh..."

She laughs. "Oh my. That sounds serious."

"It's, um, definitely...interesting."

"What's his name?"

I clear my throat. "Liam."

The man in question perks up at the mention of his name, while my mother makes a purring sound. "Rawr. Sexy."

"I'm covering my ears now."

"How's his relationship with the Lord?"

I sigh heavily. "For Pete's sake."

"Because you can't trust a man who hasn't given his heart to Jesus."

I'm beginning to regret I accepted this call. "If you must know, I'd say his relationship with the Lord is estranged."

I'm still looking at the ceiling, but I can see from my peripheral vision how Liam quirks a dark brow.

"Oh dear. Well, you work on that. Does he have a good job?"

I hesitate. "He's very wealthy."

She's immediately suspicious. "That's not what I asked."

I think for a split second about what to tell her without fibbing, because I can't lie to my mother. I can, however, stretch the truth. But I can't do it in front of Liam, so I hop off the counter and wander away, lowering my voice. "He's the CEO of an international corporation."

She makes a sound of interest. "Is his corporation in good shape? Is there a strong future there?"

"I'd say it's a growth industry." *I'm going to hell for this.*

"Would your father like him?"

I think about that. "Well, he is a gun owner. And he's definitely a 'family' man. He's very protective of me, too."

I can hear her beaming over the line. "Wonderful! And when are you and this Liam of yours gonna give me some grandbabies, honey?"

"Wow. It only took you three minutes to get there. I think that's a record."

She ignores me. "Of course, you'd have to get married first."

"Thank you for that excellent life advice."

She pauses for a moment. When she speaks again, her voice has changed. "Life is short, Truvy. Shorter than you think it will be. You can't put things on hold too long, or it might be too late."

Oh no. Not this. I stop walking near the door to the powder room and lean against the wall, closing my eyes. "I know, mama."

"It's his birthday next week, you know. He would've been twenty-seven."

We're quiet for a moment, sharing the silence and painful memories.

I say quietly, "I sit for the bar at the end of July. If I pass, I'll apply to the state public defender's office the next day. What happened to Michael will never happen to one of my clients, mama. I promise you that."

She sucks in a heavy breath. Her voice cracks. "I'm so proud of you."

"Thank you."

In the background, there's a crash and a holler. Then my mother groans in exasperation.

I say, "Go. Tell him I love him."

"I will, honey. And we love you, too."

"I know you do. Take care."

We say our goodbyes and hang up. When I turn around, Liam is standing six inches behind me. I jump and gasp in surprise.

Without missing a beat, he says, "Who's Michael?"

I press a hand over my thundering heart and take a breath. "You scared me!"

"Michael," he prompts.

I can already tell he's going to be like a dog with a bone until I tell him what he wants to know, so I go ahead and do it. Grudgingly. "Michael's my brother."

He examines my face. His voice drops. "Your late brother."

I nod, looking away, not surprised that he guessed.

He gently takes my chin in his hand and turns my head back so I can't avoid his eyes. "What happened?"

It feels like an invisible hand has taken hold of my heart and is squeezing. This is the last thing I want to discuss. I know from experience he understands that reluctance well.

Looking up into his burning eyes, I whisper, "I'm sorry, but I don't like to talk about it."

Liam gazes at me in blistering silence, a muscle working in his jaw. After a moment, he says, "Is he the reason you're going into law?"

I swallow, feeling the sting of tears welling in my eyes. "When it's too late for revenge, justice has to take other directions."

His face changes. His expression turns from hard, laser-like focus to startled understanding. To recognition, as if he's seeing me fully for maybe the first time.

Looking electrocuted, he whispers, "*Exactly.*"

We stare at each other, something huge and frightening blossoming between us. I can feel it in the air, this weird connection, an unspoken knowingness. A sameness. A shared experience that binds us in dark wrappings and has warped us in identical ways.

That experience is death.

However we might be different, in all the ways that matter, my wolf and I are alike.

He pulls me into his arms and kisses me like he's starving.

From that day on, he doesn't leave my side.

25

TRU

*U*ntethered from a normal routine that gives it shape and meaning, time slows down. Or maybe it disappears altogether. Either way, without being bracketed by work and school, my days seamlessly slip into one another. The rising and setting sun becomes the only marker of passing time, and even that is so similar from day to day that it loses its meaning, too.

Liam and I exist in self-imposed isolation, cut off from the outside world.

Cut off but not missing a thing.

We eat together. We sleep together. We talk for hours at a time. We watch old movies and avoid the news, cocooned in our bubble. He doesn't answer his phone, and I don't answer mine. Nothing interrupts our total immersion in each other. It feels like we've moved to another planet.

It feels like the invention of a whole new way of living.

There are only two topics we avoid: the past and the future.

It makes sense, in light of the rules of our time capsule. The past and the future don't exist for us. There's only now, because that's all there ever can be.

The only problem is that each morning when I wake up and see his sleepy, smiling face, my heart surrenders a little more.

I begged him to promise he wouldn't let me fall in love with him, but who can promise such a thing? Love doesn't listen to logic. Like time, love has its own physics, universal rules that we're helpless to control.

Every once in a while, I lock myself in the bathroom and give myself a stern talking to in the mirror, but even my reflection knows it's hopeless.

The heart wants what it wants, regardless.

And what I come to want more than anything is that Liam and I go on and on in our suspended time warp forever.

"Faster?"

His voice is a throaty murmur at my ear. His fingers are between my legs. I'm lying naked on my side in bed with him behind me, shuddering as he slowly fucks me, stroking my clit at the same time.

I whisper, "That's perfect. Just like that. *Ah*—"

I jerk as he pinches my throbbing clit, then tugs on it. The long, hard length of his cock slides in and out of me, unbearably slow. Through the windows I see the orange ball of the sun crest the distant horizon.

This is by far the best way to wake up ever invented.

Liam kisses my neck, sucking so hard on my flesh I know it will bruise. One more to add to the love bite collection. He increases the rhythm of his hips, biting me at the same time with a growl of satisfaction.

Every part of him is big. His cock, his chest, his hand with its rough fingers. His presence and heat, the way he overwhelms my senses with his sheer masculinity. I've never slept with such a large man before, and I find the difference between our sizes gratifying in an unexpected, primal way.

He's so much bigger than me, so much physically stronger, yet I feel more powerful with him than with anyone else.

Maybe it's because I know this beautiful brute of a man turns to putty when I look at him a certain way. All I have to do is lower my head and bite my lip and he falls apart.

Without warning, he rolls me onto my belly. Rising to his knees and keeping himself inside me, he drags my hips up and back so I'm on my knees, too, my chest on the bed and my ass hiked in the air, my cheek turned to the rumpled sheets.

He grips my hips and thrusts a few times, grunting in pleasure. I close my eyes and moan.

"Love you like this, baby," he says raggedly. "Look at you. This gorgeous ass."

He grabs a handful of my butt cheek, fondling and pinching it, then gives it a sharp, stinging slap.

I jerk, gasping. My movement drives him even deeper inside me, so deep his balls slap against my soaked folds, making me moan again.

"You like that?"

"I love it."

"My sweet, dirty girl," he whispers, his voice reverent.

I rear back to meet his thrusts, loving the shockwaves it sends through my body. My nipples are hard and aching. I'm so wet I feel it slipping down the inside of my thighs.

Liam reaches around and starts to play with my clit again, thrumming it back and forth. My groan is garbled.

"Fuck. Fuck, Tru. It's so good..."

He switches from English to Gaelic. Whatever he's saying sounds so dirty it brings blood to my cheeks, so they throb like everything else.

Then he bends over me, planting one hand on the mattress and winding his other arm around my waist. His thrusts get deeper and faster. Breathing hard, he drives into me from behind as my breasts swing and I grab fistfuls of the sheets.

Just as I'm about to climax, he slows.

When I whine in protest, he sits back on his heels, dragging me along with him so I'm sitting on his thighs. He winds both arms around my waist, plastering my back to his chest, and bends his head to my ear.

"You gonna come for me?"

"Yes."

He flexes his thighs, rolling his hips so he's seated fully inside me as I pant and whimper. One big hand squeezes my breast.

"Give me your mouth."

I turn my head and let it fall back against his shoulder. He kisses me deeply, his tongue probing and hot. He reaches down and slips his fingers into my wetness, lazily stroking my clit for a moment before sliding lower, to the place where we're joined. With gentle, searching fingers, he explores my folds, stretched tight around his thick, rigid cock.

Delirious, I moan into his mouth. I'm so close to orgasm my entire body is shaking for release.

Then, suddenly, he slaps my pussy.

It isn't hard, but it sends a shockwave of pleasure so strong through me that I cry out, arching like a cat.

He slaps me between my legs a second time, then a third.

I come, screaming.

As I convulse against him, he holds me tight with that one arm like a steel band around my ribcage and whispers words of praise into my ear.

When the violent contractions slow, I'm left limp and sweating, almost crying in relief. He kisses me again, tenderly this time, then disengages from me and pushes me onto my back.

He positions himself between my spread thighs, lowers his body so his chest is against mine, and looks into my eyes as he thrusts inside me.

"You love my cock, don't you, baby?"

I nod, too overwhelmed with emotion and sensation to speak.

"I know you do." His voice is so soft. He kisses my neck.

Against my throat, he whispers, "It's yours. That and everything else. It's all yours—I'm—"

He breaks off with a groan, thrusting harder.

I squeeze my eyes shut, telling myself he wasn't about to say *I'm yours* but desperately wanting to believe it.

I might as well believe in Santa Claus or the Tooth Fairy. Liam isn't mine, I'm not his, and this strange fairytale of ours will soon end without a happily-ever-after.

The only real question now is how hard the fall will be.

And if it will break me.

An hour later, we're still in bed. Face to face this time, his arms wrapped around me, our bodies pressed together, my toes resting on the tops of his big feet.

"Just out of curiosity, what size shoe do you wear?"

He lifts his brows. "If you're wondering if I'll try on a pair of your heels and strut around naked for you, the answer is no."

I laugh weakly at the image his comment evokes. "You're strange."

"You're stranger."

We smile at each other. He rubs the tip of his nose against mine. The sweetness of that simple gesture sends a pang of despair through my heart, and I close my eyes.

Clearing my throat, I say, "I'm guessing like a size sixteen."

"Wrong."

I open my eyes and look at him. His smile is smug. "Bigger." Then he examines my expression for a moment, his smile fading and his gaze turning intense. "What is it?"

Damn him and those sharp wolf's eyes. "Just...life."

He cups my face in his hand, his brows drawn together. He demands, "Tell me."

"I can't."

"Why not?"

I swallow, looking down at his chin to hide my eyes. "I don't want to ruin the moment."

"Too late. I'm already thinking the worst."

"I shouldn't have said anything."

His voice hardens. "Tell. Me. *Now*."

Shit. Me and my big mouth. In a small voice, I say, "Fine. Um... how many days do we have left?"

His whole body tenses. It seems as though he's not even breathing. In a husky voice, he says, "Why? You want to leave early?"

I squeeze my eyes shut and shake my head, working up the courage to tell him the truth. "I don't want to leave at all."

He's perfectly still for a long, horrible moment. Still and silent, except for his breathing, which is shallow and fast.

I whisper, "I'm sorry. I didn't mean to make you angry."

He huffs out a breath, squeezing me closer to him. He says faintly, "Angry? Jesus, Tru."

I take that to mean he's not angry, but what he might be feeling, I don't know. Except whatever it is, it's making him breathe harder, his heart pound like a hammer, and his arms crush me like a vise.

After a few moments of silence, he seems to get control of himself. Or at least his voice sounds more normal when he says, "Three days."

My heart turns over. My stomach fills with butterflies, then with a sourness that crawls up my throat, like I might have to vomit.

Three days. My god, it's been weeks that I've been here. It seems like hardly any time at all.

When I lie there tense and silent for too long, Liam growls, "Goddammit, Tru, talk to me before I lose my fucking mind."

My held breath bursts out of me, and I blurt, "I want to keep seeing each other."

He makes a soft sound of pain and releases me, rolling onto his back to gaze up at the ceiling.

Panic flares inside my chest, burning hot. I lift up onto an elbow and stare at him with wide eyes. "I know you think I won't be safe being around you because of your work, but we could keep it a secret. I'll go back to my apartment and my job and we could see each other every once in a while, or—or maybe like only on the weekends or something—"

"No."

His voice is flat and final. A knife plunged through my heart.

Glowing with shame, I collapse onto my back and cover my face with my hands, screaming at myself for being such an idiot. A pathetic, clingy, lovesick idiot.

Look at me. *Begging.* My mother would be horrified. *I'm* horrified.

I hate myself for being so weak.

I jerk upright and swing my legs over the bed, intending to run into the bathroom to pull myself together, but before I can rise, Liam grabs me.

He drags me back against his chest and pins me there so I'm sitting between his spread legs, chained by his arms.

His voice achingly raw, he says, "If there was a way, I'd find it. There's no way out for me, you understand? This thing we're doing...you have no idea what it's costing me to be away, what I had to arrange—"

"What it's costing *you*?" I interrupt loudly. Heat creeps up my neck. My pulse is flying. "How about what it's costing me?"

His voice rises. "You've got your whole life ahead of you. You've graduated law school. Soon you'll pass the bar and become an attorney. You'll be living your dream—"

This time it's my harsh bark of a laugh that cuts him off. "Stop with the inspirational speeches already! That *dream* you're talking about is more like a lifelong nightmare. It's not what I aspire to be, it's what I'm *driven* to be by the worst thing that ever

happened to my family, by the worst thing that ever happened to
me. My brother was my best friend and the best person I've ever
known and he was fucking *murdered*—"

I stop abruptly, choking on a sob.

Silent, Liam holds me.

My sense of shame intensifies, because I'm not the only
person in this room who's suffered a loss. Liam has me beat in
that awful category. I lost one brother, but he lost his parents and
six siblings.

Shaking, I close my eyes and whisper, "I'm sorry. I'm being
overly emotional. I know you've...that your family...." I take a
steadying breath. "Let's just forget it."

"Your brother was murdered?"

His voice is strange. Low and devoid of emotion, except for a
faint trace of darkness. Of danger. Unnerved by the quality of it, I
simply say, "Yes."

He waits, his body vibrating with tension. He wants more of
an explanation, but I'm loath to get into the details, so I sum it up
instead.

"That quote you told me at the restaurant, about how
freedom for wolves often meant death to the sheep..." I sigh
deeply, suddenly overcome by a wave of fatigue. "Michael was
one of those unlucky sheep."

Liam says slowly, "And you decided to dedicate your life to
avenging him."

His voice is getting more and more odd. It's fervent and
fevered, like he just discovered buried treasure. Like he stumbled
upon a pirate's chest overflowing with jewels and gold.

I turn my head and feel his burning gaze brand the side of my
face. "What did you think I meant that time I said that when it
was too late for revenge, justice had to take other directions?"

"You told your mother that you'd never let what happened to
him happen to any of your clients—I took that to mean he had a

drug or mental health problem, that he died by suicide or over-dose, that he was an attorney and so you wanted to be one, too."

"He wasn't an attorney. He never even graduated from college. He was just a good ol' boy with no money and a recreational drug problem who got on the wrong side of a very powerful man."

Behind me, Liam is still and silent again, thinking hard. I'm not sure if that's the end of the conversation, until he murmurs, "It's almost like fate had this in mind all along."

I furrow my brow in confusion. "I don't understand what you mean."

He pushes me forward off the edge of the bed so I'm standing, then stands himself. He turns me to face him, forcing me to look up into his face by gripping my jaw in his hand.

His eyes are the blackest I've ever seen them. Murderous black. Serial killer black.

Black as a bottomless pit in the darkest corner of hell.

"We're going to get dressed. We're going to have something to eat. Then you're going to tell me exactly what happened to your brother, and you're not going to leave anything out."

He pauses, eyes glittering, then adds, "Including the name of that powerful man."

26

LIAM

*T*hough Tru asks why I'd need to know his name, I don't tell her. I just steer her into the closet so she can put on some clothes, then get dressed myself and wait impatiently for her in the kitchen.

She pads in, barefoot, wearing one of my white dress shirts.

It's her uniform now. Even when she studies, she has one of them on. Sleeves rolled up her forearms, hem hanging halfway down her slender thighs. More often than not, she doesn't wear anything underneath because she knows I'll rip it off, anyway.

She takes a seat at the kitchen island. I set a bowl of cereal in front of her. I watch her eat until she sighs and sets down the spoon.

"For god's sake, Liam, stop staring at me like that. My head's about to explode."

"Patience isn't one of my virtues."

She says drily, "Believe me, I know."

We gaze at each other. It takes considerable self-control not to walk around the island, grab her, and pull her into an embrace. I stopped counting how many things we had in common a while ago, because they kept adding up too quickly. But this...

This feels less like a shared experience and more like a sign.

I say, "I'm listening."

Her eyes darken. She chews the inside of her lip for a moment, then glances down at the cereal bowl.

"If we're never going to see each other after another three days are up, why does it matter?"

Impatience claws at me, but I keep my expression neutral and my voice steady. "It's important for me to know more about you."

She looks up at me, green eyes flashing, then says tartly, "Oh, really? That must be an uncomfortable feeling."

Holding her angry gaze, I say, "Okay. I deserved that. Please tell me anyway."

I can see she's startled by the "please," and curse myself for being such a bulldozer. I make a mental note to mind my manners better in the future, then try to wait with as much forbearance as possible as she decides if she's going to do what I asked.

It's extraordinarily fucking difficult.

Finally, she drags a hand through her long, dark hair, and takes a breath. She sits up straighter, squares her shoulders, and meets my gaze head-on.

"My family is poor. I told you that. I grew up on eighty acres in a farmhouse built by my grandfather that was pretty decrepit by the time I came along, because my dad has the opposite of handyman skills. If he tries to hang a picture, he'll smash the hammer onto his thumb. If he climbs a ladder to change a light bulb, he'll fall off. He's terminally clumsy, so the house was crumbling around our ears, but he's actually good at raising crops and animals, so we had enough to feed a family of ten."

"All the kids had their chores, but my brother Michael took after my dad in the clumsy department. He was more a menace than a help. After he drove the tractor through the side of the barn the third time, my mother finally banned him from farm work for good."

She makes an impatient gesture with her hand. "Long story short, without his farm chores, and having just graduated from high school with no plans for college and no job, he had too much time on his hands. He started hanging out at a dive bar, fell in with the wrong crowd, and selling drugs to make money. Small-time stuff, pot and pills, but pot has never been legal in Texas. And getting caught smoking it was different than getting caught selling it...but getting caught selling it in partnership with the son of a local judge was the worst thing of all."

She stops speaking and looks down at her hands. Her voice drops. "Especially when that particular judge had been in love with your mother in high school, but had his heart broken when she married another man."

She's quiet for a moment. I see her working through her memories, pain etched on her face, and have to fight myself again not to embrace her.

"The judge's son had a good attorney, of course. The family was rich. Connected. The attorney argued that my brother had been the mastermind of a drug ring—as if Michael could ever be a mastermind of anything—and that he'd coerced and manipulated the judge's son. Which was a complete load of bullshit. That kid was as bad as they come. If anything, the scenario was turned 180 degrees around. But our family didn't have the money for a good attorney, so we were assigned a public defender."

Her voice hardens. "It was a bloodbath. The judge's son got off scot-free. Not a day spent in jail, not even community service. My brother, however, was given the harshest sentence allowed under the law, even though he didn't have a record."

"What was the sentence?"

She hesitates before saying quietly, "Five million dollars in fines. Plus forty years in federal prison."

Serial rapists get lighter sentences than that.

Grinding my jaw in anger, I say nothing.

"Anyway, he might have gotten time off for good behavior.

The public defender was in process of making an appeal, but never got to file it because after a month in prison, Michael was beaten to death in the shower."

I want to shoot someone. Instead I say, "I'm so sorry."

Her sigh is heavy. "Yeah. Me, too."

"Did they find out who killed him?"

She raises her head and looks at me. Her eyes are fierce with unshed tears.

"One of the men who was in on it confessed. He was a lifer without the possibility of parole, so it didn't matter to him if he had more time added to his sentence. What did matter, however, is that he didn't get paid what he'd been promised to do the job."

When she doesn't continue, my anger flares hotter. "The judge."

Swallowing hard, she nods. "But of course, the judge had all kinds of buddies in law enforcement and politics. The accusation went nowhere. A few weeks later, that prisoner was found dead in his cell. The cause of death was listed as natural."

Her voice goes flat. "Imagine that. A thirty-year-old man in good health with no underlying medical conditions suddenly dies of natural causes in his cell. A mystery for the ages."

Now I can't stop myself: I walk around the island and take her in my arms.

She buries her face in my chest, wraps her arms around my waist, and inhales a hitching breath.

I hold her until she stops shaking, then gently kiss her hair. "Thank you for sharing that with me. I know it's not easy to talk about it. Tell me the judge's name."

She lifts her head and looks up at me with wet eyes. "Why?"

"It'll be cathartic."

She studies my expression for a moment, then shakes her head. "No, Liam. I don't want blood on my hands."

I shouldn't be surprised she knows me that well, but I am. No use denying it, though. I say in a low voice, "The only one with bloody hands here is me. Give me the name."

"My definition of revenge only covers property damage and career choices."

"Mine doesn't. I want to kill him for you."

Wincing, she closes her eyes. "I'm so disappointed in myself that I find that romantic." Then she pushes me away and says firmly, "No. End of discussion."

I simply smile.

It's not like I can't find out the name on my own.

Plugged in on the kitchen counter, my phone rings. I ignore it. It stops for a moment, then rings again. Several seconds after that call ends, a text chimes through.

Ar mhaith leat tae?

It's from Declan. It means: would you like some tea?

Which is code for call me, shit's happening.

I tell Tru I have to make a call and leave her in the kitchen. I feel her curious gaze on me as I head into my office and close the door.

When Declan picks up, I say in Irish, "Yes, please bring me tea."

It's more code. If I'd said, "No, I'd prefer coffee," he'd have known it wasn't safe to talk.

He says, "Caught somebody trying to plant an IED that had your name on it."

I can tell by his tone that he's amused.

Interesting.

Even more interesting is the IED. If one of my usual enemies wanted me dead, they'd try poison or a sniper. Again. Blowing me up with an improvised explosive device is new.

"Where?"

"Alley behind Cosentino's."

Cosentino's is one of the restaurants I own. The one where

Tru celebrated her graduation with her friends. "The alley? How do you know it was intended for me?"

Declan chuckles. "Because the guy Kieran caught red-handed planting the fucking thing told him it was."

The warning Tru gave me clicks. I groan. "Let me guess. Latino kid. Good-looking. Mid-twenties. Big mouth."

"Aye. Friend of yours?"

"Something like that. Where is he now?"

"Got him in the warehouse at the docks. Had him since the middle of the night, but didn't want to, uh..." He coughs. "Disturb you. What do you want me to do with him? Fish food?"

"No. Bring him here. I want to talk to him. And not so much as a bruise on him, understood?"

"Copy that. I'll text you when we're on P1."

Declan disconnects. I lock the library door, then use the hidden door behind the bookcase to access a corridor that leads to a service elevator. Then I head down to P1 to wait.

Twenty minutes later, I'm standing in front of a handcuffed man with a black cloth hood over his head who's on his knees on the cold cement floor of my parking garage.

He's hissing and struggling like a feral cat. It takes two of my biggest men to keep him in place.

Declan stands beside me, arms folded over his chest, watching with interest.

Through the hood comes an enraged male voice. It's so loud it echoes off the walls. "I'll kill every one of you *pinche puto pendejo babosos*! Take off this hood and face me like men!"

After a pause, Declan turns to me. "Just out of curiosity, what does *pinche puto* whatever-he-said mean?"

"Fucking faggot pubic hair slugs."

Declan makes a face. "Well, that's not right. Nobody says 'faggot' anymore. It's pejorative."

"But you're okay with the pubic hair slug part?"

Declan shrugs. "It's creative. Interesting imagery."

Stifling a sigh, I look away from Declan and address my guest. "Hello, Diego."

He stops struggling. The black hood sucks in and out with his heaving breaths. "Who is that?"

"Now you've hurt my feelings. Liam Black."

"Fuck you."

"It's a pleasure to see you again, too."

His voice rises. "Where the hell is Tru?"

"Living with me. I'll tell her you asked after her. Now give me your word you'll stop trying to blow me up, and I'll send you on your way."

That seems to surprise him, because he falls still again. The black hood cocks to one side. "You're not going to kill me?"

"Unfortunately, I can't."

He cackles like a witch. "Haha! That's right! You promised Tru you wouldn't! Sucks to be you, asshole, because I'm only gonna stop trying to kill you when I actually do!"

I'm *really* starting to dislike this kid.

Declan says mildly, "He might not be able to kill you, but I sure can. Watch your mouth, or I'll stick my knife in your ribs and carve you up like a turkey."

That shuts Diego up. He kneels there, vibrating with rage. I realize the odd sound coming from under the hood is him grinding his teeth.

I make a motion for Kieran to get him on his feet and remove the hood.

When he's standing and the hood is off, he glares at me with hostile, unblinking eyes, vicious as a viper's.

"Why the hate, Diego? I thought we left our last meeting on such good terms."

He's so mad the cords on the sides of his neck stand out. His whole face is red.

He snarls, "Oh, you're real fucking funny, aren't you? This is all a big fucking joke to you. She's a joke to you, too, isn't she? You're just gonna use her up and throw her away and it'll be no skin off your back. If she doesn't get wasted by a stray bullet meant for you first, that is!"

"If trying to kill me is your attempt at defending her honor, it's misguided."

He huffs out a short, sarcastic laugh "What the actual fuck would *you* know about honor, you criminal piece of shit?"

Declan unfolds his arms and takes a step forward. I stop him with a hand on his shoulder, then move closer to Diego myself. When I'm a foot away, I stop and stare into his eyes.

I say quietly, "More than you could ever guess."

He looks like he really wants to spit in my face, but a quick glance over my shoulder to Declan makes him rethink it.

I continue in the same quiet tone as before. "You're in love with her. I understand—"

"Do you?"

"Yes. Interrupt me again and I'll have Declan cut out your tongue. I promised her I wouldn't kill you, but I never said anything about relieving you of the power of speech."

I have to give him credit. He doesn't cower or shrink away, though his fear is plainly visible in the way the blood drains out of his face and his pupils dilate.

"As I was saying. She doesn't need you to defend her."

After a moment, when he's sure I'm done speaking, he says, "She doesn't need you to defend her, either."

"Agreed."

He doesn't know what to make of that. He shifts his weight from foot to foot, looking back and forth from me to Declan, licking his lips and trying to figure out his next move.

"Listen, Diego. I want to ask you a favor."

He blinks. Then says emphatically, "No."

"You don't even know what it is yet."

"I don't want to be in your debt!"

It's a good thing this kid is good-looking, because he's as dumb as a rock. "No, *I'd* be in *your* debt."

He looks confused, then suspicious.

Without giving in to the urge to roll my eyes, I say, "Tru will be back at work in a few days and back living at her apartment. I want you to look out for her. Don't be obnoxious about it, and for fuck's sake, tone down the chest-pounding Tarzan routine. She hates to be treated like she's helpless.

"Just watch out for her. Make sure she's okay. I know I can count on you to do that."

His mouth hangs open. His expression is blank. He could be in a coma for all the reaction I'm getting.

To snap him out of it, I lightly slap his cheek.

He jumps, jerking away, then hollers, "You're asking me to babysit for you while you go away on a trip or something, is that it?"

"I'm not going away on a trip. I'm going away for good." *And leaving her will kill me.*

Diego says in stiff disbelief, "So that's it? You're dumping her?"

I grind my molars at his choice of words. When I don't respond, he says, "Does she know?"

"Just remember what I asked. Kieran, drop him off at the zoo. Maybe he'd like to visit some of his relatives."

I turn and head back to the elevators, dismissing him, but Diego isn't done with me yet.

He calls out, "Do you know she defended you to me, man? I told her you were bad news, even before I knew who you were and you were just staring at her like a creeper at the diner, and she *stood up for you*, every single fucking time. You know what that's called? Loyalty.

"I bet you don't ever get that unless you pay big for it. I told her, but she wouldn't listen, and now you're gonna dump her like yesterday's garbage, and she's gonna see you for exactly what you are."

Declan says, "Keep going, idiot. My knife hasn't been bloodied in four days. One more day and it'll be a record, and I can't have that."

At the elevator bank, I press the call button and turn around, watching as Kieran drags Diego toward a parked SUV.

Walking backward, he meets my gaze.

"At least now she'll know. You're no good, especially not for her."

Kieran opens the rear door of the SUV and shoves Diego inside.

Right before Kieran slams the door in his face, Diego leans over and hollers, "The only way you'd ever be good for anybody is if you were dead!"

Declan walks over to me, shaking his head, but I'm frozen in place as Diego's final words echo over and over in my ears.

Stopping beside me at the elevator doors, Declan chuckles. "Kid's got some balls on him, I gotta admit."

"Aye," I say, blood pounding hard through my veins.

I was wrong about Diego being dumb as a rock.

He's a goddamn genius.

27

TRU

*L*iam isn't gone long, but when he returns to the kitchen where I've been waiting, I can tell instantly something is wrong.

He's tense. His eyes are wild. His breathing is shallow. His hands clench and unclench, the way they do when he's especially agitated. I can't decide if he's furious, anxious, or something else, but whatever it is, it freaks me out.

"Are you okay?"

He heads directly for me, grabs me off the counter stool and into a crushing bear hug, and exhales raggedly into my hair.

My words are muffled against his heaving chest. "Liam? Um. It's hard to breathe."

Gripping my upper arms, he pulls away and stares down at me. His gaze is blisteringly intense. His jaw works, but he doesn't say anything.

"That must've been some phone call," I say, watching him warily. "Is everything all right?"

"No. I mean, aye. It will be. I hope."

Hope? He doesn't use words like "hope." I've never seen him this distracted and on edge. He's totally weirded out.

He looks like someone just told him he won the biggest lottery in history, but to collect the money he has to saw off his own legs with a rusty knife.

"Do you want to talk about it?"

"No."

I say drily, "Gee, what a surprise."

He drags me back into a bear hug and fists a hand in my hair. Into my ear, he says roughly, "I have to go out for a few hours. I want you ready for me when I come back. Naked, in bed, wet, and ready. No arguments."

Dear god, this man is infuriating!

I'm about to protest, but he cuts me off with a kiss. It's hard and demanding, edged with desperation, and the best kiss he's ever given me.

Instead of hollering about bossy macho men with no manners, I melt.

He releases me so abruptly I stagger to one side and lean against the island, gasping. He strides out of the kitchen to the elevator bank without looking back, disappearing through the doors the instant they slide open. Then he's gone, leaving me staring after him in disbelief.

I have no idea what just happened.

Knowing Liam, I never will.

I spend the morning studying in the library. It's just over a month now before I take the bar, and though I've been diligent with hitting the books, there's still so much more to cover.

Liam doesn't return by lunch, so I grab a container of prepared chicken scaloppini from the fridge, heat it up in the microwave, and eat alone, standing over the sink. Then I go back into the library and study for several more hours, losing myself in the work.

I'm surprised when I look up at the clock later on and discover that it's after six.

I guess Liam and I have different ideas of what "a few hours" means, because he's been gone all day.

Considering we only have three more days left, that stings.

I eat dinner, trying not to feel sorry for myself. I study some more. When I can't concentrate any longer because thoughts of where Liam could be keep distracting me, I give up and go into the living room, curling up on the massive sofa with a blanket to wait.

I must fall asleep, because I wake sometime later with the sense time has passed.

The sun has sunk beyond the horizon. Twilight paints the room in deepening hues of purple and blue. I sit up, disoriented, wondering why the automatic lights didn't turn on with my movement, and sniff the air.

I smell smoke.

Cigarette smoke.

When I turn my head and look around, I discover it's coming from the man standing with his back to me, gazing out the massive windows to the twinkling lights of the city far below.

My heart pounding, I jump off the sofa and back up a few steps, panicking. "Who are you?"

From over his shoulder, the man says quietly, "Easy, lass. It's only me."

Declan. I'm relieved for half a second, until fear blasts through me again. "What's wrong? Where's Liam?"

For a moment, he doesn't respond. He tilts his head back and blows a trail of perfect smoke rings into the air, watching until they disappear. When he speaks, his voice is even lower than before. "Get your things. It's time to go."

"Go? Go where?"

"Home."

My heart stops dead in my chest. I turn cold. My hands start to shake.

Liam isn't coming back. He's not going to say goodbye to me. He sent Declan to do his dirty work so he wouldn't have to deal with me getting emotional and making a scene.

We still have three days left.

My voice comes out raw. "I want to talk to him. Get him on the phone right now."

Declan finally turns from the window. He gazes at me across the living room, his blue eyes glinting in the shadows, his expression carefully blank.

"It's over, lass. Don't make it worse than it has to be."

I want to scream in frustration. I want to punch him in the face. I want to smash something, anything, but instead I say, "Don't patronize me, Declan. I have the right to talk to him—"

"The *right*?" His voice is a razor blade. He paces forward several steps, his posture menacing. "No, you don't have *any* rights. You're not his wife. You're not his family. You're not even his friend. Get it straight, lass: you're a skirt he's been shagging for a few weeks, nothing more."

I'm breathless with hurt. It feels like he punched me in the stomach.

He paces closer as I stare at him, wounded and horrified, unable to move. He stops a foot away and looks into my eyes. He says, "Aren't you?"

Oddly, it sounds like a challenge.

My voice shaking, I say, "No."

Examining my expression, he takes a drag on his cigarette. He blows the smoke into my face.

I *hate* it when he does that.

He says, "What are you, then?"

It must be anger. It must be hurt. It could even be defiance, but before I make the conscious decision to, I'm shouting an answer into Declan's face.

"I'm the woman who loves him!"

He doesn't move. He doesn't blink. Only his eyes change. A glimmer of emotion warms their icy depths for a moment before subsiding, leaving them even colder than before.

His tone drips with condescension. "You're a child who's confusing sex with love. Grow up."

My hand flies on its own will.

With every ounce of my strength, I slap Declan across the face. An animal's scream of rage rips from my throat as I do it.

His head snaps to the side. For one long, breathless moment, he's frozen, totally unresponsive, but then he turns his head slowly and looks at me.

My handprint glows bright pink against his cheek.

Staring him down, breathing hard, I say, "Call me a child again and I'll break your nose, you arrogant son of a bitch."

He grins.

Grabbing my upper arm, he says roughly, "Knew I liked you, lass."

He drags me away toward the elevator doors, ignoring my angry shouts and struggles.

He keeps ignoring me on the elevator ride down to the parking garage. He ignores me as he shoves me into the back seat of an SUV and buckles me in. He ignores me on the drive back to my apartment, though I pester him the entire time to get Liam on the phone and rant about what bullshit it is that he won't obey me.

He pulls to a screeching stop in front of my apartment building, drags me out of the car, and marches me silently up to my front door with his jaw set. He deposits me on the welcome mat and dusts off his hands, like he's delivered something dirty.

I'm barefoot.

I don't have on any underwear.

The only thing between me and the evening air is one of Liam's white dress shirts, because I am a romantic moron who got lost in a mobster's sad, beautiful eyes and started wearing his clothes like a crazy person.

Before Declan turns around to leave, I shout, "I don't believe he'd leave me like this, Declan! Something must have happened! Tell me what's really going on!"

Exasperated, he throws his arms in the air. "Jesus, Mary, and Joseph, woman, do you ever stop running your bloody mouth?"

"Where is Liam? Why didn't he come back today? Do you know who he talked to on the phone this morning?"

Declan stomps off, muttering, without giving me a satisfactory reply.

Then it's just me standing there alone in the empty corridor, shivering, reality starting to sink in like a creeping case of poison ivy.

It's over.

It's really over.

Liam and I are through.

I hear pounding footsteps from inside my apartment, then seconds later an angry Ellie throws open the front door. She shouts, "What the hell is all the screaming out—"

She stops short when she spots me. Her brow furrows. She looks me up and down. "Tru? What are you doing here?"

I say, "I live here, remember?"

Then I promptly burst into tears.

28

LIAM

*W*hen my cell rings and I see it's Declan calling, I almost have a heart attack.

I answer instantly. My greeting is a barked, "What did she say?"

"What *didn't* she say?" is Declan's aggravated response. "She wouldn't shut up. It was like dealing with a mental patient. Or a banshee. She screamed bloody murder all over the place!"

Imagining her upset and angry, hurt because of *me*, I groan.

"And she smacked me!" He laughs, half outraged and half admiring. "A good one, too! The stones on her, in-fucking-credible!"

When I groan again, Declan says sourly, "Oh, quit your pissin' and moanin'. She's mad as hell, but she still loves you."

I almost drop the phone. Then I almost have that heart attack again. The phone gripped in my shaking hand, I say hoarsely, "Did she tell you that?"

"Aye. Though she didn't have to. A woman only ever gets that level of thermonuclear over a man she loves."

My knees give out. I drop into a nearby chair, tilt my head back, and close my eyes.

She loves me.

She told Declan she loves me.

If I died at this moment, it would be as a happy man.

"You still there, Romeo?"

My voice is thick when I answer. "Still here."

"What's our next move?"

I open my eyes, lift my head, and look at the FBI agents sitting across the table staring back at me.

I say, "I'll let you know soon," and disconnect.

29

TRU

I don't sleep that night. I pace back and forth in my bedroom, my mind whirling. I'm sick, furious, hurt, confused, enraged, ashamed, disbelieving, and furious.

Did I mention furious?

I'm so angry it feels like I could birth a rage monster through my vaginal canal.

I want to smash every single piece of furniture in sight.

He wanted the arrangement. *He* was the one who concocted the idea of me moving in with him. *He* was the one who kidnapped me to make it happen!

And he was the one who sent his second-in-command to whisk me away like a dirty plate three days before it was supposed to be over.

He could've been a gentleman and handled it himself. I mean, I probably would've gotten teary-eyed and emotional when the time came, but I certainly would *not* have begged...

Okay, I would've begged. I'm addicted to his magical dick.

Plus—horribly, tragically, *stupidly*—I'm in love with him. So there would have been begging.

But that's no excuse for shifting the responsibility of getting rid of your willing captive to a man who doesn't have the manners to refrain from blowing cigarette smoke into a lady's face.

I hope that slap I gave Declan left him with a nasty bruise.

And if I ever see Liam Black on the street, he'll wish I hadn't.

"Who are you kidding?" I whisper to my tear-stained reflection. "Not me."

My bedraggled self stares back at me from the mirror over my desk. We both know that if I saw Liam on the street, I'd throw myself at his feet like a demented groupie, wailing for him to take me back.

So this is love.

What a nightmare.

∼

First thing in the morning, four goons in black suits show up at my door with all my things packed up in cardboard boxes. Without a word, they drop the boxes on the step and turn to leave.

"Oh, no you don't!" I holler after them.

The biggest one—his name is Kieran, I remember—turns back to give me a raised eyebrow.

I stand aside from the door and jerk my thumb over my shoulder. "In you go."

In this thick Irish accent, Kieran says, "What're you on about?"

"I'm guessing you lot were the ones who packed all my stuff up and took it over to Liam's place a few weeks ago, am I right?"

Shifty-eyed, the goons look at each other.

"That's what I thought." I step aside and sweep my arm toward my bedroom. "You know where everything goes."

Kieran laughs. When his disdain doesn't make me wilt, he glares at me.

I fold my arms over my chest and glare right back.

An hour later, my clothes, toiletries, and books are back in their rightful places in my bedroom. Kieran and the goon squad trundle out silently, looking like they're not exactly sure what just happened.

Standing in the open doorway of the apartment watching them go, Ellie says, "You know that old saying, misery loves company?"

"Yeah?"

"Tyler and I broke up again. So at least you won't have to be miserable alone. My miserable ass will be keeping you company."

I'm lying on my back on the living room floor, staring up at the ceiling, flattened with longing for a man I'll never see again. "What happened this time?"

She sighs heavily, closing the door and wandering into the kitchen. "He said he felt smothered." Her chuckle is dark. "Apparently, the girl he was seeing behind my back didn't make him feel quite so penned in."

"That's shitty. Are you okay?"

"I'll live. I've been rage eating the past few days. That always helps."

I told her the short version of Liam's heartlessness last night. Being a good friend, she was righteously angry on my behalf. I feel a little guilty that I can't muster enough outrage to return the favor about Tyler's mistreatment at the moment, but judging by my mood swings over the past several hours, later on I'll break a mirror or throw a vase off the balcony, and we can be outraged together.

Ellie grabs something out of the freezer and comes to sit cross-legged next to me. She says, "You want some pistachio ice cream? There's tons of it left. We'll probably be eating this stuff forever."

I look at her, holding out the container and a spoon, and burst into tears again.

She takes that as a no and starts to eat, every once in a while reaching out to pat me comfortingly on the shoulder.

Miserable and heartbroken, I hide in the apartment for three days. I don't go anywhere. I don't call anyone. Except for Liam, because I can't help my sad sack self, but his phone number is disconnected.

That cruel, horrible, cowardly, lying, no-good, pretending-to-have-a-heart bastard.

I miss him with every fiber of my being.

Now I understand how otherwise rational people can snap and commit violent acts. The human body wasn't designed to contain so much emotion.

On day four, I decide I'm fed up with myself. I'm still heartbroken, but lying around sobbing for hours at a time isn't helping anyone. And I've still got the bar to pass, if I can manage it.

I doubt I can manage it in my current mental state, but if I fail the first time, there's always the next.

Unless I happen to fall for another dangerous stranger in the meantime and ruin my life again.

I call Buddy and tell him I'm coming back to work. He says miserably, "Yes, dear," as if he doesn't have a choice in the matter. For whatever bizarre reason, that makes me grimly happy.

When I show up at the diner, the first person I see is Carla. She does a double-take when I walk through the door, instantly abandons the customer she'd been taking a food order from, and rushes across the restaurant to grab me in a frantic hug.

"Jesus Christ on a cracker, you look like a litter box that hasn't been cleaned in a year! I'm so glad to see you! I've been so worried about you! Are you okay? Because you don't look okay, you look like death, and oh my god," her voice rises, "*I can't believe you were living with a gangster!*"

When she finally stops for a breath, I break away from her, feeling a thousand years old.

"Thanks for letting the entire restaurant know about my romantic entanglements. It's good to see you, too. I appreciate the inspiring words about my appearance. And yes, I'm okay."

To the old guy openly eavesdropping from the table we're standing next to, I say, "Sir, mind your business."

He shrugs, turning his attention back to his pastrami on rye. "I was here first."

I mutter, "Let's take this into the back."

I head through the dining room with Carla on my heels, peppering me with questions and begging forgiveness for not calling me after my graduation dinner. I was right: Dave put the kibosh on that.

Goddamn bossy men. I should start a women's group for survivors of alpha males. There are probably millions of us worldwide, nursing bruised hopes, hearts, and uteruses.

When we get to the kitchen, Diego's at the grill, flipping burgers. For some reason, he doesn't seem surprised to see me.

"You're back." He flashes his white teeth in a smile.

"I am."

I stand there awkwardly, painfully self-conscious in my uniform, more aware of my body in clothes than I was at Liam's when I spent my days wearing his dress shirt and nothing else.

"I'd give you a hug, but I'm all greasy." Diego flips a patty, sending a splatter of fat flying onto the front of his white apron, then glances over at me. "You good?"

"Never better," I lie. "You?"

He lifts a shoulder. "Same."

He's acting strangely nonchalant for someone who threatened murder the last time we spoke. Then again, his mood swings would give mine a run for their money, so I dismiss the thought and continue walking to the break room. Carla clings to me like a baby monkey riding on its mother's back.

I shut the door behind us and fall into the nearest plastic chair, then wince in pain. I'd forgotten how hideously uncomfortable they are.

Carla pulls up another chair, sits down so close our knees touch, and grabs my hands like she's about to lead us in prayer.

"Girl," she says, all out of breath. "*Liam Black?*"

She waits with wide eyes for me to start talking.

I get choked up instead. My face scrunches up, and my voice comes out strangled. "Don't say his stupid name. I hate him."

Her voice is bone dry. "Oh, yeah, I can tell. That weepy face has hate written all over it."

I sniffle, struggling not to give in to the tears pushing against the backs of my eyeballs. In an attempt to avoid telling the story and possibly bursting into sobs, I say, "What did Dave tell you about him?"

"Only that he was the East Coast's biggest, baddest mafia dude, and I was not to have any contact with you while you were involved with him. Obviously, I won't be telling him you're back at work."

"You don't have to lie to your husband for me."

"It's not for you, dimwit, it's for me. I like this job. Besides, what the man doesn't know won't kill him." She squeezes my hands. "But if he happens to come in when you're working, even if it's a year from now, let's just pretend it's your first night back."

I say mournfully, "Oh, the tangled webs we weave."

Carla scoffs. "Stop it already. Marriage is an institution built on white lies and denial. If husbands and wives started telling each other the truth all the time, the whole system would implode. Tell me what happened since your graduation dinner."

I take a deep breath, exhale, and close my eyes. Then I tell her everything since that night, not leaving anything out.

At the end of it, I'm emotionally wrung dry, but relieved to get it all off my chest. Look at me, doing the girlie sharing thing. Ellie would be so proud.

But then something odd occurs to me.

The night of my graduation dinner, I had no idea Liam owned the restaurant where we dined. I had no idea he'd be kidnapping me from the kitchen, either. Carla and Dave left before Diego and I did, and I haven't spoken to her since. So...

"How did you know I was living with Liam?"

Carla shoots a surreptitious glance over her shoulder and lowers her voice. "Diego told me."

I frown, trying to recall what I told Diego about my situation with Liam on our phone call.

"So you're his girlfriend now or something?"

"Look, I just called to let you know I'm fine and to check in."

That call was the night after the dinner. I didn't tell Diego anything about my living situation. I haven't spoken to him since.

Even more strange: when I walked in tonight, Carla said, "I can't believe you were living with a mobster."

Were, past tense.

"How long ago did Diego tell you that?"

Carla thinks for a moment. "I dunno. A few days, I guess?"

My heart starts to pound faster. I sit up straighter in my chair. "How many days, exactly? It's important."

"Um..." She looks at the ceiling, frowning, then pronounces, "Five. I remember because it was the same day I started my period and Diego was whipping himself again over that night he made you take out the trash."

Five days ago, I was still living with Liam.

Five days ago, he rushed out of the kitchen after getting a phone call...and when he came back, he wasn't himself.

Five days ago was the last time I saw him.

Diego knew before I did that Liam and I were going to break up.

My heart pounding, I shoot to my feet. I run out of the break room and into the kitchen, skidding to a stop next to the grill.

"You talked to him, didn't you?"

In the middle of scraping the grill with a wire brush, Diego freezes. He hesitates, then says innocently, "Who?"

Heat crawls up my neck. I have to grit my teeth to keep from screaming. "Don't play games with me. *You know who.* What did you say? What did he say? Tell me right now, or I'll...I'll call the police!"

It was a totally off-the-cuff, spur-of-the-moment threat. Nonsensical to boot, because I have no reason to call the police on Diego, other than him criminally infuriating me. But his reaction is so unexpected and violent, I'm stunned.

He whirls on me and angrily shouts, "You can't prove I planted that bomb! There's no evidence!"

I stand there with my mouth hanging open and watch as Diego slowly realizes I didn't know anything about a bomb...until now.

He throws the wire brush onto the grill, turns his back to me, and says flatly, "Fuck."

My face draining of blood, I whisper in horror, "You tried to *blow people up?*"

He props his hands on his hips and exhales heavily, still with his back turned. "Not people. Him."

My hands go to my throat. I don't have conscious control over them, they just fly up to my throat and stay there, shaking. I stumble back a few steps. I want to turn and run away, but I can't seem to get my legs to agree, so I stand there, helplessly quaking like a leaf.

"Why?"

He's silent for a moment, then he turns around and faces me. His expression is hard. Suddenly, he looks years older than he is. Older and tired, and not at all like someone I know.

"Don't ask me stupid questions, Tru. You know why. And I don't regret it. The only thing I regret is that I didn't succeed."

Diego tried to kill Liam.

My heart won't be able to take much more of this shit.

Feeling faint, I pass a hand over my face. My throat is a desert. I stagger over to the iced tea and lemonade cooler on the counter in the corner, grab a glass from the stacks beside it, and pour myself a tea. I drink deeply, then turn around and lean against the counter for support.

Carla emerges from the break room. She looks at Diego and me standing opposite each other in tense silence, then hustles past into the dining room, leaving us alone again.

Before I can say anything, Diego beats me to it.

"He asked me to look after you."

Thud, thud, thud goes my heart, before stopping altogether. I whisper, "What?"

"He said he was going away for good and asked me to watch out for you."

Going away for good? What does that mean?

My question is answered when Carla runs back into the kitchen, looking gobsmacked. "Um, Tru? You better come out here. You're going to want to see this."

"See what? What's wrong?"

She points toward the dining room to where a television hangs in one corner near the ceiling, blaring a breaking news report.

"Liam Black has been arrested."

The glass of tea slips from my hand and shatters on the floor like a bomb.

30

TRU

*T*he reporter is pretty, blonde, and freakishly cheerful, with a smile like an ad for dental veneers and a manic glint in her blue eyes.

"Tonight's top story takes us into the seedy underworld of organized crime. Liam Black, one of Boston's most notorious alleged mobsters, has been taken into custody by federal agents. We learned this evening in a bombshell announcement from the FBI that a long criminal investigation of Mr. Black recently produced enough evidence to secure a warrant for his arrest. The charges include racketeering, extortion, and murder, and could come with a sentence of life in prison if he's convicted on all counts."

A picture of Liam in handcuffs being led into a government building by a squad of six armed officers in uniform appears on the screen.

He looks calm. Head held high, shoulders squared, taller and more powerful than everyone around him, despite the cuffs.

A little cry of horror slips past my lips. I think I'm going to be sick.

"*He said he was going away for good and asked me to watch out for you.*"

He knew.

Somehow, Liam knew he was going to be arrested.

Oh god—the phone call. That's why he acted so strange the morning he left. Someone called to alert him.

The reporter continues. "Mr. Black is currently being held without bail until his arraignment. Sources report he has been uncooperative with authorities. Due to his alleged connection with several international criminal syndicates and the extent and seriousness of the charges, he's considered a high security risk and is being held in an undisclosed location. We'll bring you more on this breaking news story as it develops. Shawn, back to you."

The screen cuts to another grinning newscaster, this one a man with shoe polish black hair and orange skin. He starts talking, but I can't hear a thing.

Liam has been arrested. He could spend the rest of his life in prison. Another man I love will be locked up behind bars.

And what happened to my brother Michael could very well happen to him.

I have to get out of here.

I bolt.

First, I run back into the break room and grab my purse from where I left it on the floor next to the chair when Carla and I were talking. Then, I fly out the back door and sprint to my car. I unlock the door with shaking fingers, dropping the keys twice. I finally get inside, slam the door, and rev the engine.

As I'm tearing out of the parking lot, I see Diego in my rear view mirror standing at the open back door. I turn a corner and he vanishes from sight.

I don't remember the drive to my apartment. When I get there, I can't wait long enough for the elevator to arrive. I take the stairs three at a time, my heart throbbing and my thighs burning, and burst into my apartment.

I have no idea what I'm going to do next, except it involves large amounts of alcohol.

Sitting on the sofa in the living room, Ellie's reading a magazine. Surprised, she looks up at me.

"Hey. Didn't you just leave for work a little while ago?"

When a choking noise is my only reply, Ellie shrugs. "It's good you're back early, anyway. Liam's waiting for you in your room."

All the cells in my body shriek collectively. Every muscle clenches, except in my hands. They go slack. My purse falls to the floor with a *thud*.

I stand there wide-eyed and panting, staring at Ellie, trying to decide if I heard her correctly or if my brain has finally exploded.

She sighs, sitting up. "I know, I know. You don't like the way he broke it off, and I'm supposed to be taking your side, blah, blah, blah. But there's just something about the guy, Tru! I can't say no to him! He asked so politely if he could wait for you in your room that I just couldn't turn him down!"

The front door of the apartment is open behind me, letting cool air wash over my burning skin. I manage to croak, "Did you see the news?"

Ellie frowns. "No. Why? Did something happen at Buddy's?" Her tone rises in anger. "Did that guy who assaulted you come back again?"

She doesn't know Liam was arrested. But he was.

So how the hell is he waiting for me in my room?

As if from a long distance off, I hear myself say, "Nobody assaulted me. Are you sure it's Liam?"

She makes a face. "What am I, blind? Of course I'm sure. My panties burst into flame the second I opened the door and saw him."

Holy shit. He must've escaped from prison. He escaped from prison and came here to hide. And of course I'm going to help him in any way I can.

So much for my career in law.

Clutching my fibrillating heart, my legs as wobbly as Jell-O, I make my way slowly across the living room toward my bedroom door.

Watching me go, Ellie says, "Okay, you're really freaking me out right now."

I say hoarsely, "I'm fine. Just...have a...migraine."

When I reach the door, I stand there holding the knob, sucking in deep breaths until I get the courage to push the door open. I step inside and quickly shut it behind me.

And there he is, standing at my desk.

He's in a perfectly-cut black Armani suit—what else?—and beautiful black leather shoes. His back is to me. His shoulders are wide and strong. He holds a book in his hands, and his dark head is bent toward the pages.

Without turning around, he muses, "He always did love Proust. I'll never understand it. If you ask me, it's a bunch of namby-pamby shite. Then again, he's always been the sensitive one."

Rich and throaty, with a rumble to it like a purr, his Irish brogue is exactly the same as Liam's.

So is his face when he turns around and I can finally see it.

So are his eyes, that same fine dark color, that same piercing intelligence.

Everything about him, in fact, is exactly the same. Even the tattoos on the knuckles of his left hand and the one peeking above the collar of his white dress shirt.

But it's not him.

It's not Liam.

The resemblance is so perfect someone else wouldn't be able to tell the difference, but I've been spending every moment with Liam for the past several weeks, sleeping and eating and dreaming with him, having orgasm after incredible orgasm with him, sharing laughter and quiet moments, getting his smell and the look in his eyes and the timbre of his voice branded onto my memory and my heart and every corner of my soul.

I'd know him anywhere.

And that is not him.

My knees give out. Shaking badly, I sink onto the edge of the bed and stare at this familiar-looking stranger, remembering the night I woke up and overheard Liam in his office talking on the phone.

"Who were you talking to?"

"My brother."

Not-Liam lifts his brows. "What, no hug?"

I whisper, "He didn't tell me you were identical twins."

Liam's brother purses his lips in disappointment. "Because if we're going to be family, lassie, I expect you to greet me with a hug."

I close my eyes for a moment, willing myself not to topple off the edge of the bed onto the floor.

He says sternly, "Don't go having a mental breakdown on me now, Tru. I need you clear-headed for a while longer. You can pass out from shock on the plane."

I open my eyes and stare at him. He looks very tall and imposing, all business, but I can tell he's trying to press a smile from his full lips. He's enjoying himself.

"Plane?"

He walks over to me, crouches down on one knee, and takes my chin in one of his big, rough hands. He's so large that even kneeling he's eye to eye with me.

His dark eyes alight and his Irish brogue as warm as brown sugar, he says, "I've got a question for you, lass."

My brain isn't working. Neither is my mouth. All I can make are weak grunting noises. "Uh...uh-huh?"

"If you could go anywhere in the world, where would it be?"

I close my eyes again. The room has started spinning.

He releases my chin and stands. The next thing I feel is a light tap on the bridge of my nose. When I open my eyes again, he's gazing down at me, holding out the white envelope he just tapped me with.

He says, "The ticket and passport are both under the name Ruby Diamond. *Mrs.* Ruby Diamond to be exact." He pauses. "For the record, I had no idea my brother was so lacking in imagination when it comes to fake identities. I would've named you Persnickity McFinicky or something fun like that."

I take the envelope from him, pressing it over the center of my chest, right above my throbbing heart. Very faintly, I say, "Ruby Diamond was Dolly Parton's character's name in *Unlikely Angel*, a 1996 made-for-TV Christmas movie."

"Ah. An inside joke. How sweet."

I get the sense he wants to roll his eyes, but he only says, "Now, up you go. The flight leaves in half an hour from the private terminal at the airport. I've already called you a cab."

As if on cue, a car honks its horn downstairs.

"How did you know I was coming here? I only just left work."

"I know everything." When I stare at him blankly, he smiles. "I'm a spy. It's part of the job description."

He's a spy.

A SPY?

WHAT IN GOD'S NAME IS HAPPENING?

He takes me gently by the elbow and helps me up. He brushes a lock of hair off my forehead, tucks it behind my ear, and says, "You don't need to pack a bag. Liam's taken care of everything. Just get your pretty arse on the plane and go."

I'm so confused, my eyes are crossing. I blurt the only thing that comes to mind. "I'm going to be an attorney. Here. In Boston. I'll be sitting for the bar in a few weeks."

It's ridiculous, but I think I get a pass. It's not every day your imprisoned mobster lover's spy twin brother you've never met shows up with your new identity.

"Or maybe you'll be an attorney in Argentina, lass."

All the breath leaves my body. Wide-eyed, I look down at the envelope in my hands. "*Argentina?*"

"Who knows? These things have a way of working out. Anyway, I'm off. It's been a real pleasure meeting you." His voice turns stern. "Of course, I don't have to tell you not to mention to anyone where you're going or that you've seen me."

"Of course." There. I almost sounded sane that time.

He ambles over to the bedroom door. He turns the knob and opens it. Before he walks out, I say, "Wait!"

He pauses, glancing at me over his shoulder.

I have a million questions to ask, but my brain is a pretzel. All I come up with is, "What's your name?"

He smiles. It's a dangerous smile, a secretive one, a wild and hungry one that would look right at home on a wolf.

"I'm Killian. I'll be seeing you again soon. Safe travels, Tru."

With a deep sense of shock, I realize that this time, his voice had no trace of an Irish accent.

With a wink, he's gone.

Outside my bedroom window, the car horn blares again. My taxi's waiting.

Like a flip has been thrown, I go from being frozen to moving at a million miles per hour. I don't bother to change out of my work uniform. I just run into the closet, rip a sweater off a hanger, and pull it on as I dash into the living room, clutching the envelope like my life depends on it.

I think it actually might.

Ellie's still on the sofa with her magazine. Without looking up, she says, "That's right, girlfriend. You go get that fine man and drag his ass back here. Nobody walks out on Truvy Sullivan, badass bitch extraordinaire."

I grab her and give her a quick, tight hug. "Love you, Elliebellie."

Startled, she stares at me, her brown eyes wide. "Love you, too."

I turn around and run to the front door. She calls out after me, "And if you guys are up for a threesome, count me in!"

31

TRU

*I*n the Southern Hemisphere, winter begins in June. So although I left balmy weather in Boston, when I step off the private plane onto the tarmac in Buenos Aires, it's cold and rainy.

It might as well be August in Miami for how much I'm sweating.

The flight was more than twelve hours long nonstop. I didn't sleep, eat, or drink, except for all the vodka sodas the nice flight attendant kept bringing me. Somehow, I never got drunk.

The alcohol probably burned away the minute it hit my bloodstream.

I'm on fire.

My heart, my soul, my brain, my sweat glands: all of me burns.

A uniformed chauffer holding an umbrella waits for me beside a limo parked only a few yards from where the plane came to a stop. He meets me at the bottom of the air stairs—or whatever those folding airplane steps are called—and ushers me into the car without a word.

We speed off into the gray, drizzly morning. If he's wondering why I'm wearing what looks like a hotel maid's uniform along with an expression like I've suffered several recent electrocutions, he doesn't ask.

The city center is sprawling and cosmopolitan, more crowded even than Boston with its skyscrapers and busy streets. But as we drive farther, congestion and concrete give way to green fields and rolling hills. After about forty-five minutes, we turn into a long gravel driveway flanked by huge weeping willow trees. Horses graze in the pastures beyond. The driveway meanders through the countryside until it ends at a formidable-looking iron gate.

A carved wooden sign beside the gate reads *Estancia Los Dos Hermanos*.

The driver clicks a remote. The gate creaks slowly open. We proceed about a mile up a low hill. When we crest the top, I see down into the valley below.

Off in the distance sits a sprawling ranch house with a red tiled roof and a wraparound porch in the front. A large wooden barn is nearby, along with horse stables and several other small outbuildings. A flock of geese float tranquilly in the nearby pond.

In the open front door of the house stands a man. He's tall and dark-haired, broad through the shoulders, wearing jeans, boots, and a white dress shirt unbuttoned at the throat with the cuffs rolled up thick, tattooed forearms.

Even at this distance, I know who it is.

I can't see his face, but my heart tells me.

The relief I feel is so overwhelming I break down sobbing.

I cry all the way down the hill toward the house. I don't stop, even when the limo pulls in front and the man in the doorway comes out to meet the car, his long legs eating up the distance in a run.

I cry when I throw open the door before the car has even fully stopped moving, cry as I burst out, cry as I stumble over my own feet and start to fall to my knees.

He's there to catch me before I hit the ground, of course.
Liam would never let me fall.

Probably because he so enjoys carrying me.

He sweeps me up and stands there holding me in his strong
arms as I sob into his neck, the gentle rain misting our hair, my
arms clenched so hard around him he's probably suffocating.

"Hullo, queen bee," he whispers gruffly into my ear.

Through my sobs, I manage to reply. "Hello, wolfie."

"I hear you love me."

That Declan is such a blabbermouth. "You're okay, I guess."

Liam squeezes me tight. Then he gives me a deep, passionate
kiss, which only serves to make me cry harder.

Chuckling, he turns around and walks slowly back to the
house, cradling me in his arms.

I'm too exhausted at the moment to insist he tell me how he
escaped from custody and got to Buenos Aires, and my brain is
too mushy to take it in, anyway. So I simply allow him to carry me
into the bedroom of this cozy, lovely ranch house and set me on
the bed.

He silently removes my sweater and shoes and shucks off his
boots. Then he takes us down to the mattress and holds me tight,
front to front instead of our usual spooning.

Cupping my head in his big hand, he murmurs, "How was the
flight?"

"Endless."

"You smell like vodka."

"Remind me to smack you when I wake up."

Then I fall into such a deep, dreamless sleep I could be dead.

When I awaken, the light has changed, but that's the only
thing. Liam and I are still in the same position we were in when I
fell asleep. Only now, he's asleep, too.

I take a moment to gaze at him and let my fluttering heartbeat settle, then reach up and touch his jaw. His beard is rough and springy under my fingertips. I lean in and sniff his neck, sighing in contentment.

If someone had told me a few months ago that I'd be so in love with a fugitive mob boss that the mere smell of his skin would make me shimmer with happiness, I'd have told that person she was crazy.

Liam's voice is a sleepy rumble. "If I didn't know better, I'd think you were huffing me like glue."

"I never got the appeal before, but now I can see how glue sniffing could be so addictive."

He lifts his lashes and gazes at me with warm, loving eyes. "Hullo again."

"Hi. Who's house is this?"

"Mine and my brother's."

"So that's what *Estancia Los Dos Hermanos* means: house of two brothers."

"Two brothers' ranch," he corrects, drawing me closer. He leans in and nuzzles my neck, sniffing me exactly the same way I sniffed him earlier. He makes a noise of pleasure low in his throat.

"Liam?"

"Aye, lass?"

"Does this family ranch of yours have condoms?"

He pulls back and grins at me, so handsome it takes my breath away. "I should put you on nonstop international flights more often."

"It's just that I don't know how soon the FBI will be arriving, and I want to make sure I try to fit a lifetime worth of lovemaking into whatever time we have left."

Liam kisses me softly on the lips. "The FBI won't be arriving."

"Oh. Right. They're a US agency. What's Argentina's equivalent?"

"The Federal Police Intelligence. They're not coming, either."

"How can you be sure?"

"They have no reason to be looking for me."

I crinkle my forehead. "But you're a fugitive from the law."

"No, lass, I'm not. Now about those condoms—"

I sit up abruptly and look down at him, my heart revving like a race car's engine. I say loudly, "What do you mean you're not a fugitive? I saw you on TV being arrested by the FBI!"

"Did you?" His smile comes on slow and heated. He trails a finger up the inside of my arm.

I am *so* going to smack him.

"Yes, I did! You were on the evening news! There were like six federal agents leading you up the steps of—"

When I falter, understanding blossoming in my fevered brain, Liam's grin grows wider.

I whisper, "*Killian?*"

"Having an identical twin can be incredibly convenient for that sort of thing."

"But—but—he's not in prison, either! I saw him at my apartment! He gave me the ticket and the passport, and at first he had an Irish accent but then he didn't, and he told me he was a spy..."

I gasp. "Hold on. *Are you a spy, too?*"

Liam chuckles, pulling me down by my shoulders to give me a deep, soulful kiss. When we come up for air, he says, "You're adorable."

I hide my face in his neck and whimper. "Please tell me your Irish accent isn't fake."

He wraps his arms around me and presses a kiss to my hair. "It's not fake. His isn't, either. He's just learned how to fake a lot of other accents during the course of his life. Comes in handy for the spy gig. You should hear him do an Australian accent. He sounds just like Crocodile Dundee."

I push away from him, sit up, and stare down at his face,

shaking with all the adrenaline coursing through my veins. "Okay. What's happening? Short version. Go."

Liam props himself up on an elbow and smiles at me, reaching out to caress my cheek.

He murmurs, "You're so beautiful. I've always thought so. Those eyes..." He sighs. "That's what got me, you know. Right from the beginning. I took one look into those sea glass eyes when you were helping an old woman cross the street and—"

I push him onto his back, straddle him, and shout, "Shut up and tell me what's happening already!"

He laughs, pulling me down to his chest to wrap his arms around my back. "What's happening is that we're here, we're safe, and you love me. Everything other than that can wait."

Then he kisses me, hard, his hands dug deep into my hair and his mouth demanding.

When he reaches behind me and unzips my uniform, I let him.

He's right: everything else can wait.

Several hours later, we're sweaty and sated, lying in each other's arms as rainfall patters softly on the rooftop and turns the emerald pastures into a fairyland of sparkles and rainbow mist. Off in the distance, a lone rooster begins to crow.

The sound reminds me of Texas. My head resting on Liam's chest, I smile.

Rousing to glance down at me, he says, "What are you smiling about?"

"Roosters."

His chuckle is a deep rumble through his chest. "Ouch. My ego."

"You'll live. It's just that they're so stupid. They're supposed to crow at dawn, but every rooster I've ever known has put up a racket at all hours of the day and night. You'd think they'd figure it out, the dumb things."

Toying with a lock of my hair, he says, "Maybe there's a pretty hen nearby and they're showing off."

I think about it. "That makes sense. Roosters have a lot in common with men."

Liam rolls over, pushing me onto my back and throwing his heavy leg over both of mine. Propped up on an elbow, he smiles down at me, making my insides melt.

"We're both just stupid animals, huh?"

I'm sure I have little hearts for eyes when I whisper, "Totally."

We enjoy a lazy, lingering kiss. Against my mouth, he murmurs, "If I tell you the story, I have to start at the beginning. And it's a long story."

My heartbeat ticks up a notch. "I'm listening."

He exhales slowly, then rolls to his back and tucks me into his side. He stares at the ceiling in silence for a while as the rain begins to fall harder outside.

Then, his voice low, he starts to speak.

"My father was a good man. A hardworking family man who went to church every Sunday and faithfully tithed ten percent of his income, though he barely had two pennies to his name. At that time, Ireland was in a nasty recession. There was high unemployment, hunger strikes, and a lot of social unrest. In the small town we lived in, people were starving. Nobody had any money, and there was very little food. The only people who had cash were in the mob, and they ran everything.

"I don't know what started it. I doubt I'll ever find out. But somehow my father ran afoul of a local mob leader named Eoin McGrath. He was the one who put the wooden stake through my gut."

He pauses for a moment. He closes his eyes. After a moment of heavy silence, he continues.

"McGrath and his cronies started to harass my family. They

chased my sisters home from school. Threw bricks through our windows. Killed the family cat and hung it over the front door. My mother lived in terror that one of us kids would be hurt, or worse, so she insisted we move farther out in the country to stay with her widowed sister, hoping the trouble would blow over.

"It didn't. McGrath found out where we'd gone. One night we awoke to the smell of smoke and the sound of my mother scream-ing. When we ran outside, we saw why. My father had been hamstrung, tied to a tree, and lit on fire. He was still conscious, but engulfed in flames. In agony. Burning alive.

"It was Killian who had the presence of mind to go inside and get the gun."

Liam stops abruptly and takes a breath.

I'm frozen in horror, seeing it all through Liam's eyes. His mother screaming. His father burning. His brother raising his arm and pulling the trigger, the gun pointed at his father's head.

It was mercy, but what a price Killian must have paid living with that ever since.

I can't imagine.

"We buried what was left of my father under the blackened branches of the tree he died on, then Killian and I set out to find the men who killed him. We took the gun and my aunt's car and drove back to town."

"It wasn't hard to find Eoin and his gang. They were in a bar. Celebrating. I had a butcher knife and Killian had the gun, but we were just boys, insane with grief, no match for half a dozen grown men."

Into his heavy pause, I whisper, "How old were you?"

"Thirteen."

My stomach turns over.

"They dragged us out into the street, took the weapons away, kicked us around a while for some fun. Then they tied us up and drove us back out to the farm."

His voice drops an octave. "For me, they broke off blackened branches of that same fucking tree. They cut them up and sharpened them. Then they held me on the ground and drove one through my gut and another through my shoulder, pounding them deep into the dirt with a rock so I was pinned down.

"Killian wasn't so lucky. There were five bullets left in my father's gun. They threw a rope over a high branch of the tree, strung him up by his wrists, and gave him a kick to set him swinging. Then McGrath used him for target practice. He didn't miss once."

Horrified, I blurt, "Jesus Christ."

Ignoring my interruption, Liam continues.

"At the first sign of McGrath's convoy pulling up, my mother and aunt should've run straight out the back door and taken all the other kids into the fields. It was dark. They might have escaped. But they didn't. Instead they watched from inside the house as McGrath and his gang worked me and Killian over. Then they blocked the doors, poured gasoline all over the front porch, and lit the house on fire. They drove away laughing as it burned.

"I pulled the stake out of my stomach, then the other from my shoulder. With what strength, I don't know. Then I cut Killian down from the tree. I didn't check to see if he was alive before I ran back to the house, but by that time it was consumed in flames. Through the window, I saw my mother on the floor, her arms around my brothers and sisters, all of them huddled together. So I punched through the window with my bare fists and jumped inside.

"They weren't moving. Smoke inhalation got them before the fire did. I tried to drag my mother to the window, but she was so heavy. And the smoke was so thick..."

He stops again. Jaw clenched, heart hammering, he lies still and silent, lost in memory.

After a long time, he says gruffly, "Killian pulled me out of there. Even shot five times, he managed to save my life. I don't remember much after that until days later when I woke up in a hospital bed. He was in the bed next to me."

It feels like an anvil is crushing my chest. A tear leaks from the corner of my eye, straggling down my temple to drip onto Liam's shoulder. "It's a miracle you survived."

"We shouldn't have. That's what all the doctors said. And Killian became convinced as time went on that we survived for a reason. That our family's massacre shouldn't be in vain. We were sent to live at St. Stephen's Home for Boys, an orphanage right out of a Dickens' novel. That's where we stayed until we aged out of the system.

"Then Killian joined the military, and I moved to Dublin and got a job in a book store. I met a girl there. I thought we'd get married, live a normal life. But a few years later, she was killed in an explosion. The mafia targeted an enemy, and she was in the wrong place at the wrong time.

"Julia died at a coffee shop at ten o'clock on a Saturday morning, blown to bits. They had to use dental records to identify her remains."

I gasp softly. Here ends the mystery of Julia, writer of love notes in philosophical books. Lost to senseless violence, like the rest of the people Liam has ever been close to.

No wonder he was so ambivalent about getting close to me.

Liam's voice grows rougher. "That's when I decided Killian was right when he said our family's massacre shouldn't be in vain. I decided Julia's death shouldn't be for nothing, either. There had to be a price to pay for these terrible acts men committed, and I'd be the one to extract it. That's when I joined the DMI."

"What does that stand for?"

"Directorate of Military Intelligence. It's Ireland's version of the CIA."

I sit up abruptly and stare down at him with wide eyes and a thundering pulse, remembering what I overheard the night he was on the phone with Killian.

"Eighteen years is enough. It's a miracle I've lasted this long!"

My heart in my throat, I shout, "You're undercover?"

His eyes shine with emotion as he reaches up to cup my face. "Don't be impressed. It's not a noble undertaking. I've done everything I've done for revenge, not out of any sense of duty to my country. I wanted blood. I wanted the mafia to pay for all they'd taken from me. For that, I knew I had to work from the inside."

I'm so astonished, I can hardly form a coherent sentence. "But how...all this time...how has no one found out?"

He closes his eyes briefly. "Lie down with dogs, get up with fleas."

"What do you mean?"

His exhalation is heavy. "I mean I became very good at revenge. The reputation I have for ruthlessness..."

He opens his eyes and gazes at me. The view past his pupils is endless and dark.

"It's earned. I don't just pass information along to a handler in hopes the government will gather enough evidence to build a criminal case. I'm judge and jury. I render the verdict myself. And mercy is not what I specialize in."

Trembling, I think of my brother and wonder if justice is better served Liam's way or mine.

Do the ends justify the means?

Does it ultimately matter? Or is what matters that the bad guys get what's coming to them one way or another?

Liam closely watches my expression. He leaves me alone with my thoughts for a moment longer, then goes on.

"At first, I only intended to kill McGrath and his crew and find out who'd been responsible for that book store bomb. But I realized quickly that there were far more evil actors in the criminal underworld, and their operations weren't limited to Ireland. The farther up the ranks of the mafia I climbed, the more information I was privy to, the clearer the picture became.

"I grew obsessed with finding out who was at the top. Who pulled all the strings? I wanted to cut off the head of the snake."

I fall onto my back, staring up at the ceiling and struggling to take it all in. I say breathlessly, "Declan. He knows, doesn't he?"

"He was the one who recruited me into the DMI. And he's had my back all these years."

That cagey SOB. Several things he said and did click into place, and I cringe. I think I owe him an apology for that slap.

But he *was* a jerk and kept blowing cigarette smoke into my face, so maybe not.

"Where was Killian in all this?"

"In the military, he demonstrated certain aptitudes that interested the government. He went to work for MI6 doing counterterrorism and counter-espionage. That didn't last long. Too corporate for him. He hates taking directions from anyone. So he went freelance.

"I can't tell you what his career path looked like from there, because I don't know. But he had all these crazy skills and contacts in every foreign government you can name, and we agreed to work together toward a common goal."

"Cutting off the head of the snake."

"Exactly. From inside *and* out."

"And how's that going?"

His answer is quiet. "The problem with the kind of snake we're chasing is that every time you cut off one head, another one grows in its place."

We fall silent, listening to the sound of the rain.

The rooster crows again, then he's silent, too.

"You once told me you were in enforcement. I thought that sounded so strange at the time, and even more so after finding out you were in the mafia, but now...now it makes sense."

Liam rolls to his side, lifts up to an elbow, and gazes down at me.

Trying to process everything, I turn my head and look at him. I have so many questions I still need to ask.

"So your FBI arrest...that was fake? You were working with them?"

He nods. "I gave them a few valuable pieces of information in exchange. They were very grateful."

My brows draw together. "But why fake your arrest in the first place?"

He smooths my forehead wrinkles with his finger, gently stroking the furrows away.

"Because there are only two ways out of the mob. Death or prison. I decided being killed by one of my enemies would be inconvenient..."

His voice drops. "Considering I'm in love."

I drag in a hitching breath. My eyes fill with water. My throat constricts, and my voice comes out small and strangled. "So what happens now? You supposedly rot inside a prison cell forever but in reality you have to live the rest of your life in hiding?"

Liam leans down and gives me a soft, sweet kiss on the lips. "Now it's Killian's turn to be the mafia pope."

When my mouth drops open in shock, Liam chuckles.

"He'll be 'released' from custody on a technicality and will take over where I left off. He can't wait. If you think *I'm* bossy, it's only because you don't know him well enough yet."

When I continue to stare at him with my mouth open, he chuckles again.

"The whole switching thing was his idea, actually. My original plan was to get knocked off in prison—allegedly, of course, just for the news—and retire from the revenge business so we could safely be together. But apparently Killian has always been keen on the idea of fronting an international criminal empire. I had no idea he found my work so glamorous, but here we are."

I spend a while blinking rapidly and trying to rearrange my brain cells.

"So...your brother will still be a freelance spy...but while taking over your job...which is pretending to be a mafia kingpin... while actually working for a foreign government...or two."

"Aye."

"And you'll retire from the revenge business."

"Aye."

"And we'll live happily-ever-after."

"Aye."

"And I'll have Killian to thank for that."

He's about to agree with me, but catches himself. "What? No! This was *my* idea! *I'm* the one who wanted out!"

I pretend to be doubtful, pursing my lips and staring back at him with a lifted brow.

He's outraged. "Did you or did you not hear me say that being killed by an enemy would be inconvenient because *I'm in love*?"

I can't keep up the ruse. My face breaks into a smile. I wind my arms around Liam's broad shoulders and whisper, "Yes, I heard you. I just wanted to hear it again."

Understanding dawns over his face. "Why, you little..."

He doesn't bother finishing the sentence. He simply leans down and kisses me.

It's several more hours before we come up for air again.

EPILOGUE
TRU

our weeks later

"You're gonna do great."

"I'm not. I'm totally going to fail this effing test. Yesterday was a nightmare. Today will be worse. I'm going to fail."

"You won't."

"I *will.*"

"You will if you keep thinking like that. Have some self-confidence. You've studied your arse off. You're ready."

"Remind me again why I'm bothering with this ridiculous two-day-long, twelve-hour test when my law degree has already been accredited by the University of Argentina, I've registered with the Colegio de Abogados, and I don't need anything else to practice law in Buenos Aires? Including a passing grade on the Massachusetts bar exam?"

Over the phone line, Liam's tone is firm. "Because it's a goal you've worked toward for years, you don't want to give up on that goal simply because you're living in another country now, and—most importantly—you promised your mother you would."

"Oh. That."

"Aye, *that*. I don't want to start off my relationship with her on the wrong foot."

Standing outside the meeting room door at the Hynes Convention Center in Boston where I'm scheduled to begin day two of the bar exam—like, right now—I lean against the wall and smile, picturing Liam meeting my parents. We're going to Texas in a few months for a visit.

For Thanksgiving, of all things.

It's a situation I once thought impossible, but I'm living in alternate reality land now. All kinds of impossible things have come to pass.

"Oh, crap, they're closing the doors. I gotta go in."

"Good luck. Call me as soon as it's over."

"You know I will, bossy boss man."

Liam growls, "You better, or I'll take you over my knee when you get home."

"Promises, promises. I'll see you tomorrow."

I make a kissing noise and hang up before he can make any more sexy threats. The last thing I need right now is to be distracted by the thought of him spanking my—

Too late.

I go inside, get a locking security case for my cell phone from the lady standing at the door, then take my assigned seat, forcing the thought of my gorgeous wolf and all the things he does to my body out of my mind.

Along with my now unusable phone, I've got a clear plastic storage bag holding a bottle of water, a sandwich for lunch, signed examinee agreement, and several number two pencils that I'll use to take today's part of the exam, which consists of a billion or so multiple-choice questions covering contracts, torts, criminal law, constitutional law, evidence, and real property.

Also inside the bag is my photo ID. The real one.

Because although Mrs. Ruby Diamond is a lovely name, she never applied to take the Massachusetts bar exam, so she's shit out of luck.

Everyone else in the room looks as nervous as I feel.

Six hours later, we all look nauseated. Brain dead, to boot.

I'm sure I failed, but at least I kept my promise to my mother.

I get my phone unlocked and drop the secure case into the bin on a desk near the door, then head out of the meeting room. I turn left toward the elevators that will take me to the parking garage, but stop dead in my tracks when I spot a man leaning against a nearby wall.

His head is tilted back. His massive tattooed arms are folded over his chest. One booted foot is kicked up against the wall. In jeans and a white T-shirt, he's the picture of casual cool. Like James Dean on steroids.

He's wearing mirrored sunglasses, so I can't tell if his eyes are closed, but if I could see them, I'd know their exact color.

Smiling, I walk over to meet him. "Hi, Killian."

He turns his head in my direction and sighs. "I can't tell you how disappointing it is that you always recognize me on sight. *Nobody* can tell us apart."

His Irish brogue is intact. I want to ask him to do an Australian accent for me, but get distracted. "Why is it disappointing?"

His smile is lazy. A dimple flashes in his cheek. He pushes the sunglasses up to the top of his head and gazes at me through half-lowered lids, his eyes glinting with mischief. "I keep hoping you'll throw your arms around me and give me a kiss."

"No, you don't. You're just trying to be charming."

He scoffs. "Trying? There's no *trying*, lass."

I laugh. "Oh, look, the ego runs in the family."

He pushes off the wall. Towering over me, he gazes down at me and smiles. "Aye. We're a couple of strutting peacocks, and that's a fact. You can't blame us, though." He makes spokesmodel hands at his body. "Just look at all this fancy plumage. All the other cocks are so jealous their teeth are falling out."

A young guy walks past, shooting Killian an envious look before puffing out his chest and moving on.

Seeing him, Killian's grin grows wider.

I roll my eyes. "You paid that guy, didn't you?"

He waves a hand dismissively. "Happens a dozen times a day, lass. How'd the test go?"

"Ugh. Shoot me."

"I'm afraid my brother wouldn't like that. You know he's quite fond of you."

"Fond?"

He nods solemnly. "You've grown on him. Like mold."

I laugh again, because he's so ridiculous I can't help it. "Good to know. Moving on. To what do I owe this unexpected pleasure?"

"You didn't think Liam would let you roam around Boston without an escort, did you?"

"I haven't been *roaming*—wait." I narrow my eyes at him. "I got here two nights ago. Have you been watching me this whole time?"

"Watching you?" He grimaces. "Don't make it sound so pervy."

"I take it that's a yes."

He gazes at me for a beat. I can tell he's trying not to grin.

"Were you operating under the mistaken impression that my brother isn't insanely protective of you? That he doesn't lose his mind when you're out of his sight for more than sixty seconds? That allowing you to leave your little love nest—"

"*Allowing*?" I snort. He ignores me.

"—didn't give him nightmares, high blood pressure, and send him into caveman possessive mode? Because it did."

"Actually, you would've been very proud of him. He handled it very well."

Killian chuckles. "That's what you think."

Men.

"So how's the mafia gig going? Are you enjoying being in charge of an international criminal empire as much as you thought you would be?"

He takes my hand and links it through his bent arm, leading me toward the elevators in an unhurried stroll.

"I'm *loving* it. Thanks for asking." He laughs. "But Liam collected a long list of enemies. Everyone keeps trying to kill me! There's one in particular, a young Latino kid who absolutely has it out for me. In the past month, he's shot at me, booby-trapped a car he thought was mine, and attempted to plant a homemade bomb outside a restaurant Liam owns. Excuse me —*I* own."

Oh no. My stomach sinks.

We reach the elevator bank. Killian hits the call button and continues.

"Lucky for me, he's a terrible assassin. Absolute shite. It's comical, really. I keep letting him go to see what he'll try next. It's become something of a gag for the bodyguards. I asked Liam about him, but he swears he doesn't know why this kid wants to murder him so badly."

"Um. Would you do me a favor, Killian?"

He looks at me curiously.

"Would you please not hurt him? He's a friend of mine. Was a friend." I clear my throat. "We worked together for a few years."

After a moment where he stares at me, startled, Killian starts to laugh. "Ho! It's a love triangle, is it?"

I say flatly, "Don't be annoying."

He blinks innocently. "Moi? Annoying? Never."

I heave out a sigh. "Seriously. I'm asking a favor. Don't hurt him, okay?"

He looks insulted by the suggestion. "Of course I won't hurt him. He's too entertaining. I was actually thinking of offering him a job. He's demonstrated a level of commitment I find commendable. I could use that in the ranks."

The elevator doors slide open. I step inside, but Killian doesn't follow.

"This is where I leave you, lass."

"But you'll still be spying on me, I presume."

He winks. "It's in the job description."

The elevator doors slide closed as I'm shaking my head, smiling.

As soon as I'm in the rental car and headed back to the hotel to pack my bags, I call Liam. He picks up on the first ring.

"So? How was it?"

I say teasingly, "Maybe you should call your brother to find out."

A dissatisfied grumble comes over the line. "He wasn't supposed to show his face."

"It's all right. It was good to see him. Diego's still trying to kill you, by the way."

"Really? Hmm. I'm impressed with his commitment."

"That's exactly what Killian said. He's thinking of giving him a job."

Liam chuckles. "Botching what?"

"Don't make fun of him. I feel bad."

"You shouldn't. He tried to assassinate me."

"I know, but you have to admit it's sort of romantic in a twisted way."

"I admit no such thing. I'm the only one allowed to commit murder for you."

Something in his voice gives me pause. "You say that like you have already."

His chuckle is dismissive. "No, but I'm leaving that possibility open. By the way, I moved your departure time up. The flight leaves in twenty-five minutes."

"That barely gives me enough time to pack my stuff and check out!"

"You better move fast, then." His voice drops. "Because I can't fucking wait to see you. Three days apart is three days too long."

He disconnects without waiting for an argument about his bossiness, which he obviously knew was coming.

I hurry back to the hotel, get my bags packed, and rush to check out. I would've stayed with Ellie, but she and Tyler are back together.

The more things change, the more they stay the same.

Over dinner last night, I paid her the remainder of my portion of the lease on the apartment and told her the goon squad would be by to pack up all my things.

When she asked what was happening with me and Liam, I said I had no idea who she was talking about and smiled.

She got it. After the night I left, she saw the news about his arrest and release. She heard the reporters call him a mobster. If anyone knows about complicated relationships, it's her.

She didn't ask where I'd been living, and I didn't say. We just had a nice dinner, hugged, and said goodbye.

I have a feeling I'll be seeing her again, though. Buenos Aires is incredible, but if I manage to pass the bar in Boston...who knows what the future might hold.

I mean, Killian might need to go on vacation every once in a while, right? And the mafia pope can't just leave business hanging.

He might need someone knowledgeable to step in every so often to give him a break.

The flight back to Argentina goes by faster this time because I fall asleep. I wake up as we're touching down on the runway.

When I arrive back at *Estancia Los Dos Hermanos*, Liam is waiting for me, standing in the front door.

I run to him, jumping into his open arms. He carries me into the house without a word, headed straight for the bedroom.

To his profile, I say, "Hi, honey."

He growls, "I need you naked."

I smile. "I'm getting that."

He lays me on the bed, strips off my clothes and his own, then pushes inside me with a grateful groan. I arch into him, sighing, amazed how home can be a person.

He's impatient, greedy, a little rough. His mouth and hands are everywhere. He bites my neck as he thrusts into me. I cross my ankles behind his back and take him deep.

When I come, it's with his name on my lips.

He falters, making a noise like he's in pain.

Panting, I open my eyes and stare up at him. "What is it?"

Through gritted teeth, he says, "I didn't wear a condom."

We lie there for a moment, staring into each other's eyes, our hearts pounding, until I slide my hands down his broad back. I sink my fingers into the hard globes of his ass, flex my hips, and pull him in deeper.

His lips part. A look of understanding comes into his eyes. He whispers roughly, "Baby. Are you sure?"

As an answer, I flex my hips again and kiss him.

He grabs my face in his big hands and kisses me back, hard.

"You want to have my child?" he growls against my mouth as he drives into me faster and deeper. His arms shake and his chest heaves, the thought of me pregnant driving him wild.

"More than one," I say breathlessly, making him softly moan.

My mother will be disappointed we're not married first, but I'll deal with her later.

Liam starts to buck, fucking me passionately, groans working from his throat. I'm building to another climax, too, my head tipped back into the pillow, my body on fire, my heart singing.

He gets there first. His entire body tenses. He jerks, grunting, then drops his head to my breasts and sucks hard on a nipple as he spills himself inside me, groaning into my flesh.

Feeling him throb deep inside me, I tip over the edge. The contractions in my core are hard and rhythmic, leaving me gasping.

"I love you. Baby, I love you so fucking much."

His voice is a rasp at my ear. His body is huge, surrounding me in heat. His heart pounds against mine as we rock together. I cry out, tears sliding down my temples to catch in my hair.

I was wrong, before. Love isn't a nightmare. It's a miracle. A blessing.

It's knowing you're finally home.

Afterward, we doze. I wake to the incredible sight of a rainbow arching over the distant pastures, glinting from the recent rain. The sky is clearing to patchy blue. Outside, birds are singing.

Beside me, Liam slumbers, a small smile on his handsome face.

I slip quietly from bed, tiptoeing and trying not to wake him. He murmurs something in his sleep, rolls over, then settles in again.

He's far more relaxed here than in Boston. I'd never be able to slip out of bed there without him hearing me. I put on a robe and pad barefoot into the kitchen to get the coffee started.

On the kitchen counter, beside a huge bouquet of roses, I find a small black velvet box.

My heartbeat goes haywire. My hand flies up to cover my mouth.

I glance over my shoulder, but there's no sound from the bedroom. So I creep toward the box. My hands shake as I reach for it.

Inside, nestled against the black velvet, is a gorgeous diamond ring. The center stone is huge and blinding. It's flanked on either side by a pair of fat rubies, blood red.

I stare at it, water gathering in my eyes.

Big arms slide around my waist and cinch me against a warm, solid chest. Liam whispers into my ear, "I once said I wouldn't force you to marry me, but I'm taking that back. Consider yourself forced."

Here come those damn tears again.

I whisper, "You are the bossiest, most aggravating, and by far the most wonderful man I have ever met."

"I know. Put the damn ring on."

I slide it onto my ring finger. Unsurprisingly, it fits.

I turn around, hide my face in Liam's chest, and burst into tears.

Chuckling, he holds me tight, smoothing a hand over my hair. "So when does the bar association notify you if you passed the exam?"

"Can you give me a minute to recover, please? I'm having an emotional moment here!"

Ignoring that, he says, "Because I can tell you now, if you want."

I pull away and gape at him. "How could you possibly know? I'm not supposed to get the results for two months!"

He smiles. "I know people."

"Liam!" I pound on his chest with small, useless fists. It doesn't budge him.

"Is that a no?" He shrugs, releasing me. "Suit yourself."

I glare daggers at his back as he picks up the remote for the TV that hangs on the kitchen wall, next to the breakfast nook. It comes on to a news channel. I'm about to demand more information about the test, but am distracted by the headline on the screen.

"Texas Judge Arrested for Conspiracy to Murder."

I freeze when the newscaster says a name I know all too well. It's the same judge who ordered the killing of my brother.

I listen in cold shock as the newscaster reports the story of how the FBI raided the judge's home and chambers, tipped off by an unidentified source. When I turn my astonished gaze toward Liam, he's leaning against the kitchen counter, watching me with loving eyes, his expression somber.

I whisper, "Did you do this?"

He keeps his voice low and his gaze trained on me when he answers.

"You said you didn't want blood on your hands. I figured life in prison was the next best thing."

When my knees give out, Liam's there to catch me before I fall.

As he always has been.

As I know he always will be.

Forever.

Thank you for reading! Continue with Killian's story in Cruel Paradise, the next book in the Beautifully Cruel Series.

ACKNOWLEDGMENTS

I don't know where to start with this, so I'll just begin at the beginning.

The publication of this book was delayed a few times due to several major events that happened, not just to me, but to the world.

The first was my mother's death late last year. That threw everything off kilter in my life for a long time. You can't schedule mourning, and her passing hit me harder than I expected it to. She was elderly, and ill, but it still came as a shock when she died. I was alone with her in the hospital when she went, and I'm still processing that. But very grateful to have been there, and to have had her as my mom.

I was adopted at six weeks old. I always knew I was adopted because both my adoptive parents were very open about it, and I was brought up feeling a sense of gratitude and privilege that I had been given this wonderful life. I've never met my birth mother, nor have I ever attempted to make contact with her out of respect for her privacy, but the older I get, the more I treasure the sacrifice she made to bring me into the world. Life is such a crap shoot, with luck and chance playing huge roles, and I have been astonishingly fortunate to have not one mother who loved me, but two.

So thank you to the woman who gave me life and to the woman who raised me and taught me how to live it. I love and honor you both.

The second major event that delayed publication of this book was a worldwide pandemic. The appearance of the novel Coronavirus is unlike anything I have encountered in my decades on this planet, and I hope to never experience anything like it again. My heartfelt and sincere thanks go out to all the healthcare workers, emergency support personnel, and the many largely unacknowledged and hardworking people who assisted others during the crisis.

The final thing that happened to wreak havoc with finishing this book has to do with my malfunctioning bowels.

Excuse me if this is TMI, but I have ulcerative colitis, also charmingly known as inflammatory bowel disease. When it flares, I can't eat. I can't work. I can't leave the house. I'm utterly useless. Imagine what happens when your entire colon is rife with bleeding, ulcerated sores, and be grateful for your health, if you have it. This last flare lasted two months, inconveniently while there was a worldwide toilet paper shortage due to the aforementioned pandemic.

Good times.

All of that is a roundabout way of saying thank you to my husband, Jay, who is a real life hero.

Any time I get up in the middle of the night, no matter how quietly I creep from bed to pee or get a sip of water, he instantly wakes and says, "Do you need anything?" If I do, he'll get up and get it for me. No matter what I need or want, or how it might inconvenience him, he's always there to provide it.

Even to a romance writer, that is incredibly romantic.

July 1, 2020, is our twentieth wedding anniversary. It was love at first sight. I moved in with him two weeks after we met at a restaurant where we were both having lunch with friends. We locked eyes across the dining room, he followed me out to the valet to ask me for a date, and the rest is history. We were married in a fantastically tacky chapel in Las Vegas with all our friends and family in attendance. (The only reason we didn't do the drive-through Elvis wedding chapel was because my mother was there, and she would've had nightmares for the rest of her life.)

Jay, I love you. Marrying you was by far the best decision I have ever made. You make me happy in so many ways. As of this writing, I probably will not kill you in your sleep. Just keep up the good work and you'll be safe.

Thank you to Geissinger's Gang, my Facebook reader group, for supporting my work and being so much fun.

Thanks to Letitia Hasser for her talent at making beautiful book covers.

As always, thank you to my readers. You have made my dream of being a writer come true.

Thanks to my father. I miss you every day.

Finally, thank you to everyone I'm forgetting whom I will remember as soon as this book goes to press and feel crushing guilt for not including in this section.

PS – In case you're wondering, Truvy passed the bar.

ABOUT THE AUTHOR

J.T. Geissinger is a #1 internationally bestselling author of emotionally charged romance and women's fiction. Ranging from funny, feisty romcoms to intense, edgy suspense, her books have sold millions of copies and been translated into more than a dozen languages.

She is a three-time finalist in both contemporary and paranormal romance for the RITA® Award, the highest distinction in romance fiction from the Romance Writers of America®. She is also a recipient of the Prism Award for Best First Book and the Golden Quill Award for Best Paranormal/Urban Fantasy.

She's a Southern California native currently living in Nevada with her husband and rescue kitty, Zoe.

Find her online at www.jtgeissinger.com

Join her reader group on Facebook

ALSO BY J.T. GEISSINGER

Printed in Great Britain
by Amazon

67089851R00199